JOURNEY FROM
INNOCENCE

'Now,' said Greg, 'take your skirt off.'

Without pausing to question him she obeyed, unzipping herself and letting the dark garment fall to the floor. Bending down to pick it up, she felt her bottom smart as the skin of her cheeks tautened. She folded it neatly and hung it over the back of the chair, aware that the three men would be focusing on her pubic mound, framed by her suspenders, and wondering if they could guess how moist she had become.

Greg walked over to a chest of drawers and opened the top one, pulling something out. Turning triumphantly to face the rest of the room, he showed them all the tawse.

It was large – bigger than the one previously used on her by Jack and Jenny, and its tail was slit into three strips. Greg smacked it lightly against his left palm, using minimal force, but it still made a wicked sound. Philippa gulped.

'I believe you're due a dose of the strap,' announced Greg. 'And not a light one, either. Twelve –'

'Twelve!' she exclaimed.

'– Twelve from each of us,' Greg finished.

JOURNEY FROM INNOCENCE

Jean-Philippe Aubourg

This book is a work of fiction.
In real life, make sure you practise safe sex.

First published in 1997 by
Nexus
332 Ladbroke Grove
London W10 5AH

Typeset by TW Typesetting, Plymouth, Devon

Printed and bound by
Caledonian Books Ltd, Glasgow

ISBN 0 352 33212 3

Prologue

This was the time Philippa hated, and yet loved, more than any other. The time she was left waiting. The time when there was nothing left to do and nothing to concentrate on, except for the fire in her bottom and the aching stiffness of her limbs, as she stood pinned to the wall by the chains.

In her mind's eye she could see the welts left on her bare bottom by the riding crop. Despite the blindfold, she knew it had been the crop. She understood the difference between them all, now – crop, cane, paddle, strap, cat, martinet, and although her tormentor had been silent, she was also certain she knew who had scorched her bottom ten minutes ago – Jenny.

How long would they make her wait this time, she wondered. Another ten minutes? Half an hour? Once, when it had been Jenny's turn, Jack had insisted on leaving her tied up in the dungeon for a full hour. How she had been sobbing when he and Philippa had finally returned! As cruel as the punishment itself had seemed, Philippa felt it was nothing compared to the loneliness and abandonment of this solitary confinement.

She chewed on the gag which had stifled all but the most guttural of her cries during her flogging. As she shifted her weight from one shackled leg to the other, trying not to rub her bare stomach and breasts too hard against the rough wall, she reflected on the time all those months ago when she had first entered this house. She

1

had been younger then, not only in age but in mind. She could have had no concept of the freedom gained through a locked door or a bound wrist. But it had not taken Jack and Jenny long to open her eyes to the pleasures of a blindfold. As she contemplated her situation, she became acutely aware of the moisture welling between her thighs.

The key turned. They were returning. Or would it be just one of them? Might it just be Jenny, come to finish off her victim with loving caresses and long strokes of her talented tongue? Or had Jack come alone to inspect Jenny's work, and then avail himself of the conveniently fixed victim? She could hear footsteps on the wooden stairs. Yes, they were both there. Maybe they would take her as she was, chained helplessly to the wall? Or would she perhaps be released and Jenny instructed to take her place . . .?

One

She walked down the street brimming with confidence. She was young – still only 22 – and attractive, her flawless legs accentuated by the short skirt, her full tapering hips and bust leading up to a pretty oval face with dancing brown eyes and a little nose, all crowned with a wavy chestnut mane. Her footsteps seemed to echo her self-assurance, and they had every right to, for after years of study and effort their owner was finally moving away from home and striding out on her own.

Philippa had only landed the job two weeks ago. It was her first real career move and the first to offer the financial independence she needed to strike out alone. She had applied for it because it was in London, two hundred miles from her home. It meant moving away from her family and the few friends of her own age left in her village. It was a new start, a clean page on which she could write whatever she wanted. And now there was no emotional baggage, no boyfriend whose whims and feelings had to be taken into account.

She and Paul had met at secondary school when they were sixteen. They had stayed together for most of the last six years, learning about love and sex in the few rushed moments they could find together. These had become more leisurely and enjoyable as they had grown older, and their parents had begun to think they would soon be settling down. Even Philippa herself had started to believe she could be happy with him for the rest of her life. Whether Paul had felt the same way she could not say, but he certainly had not given that impression when she had found him with her friend Tania.

She had called at his parents' house unannounced, knowing they usually went shopping on a Saturday. It was not unusual for her to visit at this time and she found herself looking forward to a couple of hours of physical release. The back door was open and she walked in. Then she heard sounds from the living room. She knew she was no woman of the world, but the noise was unmistakable – lovemaking. She slipped silently down the hall. The living room door was ajar and she peered in through it. What she saw turned her blood cold.

Paul and Tania were on the sofa. They were obviously far too wrapped up in each other to pay any attention to the world around them. The woman's naked back dominated Philippa's view, her dark brown bobbed hair jerking around wildly as her head flew back and forth. But there could be no question as to who it was – even from the back, Philippa knew Tania. And beneath her, lying stretched out on the couch was Paul, his eyes shut and his mouth closed in ecstasy as his hands reached up and seized Tania's breasts. Her thighs were spread wide over his groin, and her buttocks worked up and down, their tempo gradually increasing. Even if Philippa had walked right in she doubted either of them would have been able to stop.

But she did not even try to. It would have been even more humiliating for her to have shown them how upset and betrayed she felt. She withdrew from the house as silently as she had entered it, and ran all the way home.

She stayed in her room for the rest of the day, refusing to take repeated calls from a blissfully unaware Paul. That night she cried herself to sleep, but the next morning vowed it would be the first and last time it ever happened.

She never told Paul or Tania what she had seen, only that she did not want to see him again. He argued half-heartedly, but seemed to accept they had outgrown each other, little suspecting Philippa knew how far he had taken matters into his own hands. She told no one except her parents that she was applying for the job, or that she had got it. All she wanted to do was get away from the comfortable life which had finally betrayed her.

The company wanted her to start almost immediately, so she opted to stay in a hotel while she looked for somewhere more permanent. The hotel was good, and her new employers were picking up the bill, but she wanted to find somewhere she could call her own. Then she really could say she had escaped.

Her first morning held no great surprises. She was well qualified for the post and her new colleagues were pleasant and welcoming, but at lunchtime she declined the offer of a drink in the pub, so keen was she to start her search for a home. She began in the usual way, with the local papers. She looked at two or three places that day, but decided that none lived up to the cosy images conjured up by the advertisements. Not to worry, she thought, she would look again tomorrow; she was bound to find somewhere good in no time.

The next day's hunt, however, proved equally fruitless, and the pattern continued for some days. She began to realise how unscrupulous people in the capital could be when it came to renting out property.

She had almost given up hope of putting a suitable roof over her head when she made a sudden breakthrough, following up an innocuous looking advert in one of the papers. It had given little away about the place – *Third professional person wanted to share large house in suburbs. Must be tidy and broad-minded.* These last two words puzzled her, but she saw nothing sinister about them and telephoned to make an appointment.

She spoke to a girl called Jenny, who said she was the other tenant. Jenny shared the house with Jack, its owner, and she said that Philippa could come round and meet them both at seven.

Philippa arrived at the appointed hour – she hated lateness and always made an effort to be punctual. From outside, the house looked as if it more than lived up to the description in the newspaper, but she had seen plenty of places which looked fine externally but were only semi-habitable within.

She walked up the long gravel drive, gazing at the square grey frontage with its two rows of windows, three along the top, and two on either side of the front door. A yellow Mini was parked in front of the garage doors to one side of the house. Philippa guessed the owner kept the privilege of parking inside the garage for himself. She reached the doorstep and rang the bell.

There was movement inside, then a light appeared through the half-moon-shaped window above the door. A few seconds later the door opened and a female face peered around it. The woman was very pretty, with straight, shoulder-length blonde hair. 'Philippa?' she asked in a voice which had a slight musical quality to it.

'Yes that's right. I've come to look at the room.'

'Of course you have. Come on in.' The girl opened the door and stood aside to let her in. 'I'm Jenny. Pleased to meet you.'

Jenny took her into the lounge, a spacious room furnished with a large three-piece suite covered in floral material, and a set of wooden chairs around a small dining table. A television and video sat discreetly in a mahogany cabinet next to an electric fire. 'Do sit down,' said Jenny, indicating the couch. 'Jack won't be long; he's usually in from work by this time. He must have got held up tonight. Would you like a coffee?' Philippa accepted, and Jenny disappeared through another door to what Philippa assumed was the kitchen.

Left alone, she made the most of this opportunity to take in her surroundings. The place seemed very comfortable and homely, almost welcoming. If the bedroom lived up to this standard she would snap it up in a minute. And Jenny was friendly. Hopefully Jack would be equally as charming.

Jenny returned with two mugs and handed one to her, but before she had time to sit down there was the sound of a key in the front door. 'That'll be Jack,' she said. Philippa thought his arrival seemed to excite her more than the homecoming of a flatmate would normally have done. Was there something more between these two? Jenny had put her mug on the coffee table and was straightening her knee-length green skirt and cream blouse, as if it were important that she look her best for him.

His footsteps travelled the short distance down the hallway, then the door opened and a man in a smart business suit appeared. He was tall, about six feet, with neatly trimmed brown hair and a face most women would have described as handsome. 'Hello,' he said, in a steady and mellow voice, 'it's Philippa isn't it?' Philippa affirmed this as she rose and moved forward to shake his hand. He had a firm grip, one which imparted self-confidence.

'I've just made coffee, Jack. Would you like some?' piped up Jenny. She seemed eager, almost anxious to please him.

'No thanks, I'd better show Philippa the room first. Follow me.'

He led the way back into the hall and up the long flight of stairs. The interior of the house did indeed live up to Philippa's expectations, being pleasantly decorated, warm and bright. They passed along a landing to a door at the far end, which Jack opened to reveal a large room containing a bed, a small armchair and a wardrobe. He stood back to let Philippa inside, and as

7

she looked around, he told her about the amount of light it got during the day, assured her that it would allow her all the privacy she needed, and added that the rent included all household bills. She examined it approvingly and was about to announce there and then she would like to take it, when something caught her eye.

It was a small picture on the wall opposite the bed. At first sight it had not seemed out of place or unusual, but when she examined it properly her eyes widened in surprise.

The black and white sketch depicted three people in eighteenth-century dress, two women and a man. The women, both young, were bent over a rough wooden bench. Their long dresses were thrown up to reveal naked bottoms, and they looked anxiously over their shoulders at the middle-aged man in a black frock coat and wig, as he wielded what appeared to be a riding whip. A TYPICAL WORKHOUSE WHIPPING read the caption underneath the scene.

Philippa looked around at Jack, but he pre-empted her question. 'Left behind by a previous tenant,' he explained. 'He was a history graduate and collected them. It's supposed to illustrate the great social ills which went on in those days, or so he claimed.'

'Oh,' said Philippa, unsure whether to believe this explanation.

'If it bothers you I'll take it out before you move in. If, that is, you do want to move in.'

'Er, yes – yes I'd love to,' she answered, momentarily caught off guard by the sudden change of subject.

'Splendid,' said Jack. 'Then let's go downstairs and sort out the details.'

As she followed him back down to the living room, he explained to her how he had come to be landlord of such an impressive property. 'I inherited it from my parents. My mother died when I was nine and my father

8

passed away a couple of years ago. This was his house, but I moved out when I got a job in advertising. I was eighteen and wanted some independence. When he left it to me in his will I thought about selling it and buying something more modern, but decided that since it's such a lovely house, and the one I grew up in, why go to all the trouble of finding somewhere which probably wouldn't be anywhere near as nice? That's why the rent is so reasonable – I don't really need lodgers, but the house is too big for me. Having other people here keeps it alive. Jenny's a secretary at a city firm where a friend of mine works, and he put her on to me when I told him I was going to rent out the rooms.' They were back in the living room by now, and Jack fetched a copy of a lease from the drawer of a writing desk. Jenny appeared to have stayed in her seat all the time they had been upstairs, although she did not seem to have been doing anything to keep herself occupied – she was neither watching television nor reading. Now she smiled at Philippa in a welcoming way, and Philippa guessed that Jenny must be looking forward to having another girl move in.

'There are no real house rules,' Jack went on, 'except one. All I ask is that you keep out of the cellar. The door in the kitchen leads to it, and it's usually kept locked, but if you do ever happen to find it open, I'd appreciate it if you resisted the temptation to go down there.'

'Why?' asked Philippa, surprised by the odd request. 'What do you keep down there – dead bodies?'

'Oh no, nothing like that!' Jack apparently saw the humour she had intended in her question. 'No, I've got my photographic equipment down there – it doubles as a darkroom – and I don't want the risk of any accidents with the films and chemicals.'

'Oh, I see,' said Philippa. 'Well in that case I promise never to go near it.'

'Well, that seems to cover everything. When do you want to move in?'

'Would tomorrow be too soon?'

'Not at all. Do you want to come around about the same time? We'll give you a hand with your bags, if you like.'

'That would be good of you. OK, then, tomorrow at seven.'

As Philippa got up to go, Jenny also stood up. 'It's okay, Jack,' she said, 'I'll see Philippa out.' Having said goodbye to Jack, Philippa followed Jenny to the front door. The girl was still smiling, even more so than before. As she held the door open, she said, 'I really am looking forward to having you here, Philippa. It's been just the two of us in this rambling old house for so long. It'll be fun, just you wait and see.'

Not quite sure how she should reply, Philippa just nodded and said, 'Yes, I'm sure it will. See you tomorrow, then.' Jenny closed the door softly behind her, and Philippa walked down the drive, thanking her good fortune that she had finally found somewhere so pleasant to live.

She moved in the following day. She had only two suitcases, so it did not take long. She soon settled in and, over the next two weeks, enjoyed the luxury of cooking her meals as and when she wanted to, as well as having human company to come home to. Jack and Jenny were both delightful to be with, intelligent and chatty without ever imposing themselves upon her, but Philippa was still unable to work out whether or not there was anything between them. Of course, it would be natural for romance to develop if they had lived alone together for so long, but if that were the case, why did they feel the need to hide it from her? Surely Jenny could not regard her as a threat? On the contrary, she had gone out of her way to make Philippa feel at home. Maybe there's nothing going on after all, thought

10

Philippa one night, as she lay in bed. I lived in that village for too long, and so I don't yet know how to read city people, she scolded herself. Sleep was just beginning to overtake her when she was roused by a sound from downstairs. She sat up and listened intently, wide awake now. When she heard nothing more, she lay down and closed her eyes, and just as she did so, she heard it again. This time there was no mistaking what it was – a cry of pain.

She threw back the covers and went over to the door. Opening it a little, she peered into the gloom and listened. When she neither saw nor heard anything, she opened it slowly, then walked out on to the landing.

The house was in darkness. She considered switching on the landing light, but decided not to risk alerting whoever was down there to her presence. Then it came again, a piercing wail. This time she knew for sure that it had come from downstairs, and there had been something else – the cry had been preceded by a swishing blow.

She considered her options. She could call the police. And tell them what? That there were strange noises coming from her living room? The fear of being made to look stupid illogically overcame the fear of whatever was down there. It came again, and this time she definitely heard two separate sounds, that of something being swiped through the air, and the cry which followed.

Fighting to keep her head clear, she decided to rouse the others. Creeping slowly along the landing, trembling as she went, she gently pushed open the door to Jenny's room and whispered her name. When there was no response she called a little louder and approached the bed in darkness, reaching out a hand to wake the girl. When she made contact, however, it was with an empty set of bedclothes, ruffled as if they had been slept in, but empty none the less.

11

Seriously alarmed now, she switched on the bedside lamp. There was indeed no one in the room. Then she heard the noise again. The voice was female. Could that be Jenny down there? If it was, she obviously needed help. Running on tiptoe, Philippa fled to Jack's room. Without bothering to knock, she burst through the door and switched on the main light, opening her mouth to speak – and was met with the sight of another empty bed.

Now she was terrified. She looked around for something she could use as a weapon. Jack's room contained a large Victorian fireplace, and although modern central heating had long since rendered this redundant, a set of fire tools had been kept beside it for ornamental effect. Philippa picked up the silver poker. It was short and quite light, but would be effective enough if she were forced to defend herself.

Thus armed, she crept out of the bedroom and towards the stairs. Just as her left foot reached the top step, she heard the noises again. She paused, but steeled herself against the fear which welled up in the pit of her stomach. She continued down the stairs.

Two more screams had sounded before she reached the hall, growing louder as she got closer. She looked around, her eyes accustomed to the dark now. She saw no lights from any of the rooms. Then she heard another swish, and another yell, and this time she was able to tell where it had come from. Whatever was behind that sound was still beneath her. It was in the cellar.

Gripping the poker tightly, she padded silently into the kitchen. As her bare feet touched the cold lino she shivered but continued. The shriek came again – this time it was blood-curdlingly close, and there was no doubt as to its location. The cellar door was open, and a dim light was creeping up the stairs. No wonder the sounds had carried all the way up through the house.

12

Philippa crouched down, then got on to all fours to approach the entrance, determined not to give herself away. She crawled towards the door, then leant slowly forward to peer down the old wooden stairs, not knowing what to expect – and was hardly able to stifle a gasp when she found the key to the mystery.

There, in the cellar, were her missing flatmates. There was no doubt that it was them, but Philippa could not believe what they appeared to be doing. Jenny was lying across a stool, her toes touching the floor at one end of it, and her hands supporting her weight at the other. Her head hung forward, her long blonde hair obscuring her face. She was quite naked, her medium-sized breasts hanging over one edge of the seat. Her buttocks were in the middle of it, raised above every other part of her body. Her discarded nightdress lay on the floor beside her. She fidgeted, and Philippa heard a metallic clink. Then she saw that Jenny's ankles and wrists were manacled together by silver cuffs. The illumination came from a single light bulb hanging unshaded directly above Jenny. It was a low wattage bulb, lighting only half the cellar. In the background, Philippa could see what appeared to be furniture and objects hanging from the walls, but she could not quite make out what they were.

Behind Jenny stood Jack, but it was not the kind, polite Jack Philippa had come to know. He was wearing a silk robe and slippers, as though he too had been disturbed in the night. In his hand was a long, thin rod like a garden cane. As Philippa watched, he lined it up across Jenny's exposed bottom. She saw the girl squirm at the contact. Then he drew it back level with his shoulder, then brought it forward with a loud crack. Jenny called out, the same yell which had brought Philippa down here. She gasped again, and the couple in the cellar would certainly have heard her had it not coincided with Jenny's cry.

13

As it died away, Philippa looked more closely at the object Jack was using. It had a crook handle just above the point where he gripped it. Suddenly, she understood exactly what it was. She had never seen one in real life before, although like most people she was familiar with the shape and purpose. It was an old-fashioned school cane.

As she watched, Jack reached down with his left hand and stroked Jenny's bottom. She saw her flinch as his palm smoothed over her flesh, which was obviously sore. Then he raised the cane again. He spoke, and although she could not quite make it all out, she was sure she'd heard him say the words 'just one more' and 'reward'. Reward? What on earth could he mean by that? And something else was puzzling Philippa – though Jenny's hands and feet were manacled together, there appeared to be no restraints securing her to the stool itself. She seemed to be bent over it purely of her own volition. What on earth had persuaded her to do such a thing?

The cane swung home again, to be greeted by another cry from Jenny. This time, Philippa believed she could hear relief mixed with the pain. Jack walked over to the wall, where several more canes of various lengths hung in a rack apparently made for the purpose. Jenny lifted her head, and even at the distance Philippa was from the scene, the satisfaction on her face was obvious as she closed her eyes and let out a long sigh.

Jack walked around to the front end of the stool and looked down at Jenny, and Philippa was stunned when the girl smiled up at him. But her disbelief turned to shock at what came next.

Very slowly, Jack opened his robe. He was naked underneath it, and the act of beating Jenny had obviously excited him. Philippa had heard about men who found such things a turn-on, but she could never have imagined him to be one of them. Although she was no virgin, she had only her experiences with Paul with which to compare this. Jack's member certainly looked larger and more powerful, the purple glans already exposed. She switched her attention to Jenny and noticed the girl's smile had turned to a look of greedy anticipation. Jack was stimulating his hard-on with his hand. Without leaving the stool, Jenny reached up and brushed his fingers away, letting her own take their place. Circling the flesh, she moved it back and forth, her hands moving in harmony by necessity, being chained together. Jack's breathing gradually became audible even to Philippa at the top of the stairs.

Jenny opened her mouth and put out her tongue. Philippa instinctively knew what was going to happen, though she could scarcely comprehend that she was about to witness it. The tongue flicked over the tip of Jack's penis, making him shudder. Jenny did it again, three or four times, then began to run it along the entire length of his shaft. Philippa could feel her heart pounding and heard her own breathing becoming intense, but the pair in the cellar were too wrapped up in their little game to have heard any noise she might have made, even if she had got up and walked down the stairs to get a better look.

As it was, she could see quite clearly enough. Jenny opened her mouth and Jack slid his cock inside it. Philippa was mesmerised. She had done this herself a couple of times with Paul, and had not particularly enjoyed it, but Jenny seemed to be performing the task with relish. Jack's hips moved forward and back in a slow, perpetual motion. He raised his face towards the ceiling, his eyes closed and his breath coming in long grunts. One of Jenny's hands was now cupping his testicles, the short silver chain which connected her wrists strained to its limits, and her lips still clamped tightly around the object of her attentions.

Suddenly, Jack's jerking motions became short and

frantic and he let out a long, low moan. Jenny's eyes widened in surprise, and she gripped the base of Jack's cock with both hands, no longer moving it in or out but holding it firmly inside her mouth. Her legs parted as far as the ankle cuffs would allow, then strained against the chain. She swallowed once, twice, then a third time. Jack had come in her mouth.

They stayed almost motionless for at least a minute. Jack ran his hands gently through Jenny's hair, while her cheeks and throat contracted with more slight swallowing motions. My God, thought Philippa, Jenny actually drank the stuff! When she had tried oral sex, she had always taken her mouth away just before Paul had reached his climax – he had at least been good enough to warn her in time. But Jenny seemed to be sucking enthusiastically. How could she, after what Jack had just done to her bottom?

Finally they stirred, and Jack withdrew his now limp penis from Jenny's mouth, its tip painting her chin with a thin trail of saliva as it dropped between his thighs. He closed his robe, then put out a hand to help Jenny stand up, evidently appreciating how difficult it would be for her in the restraints. Philippa realised that they would see her if she stayed where she was, and silently crawled backwards into the middle of the kitchen. Not risking standing up yet, she crawled to the door and then into the hall, then slowly rose to her feet and tiptoed back up the stairs. She closed her bedroom door and waited with her ear pressed against it.

Sure enough, a few moments later, she heard the sound of feet ascending the stairs, and barely audible whispers accompanying them. They passed her door then stopped further along the landing. More intimate words were exchanged, then two doors were opened and closed almost simultaneously. It was only then that Philippa noticed she was still gripping the poker from Jack's room.

Hoping he would not notice and deciding to replace it as soon as possible the next day, she placed it on the floor next to her bed before climbing back in. With a pervert like that in the house, she was not sure she wanted to sleep unprotected anyway – if she could sleep at all, that was.

She lay in the dark for the rest of the night, the images replaying in her mind, time and time again. Why had Jenny not tried to escape when Jack had caned her? How had he got the hand and ankle cuffs on her? Why had she been so willing to perform that disgusting act on him? And what else was in that cellar? It was now obvious that they were having an affair, but why did they need to go down there to make love? Weren't beds far more traditional, not to say comfortable? And what should she do now – say nothing and pretend it never happened, or start to look for somewhere else to live?

The questions turned in her mind almost until dawn, when, emotionally exhausted, she fell into a fitful doze.

Two

The slam of the front door woke Philippa with a start. She rolled over and grabbed her alarm clock. 7.00 – still a quarter of an hour before she usually got up. That must have been Jack leaving – he always made an early start. Jenny would be getting up at about the same time as her. But not today. She could not face Jenny today.

She got out of bed and went to look at herself in the full-length wardrobe mirror, seeking inspiration from her reflection but finding none. All she saw was a confused girl in a white nightdress. She sat down at her dressing table and decided on a course of action for that day at least. She could no more face work than she could face Jenny or Jack, and so she decided to call in sick. That would not, strictly speaking, be a lie – she'd had quite a shock after all. No, she would take the day off and consider the situation carefully.

She waited in her room as she listened to Jenny going into the bathroom, and then downstairs to the kitchen for her morning coffee before leaving for work. Philippa feared that Jenny might be curious about her non-appearance, and that she might come to ask if she was all right, but it seemed that Jenny was in something of a hurry this morning. She had probably overslept because of her exertions last night, mused Philippa darkly.

When she knew she was alone, she left her room and went downstairs. First she tried the cellar door – as expected, it was locked. Still wrapped in her dressing gown she sat and had a cup of tea, having no appetite for food. She called the office, pleading a migraine which she said would make it impossible to concentrate; if it passed she would come in that afternoon. The receptionist was very sympathetic, and said she hoped Philippa would be better soon.

As she put the telephone down, Philippa remembered the poker. It was still in her room, next to the bed where she had left it. Well, she thought, she would never have a better opportunity to return it, and so she went back upstairs.

She opened the door to Jack's room with unnecessary caution, due, she imagined, to a feeling of guilt about invading his privacy. The room was exactly as she had seen it last night, except that the duvet had been thrown back in a typically male attempt to make the bed, and the curtains drawn to allow daylight to spill in through the window. Philippa hurried over to the fireplace and quickly replaced the poker in its slot, bending down to do so. As she was about to rise, she noticed something which had been hidden from her in the gloom of the night.

Under Jack's bed was a large brown cardboard box. Normally, she would have thought nothing of it. Most people kept things under their beds, and a box was a logical item in which to store them. But today was different. After what she had witnessed the night before, Philippa felt she had to know more about her landlord. She thought she had got to know him pretty well, but he had certainly lied to her about what was in the cellar, and arguably with good reason. Well, she might not be able to take a closer look down there, but here was the next best thing. The most likely reason for the box being stowed under the bed was to stop others from seeing its contents. She had to find out what else Jack had to be secretive about. If she rearranged everything just as she had found it, no one would ever be any the wiser. She reached under the bed and pulled the box out.

At first sight there seemed to be nothing unusual about it. She felt its contents move as she hauled it into the centre of the room, and guessed they might be books. The top was not sealed, but the flaps were folded inward. Reaching a finger into the tiny gap in the centre, Philippa pulled them apart and looked inside – and found herself staring at her landlord's collection of pornography.

She was shocked, but by now not surprised. There was a pile of about 20 glossy magazines and half a dozen videos. She picked up the top magazine and studied it carefully. *Spanker's World*, the title proudly proclaimed, above a photograph of a blonde girl in a red minidress, who was bent over the back of a chair. The dress, or what there was of it, had been folded up over her back to reveal her rounded bottom. As with Jenny, down in the cellar, a cane was lined up against the curve of the victim's buttocks. Whoever held it was out of shot. The girl was gripping the chair seat with both hands, her eyes shut and her mouth open in an expression of what appeared to be pain.

Philippa flicked the magazine open to find more photographs of the girl. These showed her tormentor to be a middle-aged man in a business suit. The pictures were arranged to tell the story of how this unfortunate young lady had come to be on the receiving end of such an undignified and painful punishment, while some text underneath them gave a more detailed explanation. She was, it said, a secretary for a building firm, who had typed an estimate incorrectly, telling the customer that the work would be carried out for one thousand pounds, instead of ten thousand. This had so incensed her boss, the man in the suit, that he had threatened her with the sack, unless . . .

So much for fantasies being rooted in real life, thought Philippa. If my boss even dared to make such a suggestion, I would have him up before an industrial tribunal before you could say 'sexist pervert'. But I suppose many men have these weird ideas. She reached down to the next magazine. It was another edition of the same publication, this time describing and illustrating the punishment of an hotel chambermaid caught stealing by the manageress. The maid was played by a pretty young redhead, and the manageress by a brunette, probably in her early thirties. She was depicted placing the girl over her lap and pulling up her black skirt. The maid wore French knickers. What a cute touch, thought Philippa. Within a couple of pages they were around the redhead's ankles, exposing another very shapely bottom to a spanking. Philippa had already gathered that some men liked to smack girls' bottoms, but had never imagined that there were also those who liked to see one girl doing it to another. Well, not only did they exist, it seemed, but Jack – charming, respectable Jack – was one of them.

Philippa carried on flicking through the magazine, and saw the maid gradually stripped naked by the older woman, who then produced a carpet beater and ordered her victim to bend over the office desk. Philippa found the whole scene vaguely comical, as the beater was applied two-handed to the girl's bottom, apparently without her making so much as a token effort to escape, but merely gripping the far edge of the desk ever tighter. The pair were finally depicted with the maid standing in the corner with her hands on her head, while the manageress sat in her chair holding the beater and gloating over her humiliated subject.

Putting the magazine down, Philippa dug deeper into the pile. There were about ten more editions of *Spanker's World*, but beneath them she found something different. *Babes In Bondage* had on its front cover a woman sitting on a sofa in an ordinary-looking room, but she didn't appear to be sitting very comfortably. She was naked and blindfold, and a gag, consisting of some

21

kind of ball, held in place by a strap which went round the back of the head, had been inserted into her mouth. Her wrists were manacled to each end of a long pole resting like a yoke across her shoulders, and another rod was attached to each ankle, forcing her legs apart and leaving her pubic area degradingly exposed.

Philippa was horrified, but also fascinated. She opened the publication and found more pictures of the girl. There was no text, but the images told the story quite adequately. *Emma Jane's Chastisement*, the title of the sequence declared. It was not really clear why she was being put through this ordeal, only that she seemed to be entering into it willingly. She was shown going into a room and reporting to a dark-haired man, who was dressed casually and probably in his mid-thirties. He ordered Emma Jane to strip, and the next two pages showed her doing so. She had long black hair and a very shapely body, with pert but not oversized breasts, and a bottom which swelled voluptuously into firm thighs and slender legs. She could easily earn a living as a glamour model, thought Philippa. Why was she appearing in perverted filth like this?

Once naked, she stood before the man with her hands crossed over her pubic region, looking up at him with apprehension. In the next frame, she had assumed an expression of shock as he held up a pair of silver handcuffs. A turn of the page, and she had been bent forward over the back of the sofa and her wrists were being locked together behind her back. Her eyes were closed, and her mouth was wide open.

The next spread revelled in her helplessness as she hung over the back of the couch. Her head was down, her hair dangling around her face, and her toes were only just touching the floor, so carefully had she been balanced. Then her captor got to work.

He was standing beside her, one hand in the small of her back, the other clasping a riding crop. Next, he was lining it up across her buttocks, then raising it above his head. Over the page, and the whip was landing across her bottom cheeks, her hair flying as she jerked her head in response to the impact.

Her punishment was depicted over the next half-dozen pages. The weals which appeared across her bottom were clear to the reader. The next couple of shots showed the man aiming at the upper part of her thighs. Then he stopped and hauled her to her feet. Either she was a very good actress, or there was real anxiety in her face.

He pointed to the corner, and then she was standing facing it, with her head bowed and her hands still shackled behind her back. A couple of gratuitous images of her punished bottom, her chained wrists resting just above the cleft of her cheeks followed, and then a wide shot of the whole room. The man had obviously been to fetch the rest of his equipment, the yoke and rods seen on the front cover, and now he was pictured beckoning the girl, as she looked fearfully over her right shoulder. The next few shots illustrated the procedure of locking her into the various implements, starting with the yoke and then the pole between her ankles, and finally, as she knelt at his feet, the ball-gag was strapped firmly in place. Then she was back on her feet, and the riding crop was in her master's hand again.

Her master? Hell, thought Philippa, I've only been reading this stuff for a quarter of an hour, and I'm already thinking like these perverts!

He began cropping the girl again, and she stood passively accepting the punishment meted out to her bottom. Then, to Philippa's horror, the girl's breasts became the target. There was no disguising the pain in her face as the tip of the crop made contact with her left nipple. Of course, Philippa had no way of knowing how severe the blow had been, but she knew it did not need to have been very hard in that area for the girl to have really felt it.

Both nipples were dealt with, and then the flesh of the breasts themselves, before he moved to the front of her thighs. Again Philippa shivered as she looked at the marks appearing on the girl's previously untouched flesh, and a close-up of the victim's face showed that her sympathy was not wasted.

Finally, the girl was left on the sofa, the last picture the same as had been used on the cover. Philippa went back to the front page and realised she had not noticed the marks on the girl's breasts and thighs. Poor thing, she thought. She decided against any further investigation of the book, believing she would not find anything more to surprise her in features such as *Manacled Merchandise*, *Lashes For A Lady* or *Paired Up For Punishment*, although a brief examination of the latter showed two naked women chained side by side so that their bottoms protruded for the lash held by a nasty-looking older man.

Philippa turned her attention to the videos, picking out two at random. They were ordinary casettes, the kind used for home taping, as opposed to commercially produced recordings. Each had a hand-written label stuck in its centre. She could not tell if it was Jack's handwriting, but assumed it must be. *Hollywood Special Delivery*, declared one, and *Les Filles Sont Punit*, the other. Her French was basic, but she recognised the words for girls and punished.

Her insides began to churn. On the one hand, she felt fear and revulsion at finding that she had been living under the same roof as a man as strange as this without even suspecting it. But this was tempered with a bizarre tingle of excitement at having uncovered his secret and unlocking a door to his private world. She felt it gave her an advantage over him. She knew, and he did not realise she knew. And she knew about him and Jenny too. Did Jenny watch these films with him before going to the cellar? Philippa needed to know more. That, at least, was what she told herself as she set off downstairs with the tapes.

The VCR in the living room was a new and expensive model, one of Jack's 'little toys', as he called the gadgets he collected. Now she understood why he wanted one which produced such a good picture. Switching the set on, she selected the video channel, then slid the first tape – *Hollywood Special Delivery* – into the machine. She pressed PLAY, and waited as the programme ran through thirty seconds of blank tape. Then it began.

The picture was poor despite the quality of the machine, and the soundtrack was equally bad, just inconsequential background jazz music. The film opened with two women sitting on a sofa filing their nails. They were glamorous, possibly overly so, one a blonde, the other a brunette. After a couple of minutes in which nothing happened, there was a knock on the door and a third woman entered.

She was younger and had straight, chestnut-brown hair, almost the same shade as Philippa's. She wore a uniform shirt and black miniskirt, and a peaked cap. She carried a small cardboard package. 'Delivery girl,' she announced, needlessly.

She handed the parcel to the blonde, who signed a form. As she turned to go, she was called back by the brunette, who pulled out a bank note and gave it to her. The girl looked at it disdainfully, then hitched up her skirt and put it in her stocking top before turning to go once more. As she went she said theatrically, 'Thanks – you cheap dykes!' At that, the blonde leapt up and seized her by the wrist. 'What did you say?' she demanded. The delivery girl protested woodenly, saying 'Get your filthy hands off me, you whore', but to no avail. With the brunette's help she was dragged back to the sofa.

She was hauled, still complaining but not really fighting, over the blonde's lap, and her short skirt was pulled up to reveal her bottom, clad in lacy black panties. The brunette sat at the end of the sofa by the girl's feet. 'Now we'll teach you to insult us,' she proclaimed in a broad Californian drawl, then raised her right hand and brought it down on the exposed bottom. The girl squealed and demanded again to be released. The blonde smacked her other bottom cheek, and the victim howled again. And so it went on, the two older women alternately slapping the girl's bottom. After about five minutes, her knickers were pulled off and discarded, and the punishment was continued on her bare flesh. After another five minutes she was allowed to get up – but only so her tormentors could bend her forward over the arm of the sofa, burying her face in the cushions to muffle her cries. This time the brunette held her still as they took turns to spank her.

Eventually the spanking stopped. The blonde disappeared, while the brunette lectured the girl on her 'terrible behaviour, rudeness and ingratitude', all the time holding her firmly in place. The girl was sobbing by this time, although something told Philippa it was not entirely genuine.

The blonde returned clutching two objects. Philippa peered closely at the screen but was not quite able to see what they were, and so she hit REWIND and FREEZE FRAME. In her right hand the woman held what looked like a table-tennis bat, although it was black. There was no doubt as to the purpose of the article in her left hand. Long, pink and shaped like an erect penis, even Philippa's limited experience allowed her to recognise a dildo.

She stared at the picture for a few seconds, unable to decide whether to keep watching or switch the beastly thing off. She considered the matter for some time before concluding that, as the film had, up until then, been so unconvincing, there was no way that the thing would actually get used. Then she picked up the remote control and pressed PLAY.

26

The blonde threw down the phallus and passed the bat over to her right hand. 'Now we're really gonna teach you,' she said, and took up position on the left hand side of the girl. She rubbed the object's surface over the target area, then raised it above her head, waited about five seconds – for effect, Philippa supposed – then brought it down squarely across the girl's already well-spanked behind. The loud slap which resounded from the television speakers made even Philippa jump, while the girl who had actually received it howled in shock and pain and lurched forward, obviously straining the tight grip of the brunette. But the blonde showed no mercy. She raised the paddle again, and brought it down with the same result. The girl was sobbing now, in between swearing at her captors and begging them to stop.

But they did not – would not – stop. The blonde delivered another four full-blooded wallops before dropping the paddle and taking hold of the girl's arms, allowing her friend to release her grip and pick it up. She took her turn to land six more stinging blows on the wailing girl's posterior, then said to the blonde, 'Hold her still while I get the last surprise ready.'

Dropping the paddle again, the brunette reached under her dress and pulled down her own panties, then picked up the dildo. Only now did Philippa notice that there were straps at its base. The woman carefully stepped into this harness, hitching up her skirt at the front and making sure that the correct part was in contact with her own sex. It was obvious what was going to happen, even though Philippa was barely able to believe it.

The brunette thrust her pelvis forward, nudging the head of the dildo between the girl's cheeks a couple of times. The girl turned to look over her shoulder at this intrusion, and her tear-streaked face assumed an expression of mock horror. 'Oh no!' she pleaded. 'Please don't put that horrible big thing in my cunt!'

'Shut up, you shit!' exclaimed the blonde who was holding her, and then said to the brunette, 'Go on, fuck the bitch!' That was all the brunette needed to hear. She took up position between the girl's parted legs – which, Philippa noticed, the girl made no effort to close – and placed the tip of the false penis at the point where the girl's vagina would be. The view on the screen was by no means graphic and close-up, so when the older woman pushed forward and the dildo disappeared there was no way of telling whether she had actually penetrated her victim. But the delivery girl gave the correct vocal response, moaning in all the right ways.

The brunette moved her hips forward and back in a bizarre imitation of the male sexual motion, while the girl being ravished turned gradually from a protesting victim to a willing participant, demanding passionately the woman 'give it to her'. What a turnaround, thought Philippa. The blonde continued to hold the girl with her left hand, but released her grip with her right and allowed it to steal under her own dress where she obviously began to play with herself. The film ended a few minutes later, with its three stars coming to a very noisy simultaneous climax. Am I really supposed to believe this, wondered Philippa, as the video ran into blank tape once again.

She hit STOP then ejected the cassette. She was about to return it to its home upstairs, when she remembered the second tape, the one with the French title. She reached for it – was there any point in looking at it? It would only be the same vile filth she had just witnessed, but in a foreign language. There was no reason to believe it would be any more convincing than the American rubbish. Or was there? The continentals had the reputation of being more risqué – was their pornography any better than the British or American stuff she had seen so far?

Loading the second tape into the machine, she hit

PLAY once again. As before, there was a minute or so of empty flickering before the opening credits rolled. Then she was greeted by a remarkable sight.

Philippa had been expecting another aimless preamble, setting the scene and telling her why the plot's victim was being punished. Instead she saw two girls, in either their late teens or early twenties, down on all fours and dressed in school-type tunics of navy blue. The camera panned to reveal their skirts pulled up and their knickers down, exposing their round young buttocks and thighs. They were shackled together at the ankles. Suddenly, something flashed into the picture and landed across one of the girls' rumps. She moaned. The object appeared again, this time on the other naked bottom, and Philippa saw it was a riding crop. The camera pulled back to reveal who was wielding it, and she was surprised to find, once again, that it was another woman. This woman was older than the two on the floor, although not by much, and dressed in a black leather miniskirt, a matching bra and thigh-length boots. Her hair was black and cut into a severe bob, lending her an air of authority, in contrast to the victims who wore their hair in girlish ponytails.

The camera angle switched again to show a close-up of their faces as they were punished. Far from writhing in agony, they seemed to be a picture of serene acceptance, to such a point that one turned and gave the other a slow, lascivious, open-mouthed kiss. The sight appalled Philippa, but at the same time she was filled with a strange curiosity. Despite the revulsion she knew she should be feeling, she wanted to know what the hell these women got out of performing in such a lewd tableau.

Having got straight into the action the film continued, allowing no opportunity for the participants – or Philippa – to draw breath. If there was a plot, it was explained, as the action progressed, by the woman

29

wielding the whip, and Philippa's French was not up to anything at this level other than the occasional one-word command barked at the girls being punished. She watched aghast as the drama unfolded.

After giving them a sound whipping, the mistress – Philippa had thought of her as such from the instant she had seen her – allowed them to get up, unfastening the leather cuffs attached to the chains which bound their ankles together. She made them lie on their backs on a sofa, one on top of the other, their legs spread wide and their most private regions humiliatingly exposed. One of them showed the usual thatch of pubic hair, but the other was completely bald and smooth. Philippa had read in more conventional magazines about women who shaved this part of their bodies, but she had never actually seen the result before. It seemed to meet with the older woman's approval, and she stroked the de-pilated pubis gently with her fingertips, crooning what sounded like appreciative words, but her voice became harsher when she moved on to the unshaved girl, and she gave a couple of sharp tugs on the dark curls to emphasise her disapproval.

She left the room and soon returned with a tray loaded with scissors, a safety razor and shaving cream. Surely not, murmured Philippa to herself. But her worst fears were confirmed; without either girl being allowed to get up, the offender was clipped, lathered then shaved smooth.

Philippa sat as though hypnotised, watching this operation with horror, and as she did so she suddenly found her hands beginning to wander. As she saw the poor girl being so horribly treated, she reached under her dressing gown and nightdress. She wore no knickers in bed, a habit she had got into as a semi-rebellious teenager. She found her own curls, and ran her fingers through them reassuringly. Since splitting from Paul she had not been averse to touching herself occasionally, even though she never masturbated as such. She told herself that what she was seeing on the screen was just creating an irresistible urge to make certain that everything she had was intact.

After the shaving the woman left the room once again, but soon returned. As in the previous film she now carried a dildo – a black one this time. But this time she was in no doubt that it was going to be used properly. The girls were still lying on top of each other on the sofa. First, the long dark shaft was inserted into the girl underneath. Philippa watched, astonished, as it disappeared between her parting lips, the skin clinging to it as it went. Then it was pulled slowly out to accompanying moans from the girl, before being forced back in again.

The mistress evidently decided that the girl on top must be feeling left out, because she began manipulating her freshly-shorn vulva with the fingers of her left hand, gently prying the vagina open with her middle and index digits. Meanwhile, her right hand kept up a steady rhythm with the dildo in the other girl's passage, and the mounting cries of both filled the room from the TV speakers.

Maybe it was that noise, or the fact Philippa had unconsciously allowed her fingers to imitate those of the mistress and was getting increasingly carried away with her instinctive reaction to the scene, but whatever it was, it stopped her from hearing the front door opening. She did not hear the footsteps in the hall, nor did she sense the presence of the face which, on hearing the sounds from the living room, had peered cautiously around the gap in the door and smiled at the discovery it had made.

The cries from the TV reached a crescendo as both girls orgasmed, and at the same moment, a familiar sensation passed through Philippa's body. A muscle in her groin began contracting violently, then a warm feeling spread through her vagina and up into the pit of

31

her stomach. Her body tensed and every pleasure zone, from her head down to her toes, seemed to be stimulated at once. Then the sensations died away and she came back down to earth, emotionally and physically drained, but realising for the first time in her life exactly what a self-induced orgasm felt like.

As she slumped down on to her knees before the TV, she pulled her dressing gown completely open and raised her nightdress to just below her breasts. The tape continued to play in front of her, the stern woman now flogging the girls with what looked like a cat o' nine tails, as they hung naked from the ceiling, suspended by their wrists with their feet just touching the ground. Philippa was not interested in their cries for mercy any more; she wanted to see what they had made her do to herself.

She looked down at her crotch. Her first two fingers were still where they had been when she had orgasmed, lodged, up to her knuckles, inside her vaginal passage. She pulled them out slowly, twitching as she stimulated the sensitive blood-filled flesh once again. Her fingers were sticky, covered in her own secretions. She held them up and sniffed them tentatively. The scent was strange; she found it distasteful, but also fascinating because of the intimate nature of its origin. She recoiled at its musky odour, coughing and snorting, disgusted with herself for her own curiosity.

'Don't you like the smell of your own pussy juice? Dear dear, how would you like it if you had to taste someone else's – Jenny's for example?'

Philippa spun around, automatically wrapping her dressing gown tightly around herself. She found herself staring straight at Jack, and felt a deep scarlet blush flood her face. He seemed totally unperturbed, as if he found half-naked girls masturbating in his living room every day. 'Mind you,' he continued, 'Jenny was just the same herself when I started training her, and now you

32

wouldn't believe the things she'll do.' Don't be too sure about that, thought Philippa, though she did not feel that now was the time to discuss it with him. But what had he meant when he had referred to training Jenny?

Completely lost for words, she got up and started moving towards the only escape route she could see. Jack had walked into the room and away from the door, but now he stepped to his right and held up his hands to stop her.

'Where do you think you're going, young lady? I'd like to know how you came to be watching my tapes. I didn't exactly leave them lying around, did I?' Philippa felt herself blush even more deeply, as if the shame of being caught naked and in the act of masturbation had not been mortifying enough. Her mouth opened, but she was not able to say anything. 'So you went into my room and rummaged around until you found them?' Jack filled in her answers for her. No, no, it was not like that, she wanted to say. But she could not. All she could do was lower her head in the deepest shame she had ever felt in her life.

'You only needed to ask if you wanted to see my films and books,' Jack went on. 'That's what Jenny did. And she's not looked back since.' Philippa gasped at the thought. Was this true, or just egotistical male boasting? Jenny seemed like such a nice girl. 'So what do you think of them?' Jack indicated the screen with a nod. She turned to see that the dominatrix was now kneeling and performing oral sex on one of her victims, both of whom were still strung up and crying. She looked back at Jack, horror and confusion written all over her features. 'Pretty strong stuff, eh? I take it you've looked through my magazine collection too? Did they give you any ideas? How about it, Philippa – would you like to atone for your sins with a good spanking?'

His words took some time to register, but then their full meaning struck her. He was proposing that he

33

spank her. She could not believe it. Was this a bad dream? It could not be happening. But his expression showed her just how serious he was. This was rapidly turning into the worst day of Philippa's life, and she was now beginning to remember unfaithful Paul in a more sympathetic light. Finally she found what was left of her voice. 'Get out of my way you – you pervert! I'm going upstairs to pack, then I'm leaving this house, and if you try to lay a hand on me I'll cripple you for life, then call the police!' She swept past him out of the living room, ran up the stairs to her room, and slammed and locked the door behind her. Jack was either taken completely by surprise by her flight, or had never intended to try and stop her, because he made no attempt to do so.

Philippa sank down on to the bed and began to cry tears of shame, shock and relief. Her pent-up emotions came flooding out for about five minutes, before she felt able to act. But what should she do first? Pack? Arrange for a taxi and an hotel? Barricade the door to keep Jack out? She opted for none of these, deciding that the most practical move would be to dress.

She slipped off her dressing gown, and had just pulled her nightdress over her head when there was a knock at the door. 'Go away!' she shouted. 'Leave me alone or I'll scream the place down!'

'There's no need for that,' Jack assured her through the door. 'I just wanted you to know I'm about to call your office.'

'You're what?' Philippa replied incredulously.

'I'm going to call your office,' he said again, 'and ask if I can speak to you.'

'Why? I'm right here. You're talking to me now.' She grasped for some kind of method to his apparent madness. His next sentence provided it.

'I'm going to tell them I'm your landlord, calling from your home – which is true – and that I need to speak to you. I take it you told them you were ill, or something like that? Well, when they repeat that little lie to me I'll say, "That's funny, I saw her leaving the house this morning. She didn't seem ill then. In fact, she was dressed up to the nines, as though she was going somewhere special, not just to work." I wonder what they'll make of that?' And his footsteps trailed off down the landing towards the stairs.

Philippa guessed what would happen if he made that call. There was no question that she would lose her job. She had only been there a month, and such blatant abuse of her employers' trust in her would never be tolerated. And what if she followed him downstairs and grabbed the telephone from him? That would create a scene which would be rather hard to explain, and which would certainly put a question mark over her character. Of course, they might give her the benefit of the doubt, but in order to check, her boss would call her at this number, and how would she get to the telephone to answer it before Jack did?

But she had to stop him from making that call and destroying everything she had worked for, and in order to do that she had to leave her room and risk whatever ambush he might be planning. Pulling her dressing gown back around her nudity, she unlocked the door and ran downstairs.

Jack was in the hall, the receiver in one hand and his personal organiser in the other, open, she presumed, at the page on which he had written her office number, which she had given to him in case of emergencies. He put the book on the table by the telephone and pressed the first button. 'Wait!' she called. He looked up at her and a wicked smile played over his lips. Unable to decide what to do next, she opted to play for time. 'What do you want?' she asked.

'I think you know very well what I want,' he replied. 'You need to be punished – for your invasion of my privacy, for your unauthorised borrowing of my tapes,

35

for playing with yourself, and for lying to your employer. In short, you need a firm spanking, and I want to be the one to give it to you.'

Philippa stood in the hallway, clutching her robe about her even more tightly, as if she were hoping to disappear into its folds. She felt her cheeks burning with embarrassment, in strange contrast to the spreading chill in her bare feet. She ran through the options in her mind. This did not take her long – she did not have that many, and none of them were particularly pleasant. 'OK,' she said bitterly. 'You win. So long as you promise not to call my office. And,' she added, 'I'm out of here this evening, I don't care where I end up staying.'

'I'm sorry to hear that,' Jack replied, 'but if it's how you feel, then so be it. But you must be punished. And once it's done, that's it. I won't rat on you – you have my word as a gentleman.'

Philippa let out a snort of contempt at this remark, and noticed that Jack raised an eyebrow on hearing it. 'So, let's get it over with,' she declared, a challenge in her voice. He might, for all she knew, be intending to humiliate her further, but she was damned if she would give him the satisfaction of seeing her behave like a pathetic little girl. 'How am I going to be spanked? Across your knee, I suppose.'

'However I choose to position you,' he replied curtly, 'and in the living room.' There was no questioning the tone of command in his voice, and Philippa found herself obeying him and walking into the lounge, despite the anger and resentment she felt.

The television had been switched off, and the two tapes now sat next to the VCR. Looking at them she could not help but reflect on how much trouble they had got her into. 'Now,' said Jack, following her into the room. It's very important you answer this question truthfully. Have you ever been spanked before?'

36

Philippa turned on him, shock and rage in her eyes. 'Of course I bloody well haven't! What kind of girl do you take me for?'

'OK, calm down. I need to find that out so I know how hard I can be on you, and since I believe this is your first time, I'll be a bit more lenient than I would usually be. Jenny certainly wouldn't get away with just a smacked bottom for what you did – she'd be getting the cane by now.' Philippa looked away self-consciously, not wanting her eyes to betray the secret she kept about seeing the previous night's events.

'Now – how does one position a complete novice?' said Jack, more to himself than to her. 'It's so long since I spanked a virgin bottom. In fact, I do believe Jenny was the last girl I broke in, and it was in this very room. Let's see, how did I have her? Ah, I remember.' He walked over to the coffee table and cleared the collection of magazines and coasters from its surface, then perched on the edge which faced away from the sofa. He looked up at Philippa and crooked a finger, beckoning her to him.

She swallowed hard and took a deep breath, then began walking towards him. It was only a few steps, but her feet were still none too steady. When she was beside him he took her by her left hand and guided her down over his lap, and she felt the blood rush to her face as well as to her head. Waves of humiliation washed over her, and she closed her eyes to try and block them out.

As Jack clamped his right leg over both of hers, and used his left hand to grip the right side of her waist, his arm resting across the small of her back, Philippa had to suppress a shudder of apprehension. She was beginning to doubt that the spanking itself could be much worse than the build-up to it. Nevertheless, it took her completely by surprise when Jack took the hem of her dressing gown in his right hand and pulled it up over her back. She was, of course, naked underneath it, and

this evidently amused him, as he gave a malicious
chuckle as her bare bottom was exposed to his view.
'Hey! Don't you dare! Cover me up, you bastard!' she
wailed, and began to struggle. But it was no use. Jack
had worked his tactics out perfectly. He had not
touched her clothing until he had made sure she was
completely helpless, held in position by his leg, his arm,
and her own precarious balance. She was trapped and
he could do almost anything he wished with her in this
position.

'Come now,' he chided her. 'You saw the tapes and
magazines. You didn't really expect me to waste my
energy beating the dust out of your clothes, did you? A
traditional spanking is always administered on the
bare.'

The first blow landed, a loud, crisp smack which
echoed around the room as Jack's palm connected with
Philippa's right buttock. At first she thought it was not
as bad as she had been fearing, but half a second later
the pain registered fully. God, it hurt! Had she been
asked, she would have sworn it was the worst pain she
had ever experienced. All the pain she'd felt in the past,
even that which she'd felt on breaking her wrist as a
child, was only a distant memory. This was fresh and
immediate – all she knew now was the burning agony in
her bottom.

A few seconds later, however, Jack took her mind off
it by administering an equally hard slap to her left
buttock. The first blow had come as such a shock that
she had only gasped, but this time she let out a lusty
yell.

Jack was unmoved by it. He laid another slap on her
right buttock, a little higher this time, eliciting another
yell from her. She was wriggling like an eel by now,
desperately trying to shake herself free of his grasp as
the next blow landed on her left cheek. She felt tears
begin to well in her eyes and she knew she was losing

control. What had happened to the iron-willed woman who had been going stoically to accept whatever this pig wanted to hand out?

She tried to pull herself together. As the smacks continued to rain down upon her unprotected rear, she reached forward and dug her fingers into the pile of the carpet, then took a deep breath and concentrated on the pattern in it. For a time it worked; she bit her lip and held back the cries. But it did not take her long to work out that she was being spanked by a real expert, as if she could not have guessed before. His slaps were landing at regular intervals, were all of more or less the same strength, and covered the whole surface area of her bottom. Jack seemed to be taking care not to land a blow on any spot which had already felt his hand, but eventually he would run out of unmarked skin, and would have to return to a part which was already sore. And Philippa did not need to watch any videos or read any magazines to work out how much that was going to hurt.

Gradually the whole area from the top of her bottom cleft to the curve where her buttocks met her thighs was throbbing. She started to find that the pain in the areas which Jack had spanked first was beginning to deteriorate into a tingling sensation, which in comparison to the sting of the slaps he was laying on other parts of her bottom did not feel unpleasant. Her relief, however, was short lived, as it soon became obvious that Jack had covered his entire target area. A brisk smack landed on the centre of Philippa's right buttock, followed by one to her left, and unable to help herself, she threw her head back and let out a long, low moan. By now her tears were flowing freely and, as the spanking continued over her already sore flesh, she wondered for how much longer she could hold back from sobbing out loud. She had already given up on trying to retain any semblance of modesty – at first she had been appalled by the idea of what Jack might be seeing, and had kept her legs clamped tightly shut, but now she did not care any more and let them fall open, as she wriggled and kicked in an attempt to get some relief – any kind of relief – from the pain which scorched her bottom. Her eyes were blurred with tears, and her vision was also obscured by her hair, which was now flying around her head as she finally broke down and wailed like a child throwing a tantrum. But Jack carried on spanking her.

She had no idea how long it went on. Eventually, all she could hear was the rhythmic slapping of his palm on her rear, and her own moans, which sounded to her as though they were being made by someone else. Was it really her? Maybe it was the physical discomfort or the emotional overload of the whole situation, but somehow she seemed to float away from reality.

Finally Jack stopped. At first, Philippa hardly dared believe that her punishment was over and done with, and assumed that he was only taking a break. But he did not start again. Instead, she felt the tail of her robe being replaced over her burning bottom. She winced at the contact of the rough towelling, but was still grateful for the return to decency. She felt him loosen his grip on her waist and raise his leg to free hers, and then found herself being hauled back to her feet by firm hands on her shoulders. Jack stood in front of her, still gripping her shaking body by the shoulders. She could not bear to look at him, but brought a trembling hand up to wipe her eyes, all the while trying to regain some vestige of dignity. Jack spoke, saying the last words she had expected to hear from him at that particular moment. 'Well done. For a first-timer you did very well. It'll be a shame if I never get to deal with that pretty bottom again. Now I'll collect the file I came back home for, then leave you to pack. But if you change your mind, you're more than welcome to stay. You could be a great addition to the household.'

He released his hold on her and left the room, and she noticed that he blew on his right palm and rubbed it against his left as he went. Feeling suddenly dizzy, she sank to her knees then put her head in her hands and began to weep again. Why had she let him treat her like that? What on earth had she been thinking of, backing down so easily? And what was she going to do now?

She heard Jack taking the stairs three at a time, and then the door to his room being opened and closed again. Then, true to his word, he ran straight back down them again and out of the front door, pausing only to shut it behind him. Philippa was alone again. Seeking some kind of security she clambered back to her unsteady feet and sought the refuge of her room and her bed. Completely drained, she passed out rather than fell asleep.

Three

Philippa was woken by an insistent knocking at her door. She struggled back to reality, unable for a moment to remember where she was or what had happened. Then, as she rolled over on to her back, a sudden, sharp pain in her buttocks brought everything back to her.

The knocking came again. She threw back the covers and got to her feet, rubbing her bottom as she did so. The pain was not as bad as it had been, more an insistent ache than actual soreness, but it was enough to remind her of why she needed to get out of this house as soon as possible. Another reminder was the sound at the door. Was it that pervert back for another helping? Well, she was damned if she was going to let him in. He could do what he liked, he was never getting her over his lap again.

When, however, the knocking started again, Philippa noticed it was not the firm, assured sound she would expect to be made by a smug, self-confident bastard like Jack, and the voice she heard when it stopped was certainly not his.

'Philippa?' It was Jenny. 'Philippa, are you still there? Please answer me. I know you must be, the door's locked on your side. We have to talk.' Philippa looked at her alarm clock. She had been asleep for an hour and a half. Should she let Jenny in? Though her anger was directed, for the most part, towards Jack, her feelings

42

towards the other girl were ambiguous. Jenny was Jack's co-conspirator in these kinky games, if what Philippa had seen the night before, and the boasts Jack had made were anything to go by. Unsure of what to do, Philippa said nothing.

'Philippa, please,' said Jenny softly. 'Jack called and told me all about what happened this morning. He said you were threatening to leave, so I took the afternoon off straight away so I could come home and try to talk you out of it. Please let me in, I'm not going away until you do.' Her hands trembling, Philippa unlocked the door.

Jenny stood before her in a black business two-piece and white blouse, her legs clad in black stockings and her feet in matching high-heels. Her long blonde hair hung loose, but neatly groomed, around her shoulders, and her face was a picture of concern as she stood in the doorway. 'Oh Philippa,' was all she said.

Philippa stood aside to let her in, and she walked over to the bed and sat down on the rumpled covers. Philippa followed and gingerly sat down next to her. Jenny took her by the hand, and reached up with her other to wipe Philippa's tear-stained cheeks and sweep her tousled hair back from her face. 'I'm so sorry I wasn't here to help you when it happened,' said Jenny.

'So am I. Together we might at least have been able to make him think twice about imposing his filthy ideas on us.' Philippa realised she had included Jenny in this sentence before letting on that she had seen her with Jack in the cellar, and also that she was suggesting that Jenny had not willingly submitted to being caned. But Jenny's expression did not change.

'Never mind, I'm here now, and I reckon I've got just the thing to make you feel better. When I get sunburn I often put some moisturiser and cold cream on it – do you think your bottom would feel any better if I did that for you?'

You mean when Jack has tanned your hide, thought Philippa, but said nothing. At least Jenny was trying to be kind. Although Philippa's initial reaction was to hide the embarrassing results of her humiliating spanking, she wanted to keep Jenny as an ally. Besides, Jenny was another girl – there was no sexual threat. Philippa smiled and nodded.

'Pull up your robe and lie down,' said Jenny, rising to her feet, 'and I'll go and fetch the stuff.'

When Jenny returned, Philippa was face down on the bed, her bottom on display. Philippa looked over her shoulder to see that Jenny had taken off her jacket and was rolling up her sleeves, a large pot in her left hand. Then she heard the girl let out a gasp as she saw Philippa's rear. 'Oh my God! He really gave it to you, didn't he?' Philippa could only nod in reply. 'Never mind. We'll soon have it cooled down,' Jenny said, and perched on the edge of the bed next to the prone girl, who wriggled aside to give her more room.

Philippa looked ahead, staring at a spot on the wallpaper, trying to forget her acute shame at having to let another person see her in this condition. She heard Jenny unscrew the lid and set it down on the floor with the pot, and was surprised, having expected the girl to start rubbing in the lotion immediately, to feel a pair of dry hands on her bottom cheeks.

'Ooh!' she groaned, as Jenny placed her palms on the crest of each of her buttocks, and moulded her fingers to their shape. 'What are you doing?'

'Don't worry,' answered Jenny, 'I'm just testing to see how sore you are. You really do need something to cool you down, don't you?' Philippa could tell that Jenny's touch was actually very light, and yet it was still causing her sensitised bottom to smart. 'Now, let's see what we can do about it, shall we?' Jenny said, taking her hands away and reaching for the pot of cold cream.

Philippa buried her face in her folded arms to hide the

fact that it was now as red as her backside. A second later and she looked up again, as the sensation of the ice-cold cream on her flesh registered.

Jenny had started with Philippa's right cheek and was gently massaging the cold cream into its crown in a circular motion, all the while moving slowly outward to cover the whole buttock. Philippa sighed as the relief flooded through her, although it made the pain in her untreated cheek seem all the more intense. But that would soon be remedied, she told herself. Jenny was a talented masseuse – probably another little game she played with Jack – but at that moment Philippa did not care. Her bottom was feeling ten times better, and that was all she could be concerned about.

Jenny gave her right buttock three generous helpings of cream, each one smoothed in with the same gentle touch. Then she turned her attention to its neighbour, and the anaesthetic effect was immediate. Philippa sighed, and her eyelids began to droop as she tried to forget everything that had happened earlier that day.

She had slipped into a half-doze and was not really listening properly when Jenny started talking to her again. 'You really do have a fine bottom,' she mused. 'Well, your whole body is gorgeous from what I've seen of it. And Jack obviously enjoyed turning your bum red, even if he was a bit over-zealous. He gets so carried away, you see; he thinks everyone can take as much punishment as I can.'

What was that? Philippa snapped awake. Jenny was actually admitting she did this sort of thing with Jack, and though Philippa had been mortified by her own experience, she was curious as to the nature of Jack and Jenny's relationship. So she said nothing as Jenny went on.

'I guess it must have come as something of a shock to you when you found out about our little games, but they're quite harmless really. Oh sure, they hurt at the time, sometimes they hurt a lot – you've no idea how painful a caning can be – but the excitement and adrenaline rush feel so good, I just couldn't give them up now.'

Philippa could hear her own breathing becoming deeper. Was she getting excited by the details of this woman's sex life? Already, she could not believe what she was hearing, and yet she was desperate to find out more.

'My introduction to corporal punishment came from Jack too,' Jenny went on, as she continued to rub the slippery ointment into Philippa's bottom, now using both hands, one on each cheek. 'It was about three months after I moved in, when just the two of us lived here. I've never been terribly good with cash, and well, one month I managed to spend the money I should have used to pay the rent on other things. I didn't think Jack would mind that much – after all, he doesn't have to pay a mortgage on this place – so I asked him if I could give it to him the following month. He was very sweet and agreed, but of course the next month I couldn't find one month's rent again, let alone two. He gave me another month, but I suppose he must have realised I'd never be able to catch up. When I owed three months' worth he told me things couldn't go on like this, but that he didn't want to lose me as a lodger since we got on so well. I thought he was going to let me off the debt altogether, but no, he had quite a different idea. He told me I could pay it – in a rather unusual way.

'At first I thought he meant he wanted me to have sex with him, and I'm not sure I would have refused – I mean, he's a good looking bloke, isn't he? I'd often wondered why he didn't have a girlfriend. Then he explained that he wanted me to pay the back rent with my bottom – I couldn't believe the way he came straight out with it! He proposed a spanking, followed by a caning – six strokes for each month I owed, eighteen in all. I was stunned, as you can imagine, but I didn't say no straight away. He let me think about it for a couple of days, and I soon decided it was a price worth paying. I'd realised how much I enjoyed living here, and how much I liked Jack despite his outrageous suggestion, and that at the end of the day all I would have would be a sore bottom and no more debts. I also knew that if I decided not to take the punishment I would have to move out, find somewhere else to live, and still have to pay Jack the back rent. The spanking and caning seemed the simpler option, and I even managed to convince myself that it would buck up my ideas when it came to handling money!

'So I told Jack I'd go for it, so long as he promised it would just be between us, and that he would do no more to me than he had told me he would. He agreed, adding that the punishment would be on the bare – and it wasn't hard to work out what he meant by that! I was a little worried about this – it honestly hadn't occurred to me that he'd want to take my knickers down – but he promised it would be no more than was strictly necessary. I agreed, and we set a time and date – that Friday, three days away, at 7.30 in the evening.

'I'll happily admit that I was pretty nervous throughout the following three days. Sometimes I'd get jittery at work, when I suddenly remembered what was going to happen to me. I'd be sitting at my desk, and would surreptitiously slip my hand down to feel my bottom, wondering if I'd be able to sit down again by Monday. But those butterflies in my stomach were also a little exciting, and I found the tension quite stimulating. I was dreading the pain and the humiliation, but at the same time, I could hardly wait to get on with it. I still think Jack deliberately set the date for a couple of days ahead so that I'd get wound up about it, even though he reckons he chose the Friday because he knew I wouldn't have to go to work the next day, and therefore wouldn't

47

have to explain why I was so stiff and sore. But even now, he sometimes keeps a punishment hanging over me for a few days just to build up the dramatic tension. It's delicious, believe me!'

Philippa found herself wondering silently how many times Jenny had been punished in the weeks since she had arrived.

'Anyway,' continued Jenny, 'Friday came. I was in a bad way at work all day, making mistakes with my shorthand, and totally unable to concentrate on my typing. I was glad when five o'clock came, even though I knew I was going to be getting a very sore bottom. It's funny – like so many girls, I must have fantasised about it sometimes, but now that I was facing the reality I wasn't sure what I felt most, fear or excitement. I got home before Jack did, as I usually do since I leave work earlier. As you know, I normally have something to eat and then get ready to go out or plan an evening's TV, but tonight was different. I'd cancelled all my other plans and I really had no appetite. I was mad with nerves, and wondering if I should change my clothes. Jack hadn't mentioned wanting me to wear anything special, and I was wary about dressing too sexily – I didn't want to look like I was trying to lead him on. On the other hand, it's against my nature to look sloppy, so I decided to stick with my office clothes. At least, wearing them, I could pretend I was keeping some kind of control.

'I sat in my room to begin with, then thought how much more embarrassing it would be to be called downstairs for my punishment. So I went and sat in the living room, trying to read a magazine, and trying even harder to compose myself, but actually fidgeting and getting more and more agitated as time went by.

'Eventually Jack arrived. It was 7.15, a good hour after he usually gets in. He said his train had been delayed, signal failures at Clapham Junction and so on, but I suspected he'd deliberately left his office late to turn me into a nervous wreck. Anyway, he was here now and almost ready to begin my punishment, but first he was going to make himself a cup of tea – can you believe that? But that is exactly what he did. I asked him what he wanted me to do, and he said nothing yet, it wasn't 7.30. I just had to be on time for my spanking!

'As you can imagine, I was in a bit of a state by then. He went through to the kitchen to make his tea – I declined the offer of a cup, by the way – leaving me to get even more worked up. It was clear that he was going to stick religiously to the rules he'd set, and I suppose that I was grateful to him for that.

'All I could do was sit and wait for him to come back, watching the minutes tick by on the mantelpiece clock, checking it against my watch. Honestly Philippa, I've never known ten minutes move so slowly. But eventually the time came. At precisely 7.30, the door opened and Jack appeared. He'd taken off his jacket, but was otherwise still perfectly dressed for a day at the office. In his right hand there was a thin, whippy-looking stick, about two-and-a-half feet in length. I'd never seen anything like it before, but guessed what it was straight away – the cane he was going to use on me.

'He looked at me with a stern, unflinching expression. "Well now, Jennifer," he said, "are you ready for your punishment?" Jennifer? No one had called me that since I was eight. I was about to ask him what he meant, but he was clearly in no mood for frivolity. "Stand up," he ordered. "It's time for you to get your just desserts." Well, I'd consented to participate in this little scenario, so I just went along with it.

'I got up, looking at the floor, with my hands clasped anxiously in front of me. I must have looked the perfect image of a contrite schoolgirl, which I suppose was what he was hoping for, since it inspired him even more. "You know why you're here, don't you Jennifer?" he asked.

' "Yes Jack," I replied meekly, hoping that if I convinced him that I was sorry enough, he'd be more lenient with me.

' "Did I give you permission to call me Jack?" he asked, with a kind of sneer in his voice. "For the duration of the punishment it's *sir* at all times. Is that clear?"

· ' "Yes, Jack – I mean, yes, sir," I whimpered. Now I'm not exactly inexperienced, and I'd tried a couple of role-playing games with some of my previous boyfriends, but I'd never taken that kind of thing too seriously. Jack, though, was clearly completely absorbed in the character he wanted to be at this moment, some kind of headmaster or authority figure, and he wanted me to be the subservient little girl. OK, I thought, if that was what he wanted, that was what he was going to get. And I'd be the best submissive partner he'd ever had!

'He told me to stand in the middle of the room then walked around me, lecturing me about my inability to balance my housekeeping and find the money to pay the rent, and telling me, as he insisted on putting it, that it simply wouldn't do. As he did this, he also shook his cane for emphasis, so the tip vibrated with a slight swishing noise. That frightened the life out of me, I can tell you, but I had no intention of giving in, having come this far. I kept my eyes lowered and my hands together, answering with the occasional "Yes sir" or "No sir" as and when I was required to. I'd expected him to begin the punishment right away, and had been looking forward to finally getting on with it, but, to be honest, this stay of execution was turning me on because of the heightened anticipation. Finally, though, Jack decided I'd been verbally castigated enough.

' "I think it's about time I gave you your lesson, don't you?" he finished. "Upstairs, to your room." To my room! He'd said nothing about that. At least the living room was neutral territory. I opened my mouth to object, but he was one step ahead of me. "It'll be much more cosy in there. Anyway, didn't you know it was the custom a hundred years ago to punish naughty girls in their bedrooms to save their blushes from the rest of the household?" Quite who he thought he was saving my blushes from I wasn't sure, and of course I had no way of knowing whether or not he was making the whole thing up – did you know he did history at university? – but I could see that there was no point in arguing. Anyway, what difference did it make which room he caned me in – it was still going to hurt. I turned around and walked into the hall, then climbed the stairs.

'He followed at about five or six paces behind me holding the cane in front of him as if to let me know that he was ready to use it if I decided to turn around and make a run for it, even though that was the last thing I was going to do. We reached the door of my room, and I opened it and stood aside to let him in. I always make an effort to keep it tidy, and at that moment I was very glad that it was presentable, not only because it saved me the embarrassment of Jack seeing a complete mess, but because I honestly believed he would have used it as an excuse to give me a harder spanking or caning.

'As I closed the door behind me I could see him glancing round approvingly. I just stood by the door waiting for his next orders, which he soon gave to me. He pulled the straight-backed chair which I use with my writing-desk into the space in the centre of the room, hung the cane by its crook handle on the back of it, then sat down.

'It was the moment of truth, the one I'd been dreading for three whole days. He asked me if I'd ever been spanked or caned before.' Philippa thought back to that morning, when she had been asked the same question, but she said nothing. 'I told him that I hadn't, and he said I'd been very lucky in avoiding corporal punishment for so long, as I was so obviously in need of a good dose of it. 'Anyway,' Jenny went on, 'Jack beckoned me to him and I walked over with as much dignity and composure as I could muster.

'Taking my left wrist, he pulled me over his lap in one go. One second I was on my feet, and the next I was lying across his knees, my bottom thrust up at him, and my hands spread on the carpet in front of me. My head swam as the blood flowed into it. My toes were only just touching the floor on the other side of his legs, and I definitely remember thinking I would have been more comfortable if I'd taken my shoes off – what a ridiculous thing to think when you're about to have your bottom smacked, eh?' Once again Philippa said nothing, but mused on the crazy and apparently random notions which had gone through her head when she had been in the same position a few hours earlier.

'I felt him smooth his right hand over my bottom,' Jenny continued, 'while his left went across my back just above my waist, presumably to hold me in place, although I had no intention of getting up and making a run for it – not at that stage anyway. Then he took the hem of my skirt in his right hand. I'd prepared myself for this, but it still took me by surprise, and I was pretty embarrassed when he lifted it and folded it back. I was down to my knickers and hold-up stockings, and I knew my panties wouldn't be in place for much longer. I expected him to remove them straight away, so when his hand left my bum I was a little surprised and had no idea what was about to happen.

'I soon found out; his hand landed with a crisp slap on my bottom through my knickers. I squealed with shock more than pain. My first proper hand spank, and he hadn't even warned me it was coming! The second soon arrived, landing on my left cheek after the first had hit the right. I know now he wasn't smacking me as hard as he could have done, and of course my cotton panties gave me some protection. But it still began to

52

smart like hell as he carried on whacking me about every two seconds. I struggled to keep control. The pain was not unbearable – we girls have quite a high pain threshold, you know – but it was the indignity of being in this position which caused me more distress. Then again, I'd made the decision to let him spank me, and I was determined to see it through to the end.

'He carried on spanking me for about two or three minutes I guess, then stopped and allowed me to get myself together. When my breathing had become normal again, and I'd stopped wriggling, he spoke: "Now, Jennifer, that's got you nicely warmed up, so I believe we can move on to the serious business." I knew what this meant and I shivered a little. My panties, already damp with perspiration, were peeled back from my skin, and pulled halfway down my thighs. Suddenly my bottom, which was rather sore from the walloping I'd already received, felt very exposed and vulnerable, and hard though it was for me to believe it, the feelings of embarrassment and apprehension were definitely beginning to turn me on!

'His hand smoothed over my cheeks again, this time making me sigh in pain as his palm rubbed my sore flesh. Then he took it away, and I knew my punishment was about to begin in earnest. I closed my eyes and held my breath.

'There was a loud crack as he slapped my right buttock. I didn't realise quite how much protection my knickers had afforded me up until then – it stung like hell on my naked skin. Then he smacked my left buttock, and I howled out loud. But he was deaf to my shouts, and just spanked my bare arse for some time. I'm not sure how long this went on for – well, I bet you didn't keep time when he was doing that to you, did you? – but it must have been at least ten minutes. The slaps became gradually harder, too, although I stopped feeling them so much as my backside got more numb.

53

'Eventually, I convinced myself I could take no more, and was starting to consider ways in which I might struggle free from his grasp and escape from the house, even if it did mean having to find a new home. But then he stopped. In between my sobs I heard him above me. It sounded like he was rubbing his palms together and breathing almost as heavily as I was. "There's no question that your bottom's warmed up now, Jennifer," he said in his authoritarian tone, "I think you've earned yourself a little break before you get your caning," and he pulled me back up on to my feet just as easily as he'd placed me across his lap.

'I reached down to hoist my panties back up, but stopped when a sharp slap landed across the back of my left thigh, making me cry out again.

' "Now, now, I didn't say you could pull them up, did I?" he scolded.

' "No, Jack," I said, then "Ooh! I mean, no, sir!" as my right leg was slapped for the second mistake. He walked around behind me and tucked the hem of my skirt into the waistband, then came back round to face me again.

' "Just to make sure you don't forget this is a punishment session, I think you'd better go and stand over there with your hands on your head," he said, and pointed to the corner of my bedroom nearest to the door.

'I couldn't believe it. He was actually telling me to stand in the corner. He might have been acting out some fantasy of treating me like a naughty schoolgirl, but this was taking things a bit too far! I stared at him in disbelief, with my mouth wide open, but not a flicker of doubt crossed his face. He really expected me to do it.

'So what else could I do, Philippa? I hobbled over to the corner, my legs sore and stiff and my clothes all over the place, and, of course, my bottom on display, and took up the position. I linked my fingers together and placed my palms on the top of my head. I'd honestly never felt so terrible in my entire life, and yet there was something else, something I couldn't quite put my finger on. Often during sex I'd taken control of my men, just like all the women's magazines say you should, telling them what I wanted, and even tying one poor bloke to the bed! I was usually disappointed when they couldn't deliver exactly what I was looking for. Now this wasn't strictly speaking a sexual situation, but I was certainly getting the same kind of adrenaline kick out of it, without having to work to get it. Jack was in total control. He was the one who was having to make the effort, and having to keep me on my toes, so to speak. And on another level, away from the pain and humiliation, I was beginning to find the whole idea incredibly exciting.

'My embarrassment eased slightly when Jack left the room. I heard him go downstairs towards the kitchen, presumably to make himself another cup of tea, and I used this opportunity to take my hands down from my head and rub my aching bottom. I'd been dying to do this since being allowed to stand up, but thought Jack would disapprove, and as it turned out, I was right.

' "What the hell do you think you're doing, Jennifer?" he said, suddenly. I looked round. I had been so engrossed in what I was doing I hadn't heard him come back. "Were you given permission to rub your bottom?" I didn't answer. "Well, were you?"

' "No, sir, I wasn't," I finally managed to say meekly.

' "So why are you doing it?" he asked sarcastically.

' "Because it hurts so much, sir," is all I could manage.

' "Well, at least the punishment is having an effect," he said, more to himself than to me. "Ordinarily, that little crime would merit three across each palm with the cane." I gasped, but was relieved when he went on, "But since this is your first session with me, I'll allow you some grace." So he had a heart after all, I thought. "I'll just add two to the total you'll receive on your bottom, one for each hand. That makes twenty, I think." Maybe I'd been right in assuming he didn't.

'I didn't think to argue. All I was able to do was put my hands back on my head and turn my face to the wall again. I heard Jack walk to the chair and unhook the cane, and then I heard a couple of loud swishes which I took to be practice swings. The sound made me jump and gave me butterflies. My sore bottom twitched in dreadful anticipation. Was he going to make me wait much longer?

'Fortunately, or unfortunately, depending on how you look at it, he seemed as eager to get on with it as I was. "Jennifer," he barked, "come here." The time had arrived.

'On very unsteady legs, I went to him. I didn't take my hands away from my head. I'd learnt by now that I wasn't to do anything unless I was told to. I looked at the chair and assumed that I'd be ordered to bend over it at any second. Jack saw me look at it, but he had other ideas. "I think you'll be a lot more comfortable on your bed, don't you?" he said. I looked at him, completely lost for a moment. "Just go and lie face down on it, with your legs over the end and your bottom raised as high as you can." Well, his orders were pretty specific, so I tried to obey them to the letter. I took the two or three steps to the bed, which was in the corner of the room furthest from the door, and stretched out on it as gracefully as I could in my state of undress. He came and stood behind me. He tapped the inside of my left thigh with the tip of the cane, and told me to open my legs a little further. I did so, aware of just how much I must be putting on display in this lewd position, but my senses had been sharpened to such an extent it was honestly the last thing I had to worry about.

'Jack took hold of my panties and eased them down

56

until they were just below my knees. I noticed that he took his time with this straightforward task, arranging my frillies with undue care, and probably enjoying what he saw while he was doing it. When I was displayed to his satisfaction, he stood back and took what I assumed to be a gloating look at me, his victim.

'I must have seemed delicious to him – vulnerable and submissive, but not really afraid he'd hurt me any more than he'd told me he would. I buried my head in my arms. In my helplessness, it was all I could think of to do. Then I felt the cane being lined up across my bottom.

'I flinched when the wood touched me, but with a supreme effort of self-control I steadied my limbs and prepared to meet my fate. I was going to take it like a man, if you see what I mean. The cane was lifted from my buttocks, and I held my breath as in my mind's eye I saw it being raised up behind Jack's head. Then I heard a high-pitched whistle, and it bit home.

'It landed squarely across my buttocks, scoring a streak of pain which it took me a fraction of a second to fully register, but when I did, I did so with a vengeance. "Ouch! That bloody well hurt!" I yelled, unable to help myself. I clutched both hands to my bottom and rolled over on the bed.

'Jack didn't react to that straight away, he just waited patiently as I wriggled and squirmed, flexing the rod in his hands. When I'd calmed down enough to look at him, he just said coldly, "I'll allow you that one, but if you move again during the rest of the punishment I shall add another one, then two for the next offence, then three for the third, and so on. Resume your position, Jennifer." Was this really my gentle-natured easy-going landlord? I could have refused, but any fight I'd had in me before was long gone by now. I just rolled back into place and took my arms away.

'Once again, I felt the cane being positioned against

my bottom, a little above where I could feel the sting left by the first stroke. Then it was drawn back, and then a few seconds later there was that horrible swishing noise again, and it landed almost exactly on the spot he'd been aiming at. I cried out again, tears beginning to run down my face, but I didn't dare try to move. The threat of more than twenty strokes had seen to that.

'Honestly, Philippa, I don't know how I did it. He went on caning me at about five- to ten-second intervals, and each time the bite seemed to get worse. Even though my whole bottom still ached from the spanking I'd had, the sting of the cane was something different. It felt like a fire was being lit in my arse at every whack, and though he tried to land each blow on a different part of it, they sometimes crossed over a previous one, making the pain at that particular point so much more intense.

'I tried to detach myself from what was happening, but that can be difficult when someone's caning you like there's no tomorrow. In the end I heard my screams – and believe me, I did scream – as if they were being made by someone else, but there was no way I could pretend it was someone else feeling the bloody thing. I hadn't been told to count the strokes out loud – I later found out that was something else I was let off doing because it was my first time – but I ticked each one off in my head as it was laid on me. We got to nineteen – one more to go, and *boy* did he make me wait for it. He must have left it a good fifteen seconds, I reckon, but when it finally landed, it made up for lost time. It was a real corker, and landed almost exactly across the line of the first. It was too much. I didn't try to get up, even though the caning was over as far as I could count. I just fell apart and buried my face in my hands, crying my eyes out, and, perverse as it may sound, pushing my bottom out even further.

'But Jack had finished with me. He didn't say anything, he just walked away from me – he'd caned enough girls to know that you leave them alone after the first time. He went out and closed the door, then I heard him make his way downstairs, leaving me alone with my churned-up feelings and a very sore bottom.

'Standing up very gingerly, I wiped the tears from my eyes then, without bothering to pull my knickers back up or lower my skirt, I stumbled to the mirror on the wall to see how much of a mess had been made of my make-up – what a typically female thing to worry about, eh Philippa? Then I took a look to see what damage had been done to my rear end.

'I turned my head as far as I could, raised my right arm, and looked back under it. I could see a glowing redness at the upper edge of my bum, but nothing really substantial. I don't have a full-length wardrobe mirror in my room, so I decided I would have to take the wall mirror down. I did this very carefully – the last thing I needed was seven years' bad luck and another excuse for Jack to cane me – and propped it up against one side of the fireplace. It was a round one, not particularly heavy or large, but big enough for my needs at that moment. Angling it upwards, I turned and crouched down a little. Then I looked behind me again, and was appalled at what I saw.

'My whole bottom was one deep scarlet blotch. As you can see I'm very fair-skinned, so I suppose it showed up all the more, but there was no denying he'd done a good job. Against this background, there were some even darker marks, clear lines criss-crossing my cheeks. If I'd had time I could probably have counted each of these and come up with twenty, but I wasn't really in the mood to do that. I ran my hands gently over the skin, wincing but gradually kneading them a little harder, as this seemed to bring some relief. I sighed, moaning occasionally, whenever I rubbed too hard. I closed my eyes and took several deep breaths. This must have been why I didn't hear Jack returning.

' "They always want to look at their stripes," he said.

"It doesn't matter if it's their first caning or their hundredth." I opened my eyes and stood up, dragging my panties up to cover my shame. "I thought you might like some of this," he went on, holding up a bottle of baby lotion. "It's OK, the punishment's over. This is your reward for being such a good girl and taking it so obediently." I didn't know whether or not to believe him, but he'd been nothing but honest with me up until then, so I gave him the benefit of the doubt. "I think we'll both be happier on the bed," he said, and sat down.

'Uncertainly, I went over to him, my clothing still a mess. He looked up at me and patted his lap. I wondered if this was some kind of trick, but then I decided it wasn't, and in any case, I thought, my bum couldn't possibly get any more sore than it already was. For the second time that evening I laid myself across his knees, and this time he went out of his way to make sure I was comfortable, letting me rest my legs upon the mattress and my arms and head upon the pillows. I was lying practically flat, save, of course, for my bottom, which was sticking up in the air.

'Then I felt a generous squirt of baby lotion being squeezed on to my left buttock. It was cold and so I shivered a little at first, but it doused the fire in my arse almost immediately, which felt so good I just wanted more of it – I'm sure that you can appreciate what I'm talking about. Gradually, Jack smoothed the lotion over my entire bottom. He'd probably put the bottle into the freezer as soon as he'd got in, the stuff was so cold, and it was just what I needed. I lost myself so completely that at first I didn't notice where he was putting his fingers, but I opened my eyes with a start when I felt a gentle prod against my pussy lips.

'I know what you're thinking. I should have jumped up there and then, slapped him round the face, and marched out of the house announcing that I was going to have him arrested for indecent assault at the very least. But to tell you the truth, Philippa, I was actually enjoying it. I was finding the gentleness of his touch both soothing and exciting.

'He must have taken my passive acceptance as a green light, because he then slid his first two fingers a good inch into my cunt, which was moist but not wet, if you know what I mean – oh, you must know what I mean, Philippa!' Philippa started as Jenny administered a playful slap to each of her buttocks, but then, to her surprise, she felt a conspiratorial smile begin to steal across her face. 'The room suddenly became totally silent,' Jenny went on, 'except for the sound of his hand moving in and out of the cleft between my buttocks, and my breathing becoming more intense as he sped up little by little. He increased the tempo at just the right pace – I couldn't have timed it better myself. A lot of men will just ram their fingers in up to the knuckle without giving you a chance to get used to it, but he wasn't like that. He rubbed rather than shoved, and took his time before moving on to the magic button.

'By the time he finally got around to playing with my clitoris I was panting heavily, my fists screwed up and my bottom twitching like I had Saint Vitus' Dance. It's just as well that he was holding me by the waist again with his other arm, or I would have fallen on the floor. He rolled my little bud between his fingers, not roughly but incredibly lightly, giving me the most delicious sensations. You know how it is when you're playing with yourself and you're on the brink, so you ease off and do it just enough to keep yourself there?' It was obviously a rhetorical question, and in spite of herself, Philippa nodded and muttered, 'Uh-huh'. What the hell did it matter what she said? They were all girls together as it were, and she would soon be leaving this house anyway. So what if Jenny thought she masturbated regularly? The fact that Philippa's first real experience of it had been a couple of hours ago was none of Jenny's concern.

'It was amazing,' the blonde girl went on. 'I didn't think anyone else could do that to me, finger me like he knew exactly what I was feeling, almost as if he had a psychic link with me. He did it, though; Jack kept me on the edge for as long as he could. It could have been ten minutes, fifteen or even twenty, but it went on until I could physically stand no more. I started sobbing, and as I orgasmed all sorts of thoughts rushed through my head. In my mind I could see myself lying across his lap, with his fingers buried deep inside me. Then I saw myself over his knee in the middle of my room getting my bottom smacked, and then over the end of the bed being caned, as if the last hour was replaying itself just for me. And I couldn't believe how turned on I was getting. Even after I had come down from my climax, I was still experiencing some of the most intense feelings I had ever known.

'For a long time I just lay limp, totally spent. I rested my head on my arm and only moved when my neck got too stiff. Jack had taken his fingers out of my pussy by then and was gently stroking my buttocks. The first thing I noticed when I lifted my head was how the pain in my bottom had become nothing more than a throb. It was insistent, and when I moved it still burnt a little where I guess I had cane stripes, but overall, the feeling was more of a tingle which I actually found rather nice. At the time I assumed this was all part of the afterglow you get from really good sex, but now I know it was more than that.'

Philippa suddenly realised that she knew exactly what Jenny was talking about, and she told her so. 'You're right,' she said, 'my bum doesn't hurt as much now as it did before you put that stuff on.'

'It's good, isn't it?' said Jenny, smoothing another dollop on to each cheek then rubbing them simultaneously in opposite circular motions. 'But it won't make you feel anything like as good as this will.' Philippa was puzzled for a second, then a shock wave hit her. Jenny was beginning to finger her!

At first she did not want to believe it was happening, but after a couple of seconds she was left in no doubt. Jenny's right index finger had burrowed furtively into her vagina, and was wriggling about inside it. Philippa looked around at her, her face a picture of shock and astonishment. She wanted to say something, but found herself speechless. She wanted to do something, but was unable to move. For whatever reason, and there was none she could think of at that point or even after the event, she did not try to move Jenny's hand away.

As Philippa turned her head, Jenny's left hand reached up to clasp her shoulder. 'Now, Philippa, don't struggle. Just relax and you'll get far more out of it. I can't promise to be as good at it as Jack, but if one girl doesn't know how to please another there's no hope for any of us, is there?'

'Jenny – please – let me go,' Philippa finally managed to whisper hoarsely. But her heart was not in it. She remembered what she had done to herself in the living room, what Jack had seen her doing. Before his interruption that had felt good. Now this felt twice as sweet, mainly because it was not her hand doing the dirty work. But she was still fighting the feelings of guilt which had held her back all her life, those which she had had to overcome when she'd first started seeing Paul, and then when she had applied for the job which had brought her here. She had fought them all her life, and she was still fighting them. Even now, something was telling her it was wrong to allow someone to do this to you, and even more wrong if that person was another woman. But as the warm sensation in her groin grew and spread, none of it seemed to matter for this one moment in time. She buried her face in the pillow and tried to relax her limbs.

This proved an impossible task, because of the frightful state of agitation Jenny's manipulation was putting her body into. The girl worked quickly, tickling her clitoris for a few moments, then resuming the in-and-out motion a penis would use, stimulating the walls of her canal, then returning to the centre of her sex. The result was inevitable and fast. Philippa closed her eyes and gritted her teeth, her fingers clawed into the pillow, and her breath hissed out her release. It was not as intense an orgasm as she had experienced in the living room, but it lasted a little longer and she was able to enjoy it all the more. For a few seconds she forgot where she was and who she was with, and just sank into the bed, feeling the tension flood out. Her bottom was still rudely exposed but she did not care. All she was aware of was how good her second climax had felt.

Jenny withdrew her fingers as soon as Philippa stopped twitching, and then Philippa felt the girl's hands on her shoulders, pulling her up into a sitting position. Her head swam as she raised herself up, but it cleared in a few seconds, and she perched on the edge of the bed next to Jenny. Jenny put her left arm gently around her, giving her a sisterly hug. 'Now you're just like me,' she murmured, and she leant over and kissed Philippa on the forehead, then stood up and walked out, leaving a very confused girl alone with her thoughts.

Jenny closed the bedroom door behind her and crept silently down the stairs, and when she went into the living room she took care to shut that door too. Jack handed her a drink. 'How did you get on?' he asked.

'Famously,' replied Jenny, taking a large sip of the brandy he had given her. 'I think I planted a seed in her pretty little head. But did you have to spank her so hard the first time?'

'Cruel to be kind, Jenny – you of all people should know the value of that. How did she like your little story, by the way?'

Jenny sidled up to him and circled his waist with her right arm. They kissed deeply before she whispered her answer. 'She loved it. Just like you said she would.' Their glasses clinked and they kissed again.

Four

Philippa had no appetite that evening so she stayed in her room, which also suited her plan to avoid Jack. She feared the prospect of having to look Jenny in the eye, too, and so she left getting up for work until a little later than usual the next day. After the previous day's events she thought it best that she go in, if only to take her mind off what had happened and to avoid any awkward questions about a prolonged absence. As it was, all she got were a few concerned enquiries which were quickly and easily dealt with.

All the same, she found it hard to concentrate, due to the soreness lingering in one or two parts of her bottom, towards the centre, where Jack had spanked her hardest. And every now and then, even when she was performing the most mundane of tasks, she would be aware of a vague memory of the soaring ecstasy which had exploded through her vagina and caused her legs to tremble.

And there was something else. She found herself looking at other women in the office, women she had seen every day for weeks, and to whom she had not previously paid any real attention. Now, though, she began to wonder what they looked like underneath their smart, starchy office clothes. She could not understand it.

She was honestly able to say that she had never previously had any sexual feelings towards another woman, regardless of the fact that she had read in numerous magazines that most women did at one time or another. Maybe it was seeing the girls in the videos, or perhaps her intimacy with Jenny, but now it was different. She did not feel any attraction to them as such, she was just curious as to what shape their bottoms were, or how they would look bending over. Would they look anything like she had looked? Would their buttocks turn the same colour if they were smacked as hard as hers had been? She could not drive these images from her mind, no matter how busy she tried to make herself.

That evening, she caught her usual train home and walked back from the station. As she reached the drive, she noticed that Jenny's Mini was in its place beside the garage. She assumed that Jack's car would be inside the garage, but this did not necessarily mean that either of them was home as, like her, they commuted by rail during the week.

She slid her key into the door as quietly as she could, hoping to slip in unnoticed, and was at the foot of the stairs and congratulating herself on succeeding when she heard Jack's voice calling her from the doorway of the living room.

She turned around, uncertain as to what attitude she should take with this man, who had so cruelly assaulted her the day before. After a second's deliberation she decided to let him set the tone, but swore to herself that if he tried it on again, she'd make him sorry he had been born.

'Philippa, I just want to say how sorry I am about the way I acted yesterday.' So it seemed he had come to his senses. 'It was unforgivable of me to treat you the way I did, and as a gesture of apology, and in the hope you'll stay under my roof, I've taken the liberty of cooking enough dinner for us both this evening. Would you agree to join me in eating it? As my guest?' He opened the living room door and stood aside.

Was this another trick? Philippa decided to give him the benefit of the doubt, based on the Jack she had known before yesterday. And, in any case, whatever it was that he was cooking smelt absolutely delicious. She dropped her bag and raincoat in the hall and walked cautiously into the room, watching him all the time, and readying herself to duck and evade his grasp if he made any attempt to grab her. But he just smiled as she walked past.

If it was a trap, she mused, then he had gone to a lot of trouble to set it. The room had been thoroughly swept and tidied, and the furniture rearranged to make the dining table the centre of attention. One chair had been placed at either end of the table, which had been laid restaurant-style, with a starched linen cloth and silver cutlery. The curtains had been drawn and the lights switched off, so that the only illumination came from a large blue candle in an elaborate stick in the centre of the table.

So that's his game, thought Philippa. Now the bastard's going to try to seduce me. Well, let him try. It won't work. But why say no to what smells like a damn good meal?

She let him take her jacket, then waited by one of the chairs. When he had returned from hanging the garment in the hall, he pulled the seat out and she sat down. She winced a little as she did so, but whether it was merely due to the fact that she was in the same room as the man who had spanked her, or because she was still genuinely sore, she could not tell.

Jack went into the kitchen, and quickly returned with two small dishes. 'Prawn cocktail with a homemade dressing for starters,' he announced. 'I hope that's okay.' It was more than okay, thought Philippa, when she tasted it. He was obviously a far better cook than she'd given him credit for. Either that, or someone else had helped him to prepare it. In all the time she had been in the house, she had never seen him tackle anything which did not involve using ready-made ingredients.

They moved on to the main course, a simple but delicious Spaghetti Bolognese. Throughout the meal, what conversation there was was awkward, although Jack did his best to keep it flowing. He asked Philippa about her job and how it was going, about her home village, why she had decided to move to London, and other equally innocuous questions. She replied to them as politely as possible, but always tried to maintain a façade of indifference, making sure that he knew he was not forgiven for what had happened the day before. She also left out any mention of Paul, feeling that what had happened between them was nobody's business but her own. The events of the previous day were, mercifully, not mentioned, but she still found herself squirming uncomfortably in her seat a few times, and decided that her bottom must still be retaining some kind of physical memory of the beating. And as for the thought of what Jenny had done to her afterwards – hard though she was trying to forget it, the recollection of how good the girl's fingers had felt when they had entered her sex could never be far away.

At least the food is giving me something else to think about, she pondered, as she wiped up the last of her sauce with a piece of garlic bread, and washed it down with a second glass of the excellent red wine Jack had provided to complement the meal. 'That was wonderful,' she told him, seeing no reason to withhold that particular compliment.

'Thank you, but I must confess, I didn't prepare it entirely on my own,' he replied, confirming her earlier suspicions. 'But don't worry,' he went on, as her face clouded, 'the other cook also has a debt to repay you, so the sentiments are all genuine.'

'Can I clear the dishes away for dessert now?' The

voice from the doorway made Philippa spin round, and she stared in shock at the sight which greeted her.

There stood Jenny. Philippa had recognised her voice instantly, but she could not believe the costume the other girl was wearing. It was a French maid's outfit, complete with a little white lace cap and apron. The black skirt was impossibly short, exposing at least an inch of creamy thigh above the tops of Jenny's black stockings, which were clearly held up with suspenders. On her feet she wore spiky black stilettos, the five-inch heels forcing her to stand completely erect. The short sleeves were puffed at the shoulders, which accentuated the beauty of her long, slender arms, while the low cut of the neckline displayed her ample cleavage to perfection. She wore very simple make-up, and her hair had been plaited into two neat pigtails, which made her look much younger than she actually was. In front of her, she held a large, empty silver tray.

Philippa gawped at her for a few seconds, her mind racing as it took in all the details. Jenny was a pretty girl, there was no doubt about that, and she filled the sexy outfit well, but to Philippa she presented an obscene stereotypical image straight out of a male fantasy.

'Yes, Jennifer, you may clear away the plates and serve dessert.' Philippa turned to look at Jack, unable to believe the way in which he had just addressed their flatmate. Jenny, however, remained unperturbed and walked carefully over to the table, placed the tray down on it, and gathered up the used dishes. Then she picked the tray up, turned around, and walked back out to the kitchen.

'I can see you're shocked by our little surprise.' Jack's voice cut into Philippa's mind, as she watched Jenny's bottom wiggling its way out through the door. Philippa stared at him. Shocked? Shocked did not come close. She waited for an explanation, and true to form, Jack came up with one. 'Jenny felt a little guilty for taking

70

advantage of you in the way she did yesterday. Didn't you feel that was what she was doing?' he added, when he saw her questioning glare. 'She went to you purely to give you a little sympathy, and something to soothe your delectable bottom, but when she saw it, all red and sore from the spanking I gave you, she couldn't resist going a little further than she had originally intended. She said you enjoyed it – you did, didn't you? – but that's still no excuse for exploiting an innocent young girl.' Philippa could not believe what she was hearing. Her face flushed red with embarrassment and anger. So Jenny had told Jack everything – and how the lecherous bastard must have drooled, as she recounted every juicy detail!

'So, you see, we both felt we had something of a debt to pay you,' he continued, as if he were talking about a bank loan. 'My part of the deal was to cook the meal – well most of it anyway. And Jenny decided it might be quite fun to play serving girl for the evening. It's one of her favourite fantasies, and she does it very well. Ah, here she is now.'

Jenny had reappeared, her tray now loaded with two dessert bowls, each filled with ice cream. She smiled sweetly at Jack and Philippa, then walked to the table and laid a dish in front of each of them. Philippa gave her a long hard stare, intended to show her exactly what she thought of her, but Jenny seemed oblivious to her anger. Indeed, there even seemed to be an extra spring in her step as she performed this ridiculous and menial task in her demeaning costume. 'Is everything to sir's and madam's satisfaction?' she asked, cheekily.

'Yes, thank you, Jennifer,' replied Jack. 'You may go and wait in the kitchen until we need you again.' Need her again? What on earth was that supposed to mean?

But Jenny did not seem at all perplexed. 'Very good, sir,' she said, and made her exit, even stopping to drop a little curtsey as she reached the door.

'What's going on?' Philippa had finally rediscovered her voice. Jack had already started to eat his dessert, but she was in no mood for ice cream. She wanted answers, and she wanted them now.

'Just what I told you,' he said. 'We both feel we have something to make up to you, and this is our little way of doing it.'

'Well, you can damned well forget it,' said Philippa, getting up from her chair.

'Oh, I see. You're going to go stamping off to your room again, are you?' His voice was calm but authoritative, perhaps even mocking.

'What do you mean?' demanded Philippa, angrily.

'You know exactly what I mean. You use my tapes without asking, and get caught bunking off work, and then, when you have to pay the penalty, you go and lock yourself away. I know a bare-bottom spanking is painful and humiliating, but that's because it's meant to be. Jenny was good enough to soothe your bum, but she got carried away. Now we're trying to make it up to you in the way we know best, and all you do is flounce around like a spoiled brat.'

Philippa's chin almost hit the floor. She could not believe she was being spoken to in this way. Who the hell did this guy think he was? Her first instinct was to slap his face and walk out, making sure to slam the door good and hard on the way. But was that not exactly what he was trying to goad her into doing? Yes, it was, and for all she knew, she would find herself being hauled back over his lap for another spanking, possibly with that bitch Jenny's help. No, she would show him how wrong he was about her. Drawing a deep breath, she picked up her spoon, sat down, and began to eat her ice cream, doing her level best to present an equally cold exterior.

Jack carried on eating, all the while studying her, apparently looking for any change in her countenance.

Once or twice she caught his eye, and tried to give off an air of nonchalance which she knew she did not really feel. But how was he to know that, so long as she did not let the mask slip?

In time they finished their dessert, and laid down their spoons. Jack sat back and smiled. 'Did you enjoy your dinner?' he asked.

'Yes, thank you, it was delicious.' If he wanted to sit and exchange pleasantries, as though nothing had happened, Philippa was not going to disappoint him.

'Good. But I think you're going to enjoy what's coming next even more.' So what was going to happen now? Philippa did not have time to think before Jenny reappeared in her outlandish garb. She wiggled over to the table and collected the empty dishes, making a brief enquiry as to the quality of the dessert, which was met with equal brevity by Jack. Then, however, he added, 'It's time for the rest of your penance, Jennifer. Come straight back when you've cleared away the dishes. You know what to bring.'

'Yes sir,' she replied, picking up the tray and heading back to the kitchen. Had she found herself in this situation 48 hours before, Philippa would have run screaming from the room. But events had conspired to turn her world upside-down, so instead she found herself calmly sitting and awaiting whatever was going to happen. Let Jack and Jenny do their worst – she would not budge.

Jenny left the room and Jack stood up, dabbing his mouth with his napkin before dropping it on to the table. He took hold of his chair and carried it to the fireplace, the open fire long since replaced by an electric one. Turning the chair around, he positioned it so that the seat was facing the fireplace, and its high wooden back was towards the table. He adjusted it carefully, stepping back a couple of times to make sure it was as perfectly centred as it could be. Philippa

73

watched intrigued. She had no idea as to what he was playing at. Then she heard Jenny coming back.

Philippa turned and was greeted by a most shocking sight. Jenny was still carrying the serving tray, but now, instead of dishes, it bore a single object. A foot-long leather strap.

The strap was brown, each end of it slightly overlapping the tray. A cord loop hung from one end, while the other was slit into two separate tails. As with the cane two nights before, Philippa had heard about straps being used in schools, but had never seen one up close. She seemed to recall that this type was used in Scotland, and that it had a special name. Suddenly it came to her – the strap was called a tawse.

Jenny held the tray in front of her, as though oblivious to the threatening-looking item. She looked straight at Jack, obviously waiting for instructions. Finally, he spoke. 'Approach the chair please, Jennifer.' His voice was calm and passive, betraying no trace of excitement. 'Place the strap upon the chair.' Jenny obeyed without hesitation, bending exaggeratedly as she carefully laid the tray down, and allowing her skirt to ride up and show a pair of frilly white knickers to Philippa, before standing upright once again, and folding her hands in front of her. She looked at Jack submissively. 'Over the back of the chair if you please,' he said.

Jenny walked slowly around the chair, then, reaching forward, very deliberately rested her stomach on top of the back of it, and put her hands down to clasp its sides. It was a relatively tall piece of furniture, and had she not been wearing the high heels, she might have had difficulty in assuming this position.

Jack watched her settle into place, his arms folded and his face a mask of indifference. He might as well have been giving a puppy obedience lessons for all the emotion he displayed. When Jenny had stopped wiggling and was as comfortable as she could make herself,

74

he took his place next to her. Seizing the hem of her skirt, he raised it up and folded it back. Her white knickers were indeed very pretty, fitting snugly around her bottom cheeks, a set of black suspenders passed underneath them. He tucked the hem carefully into the waistband of her pinafore to make sure it stayed out of the way, then took hold of the elastic at the top of her knickers and began to inch them down.

Philippa watched this performance with an increasing feeling of fear. It was obvious now that Jenny was in for another beating – surely that didn't mean . . . ? Through her confusion, she suddenly remembered Jack's comment that he and Jenny both felt they had a debt to repay her, and that this little scenario had supposedly been arranged for her benefit. Something, she was not sure what, was telling her that she was, for the moment at least, in no danger.

But what about Jenny? Should she allow this to continue? She was clearly about to get hurt. But there had been no physical compulsion. She had walked back into this room and bent over the chair apparently of her own free will. Hell, she had even carried the strap in with her! She had had ample opportunity to escape. It seemed she just did not want to.

Jack had, by now, pulled Jenny's undergarments down to mid-thigh level. Her smooth bottom was fully exposed, the roundness of its cheeks framed perfectly by the suspender straps. Her legs were ramrod straight, obviously the result of plenty of practice in this position. Jack leant back to check everything was set up to his satisfaction, then he spoke to his victim again.

'Now Jennifer.' His tone was once more commanding and powerful. 'Will you please tell us why you are about to be punished?'

'Because I – I went too far with Philippa yesterday, sir.' Her voice was a little-girl-lost kind of whimper. Was she really frightened? Philippa was not sure. From what she had seen over the past couple of days, these people were not only perverts, but very good actors.

'That is correct,' Jack intoned, 'and how exactly did you go too far with our new flatmate?'

'I – please, sir, I went up to her room after you'd smacked her bottom and rubbed some lotion onto it for her, sir. I only wanted to help.'

'And I'm sure you did, Jennifer. But you did a little more than that, didn't you?'

'Yes, sir. I did.'

'Well? Tell us what it was.'

'Oh, sir! Please don't make me say it!'

'Come now, Jennifer. You know the rules of this house. Before a public punishment, a girl has to tell the audience exactly why she's being dealt with.'

'Oh, sir! I – I felt her up.'

'A little more than that, I feel.'

'I used my fingers in her – in her pussy sir. I made her come with my fingers.'

'And had she asked you to perform such a task for her?'

'No, sir, she hadn't.'

'Well, that would be my definition of taking advantage of a vulnerable young girl, Jennifer, so I think you'll agree that the walloping you're about to get is well deserved.'

'Yes sir, it is.' Jenny was sniffing by now, and sounded as if she were already in tears. But what a hypocrite that man is, thought Philippa. If anyone had taken advantage of a young girl in this house, it was him. It seemed to her that Jennifer's impending fate was more than a little unjust, but she also realised that any sympathy would be wasted upon her. The girl almost certainly wanted what was coming to her.

'So, my sentence is this,' said Jack, placing his left hand in the small of Jenny's back. '24 hand spanks to warm you up, followed by a dozen lashes with the strap.'

'Twelve? Oh no, sir, please not that many!' Jenny's acting was good; Philippa was prepared to concede that.

'Twelve it will be, Jennifer, unless you don't stop whining, in which case it will be fourteen.'

'Oh sir, please sir, I'll be good, sir.'

'Very well. Shall we begin?' And without waiting for her to agree, he raised his right hand and brought it down on her left cheek. There was a sharp slap, and the injured girl yelped and jerked up on her toes, but she quickly came back down to rest and made no other complaint. A similar spank landed on her right buttock to exactly the same effect. Philippa stared at the vivid handprints which had appeared on each mound, and the outlines slowly turned a darker shade of red as she watched. A few seconds later, another smack landed on Jenny's left cheek, followed by another one to the right. Jack was certainly giving her no quarter.

However, the poor girl took it well. As the spanking wore on, the blows sounded as if they were becoming much heavier. Nevertheless, the only sounds she made were the sharp little squeaks which greeted each one, and her legs never once buckled or bent. They were pressed very tightly together throughout the ordeal, not allowing Philippa a glimpse of the treasures between them. What? Did she find herself wanting to see another girl's private parts? She kept telling herself she was not a lesbian. Or was it something to do with the predicament Jenny was in? My God, was she actually enjoying seeing her suffer? Did she want to see her humiliated even further?

Banishing such thoughts from her mind, she concentrated on the scene before her. Philippa had not been counting, but obviously Jack was doing so. Finishing with two really hard cracks, he stopped. His breathing was slightly more irregular, although he was by no means panting with exhaustion. He ran his hand gently up and down Jenny's untouched thighs, then made her wince as he let it brush over her sore flesh. 'And now my dear,' he announced theatrically, 'the strap.' Philippa realised that Jenny had been staring right at the dreadful implement all through her spanking, lying as it was on the tray on the seat of the chair. That must have made the spanking even harder to bear, having that horrid thing stuck under her nose, reminding her that she was only being warmed up before it was used. And she had to take twelve!

Jack reached down and picked it up. Holding it in his right hand, he ran it across his left palm a couple of times, apparently to test its suppleness, but probably to alarm the two girls as well. It certainly worked on Philippa, but Jenny, who was after all about to receive the strapping, seemed to be perfectly composed and did not flinch.

Jack took his time, prolonging the agony for the pair of them. He carefully readjusted Jenny's skirt, as though the exertions of the spanking had partially dislodged it from up around her waist. He also pulled her knickers down a fraction further, not really achieving anything, but making her twitch just a little as he touched her. Then he tapped the insides of her thighs with the tail of the tawse. 'I think we should have these a little wider,' he said, matter-of-factly. 'You had a good look at Philippa's pussy, it's only fair that she should see a little of yours.'

Jenny obeyed, shuffling her feet to expose the cleft of her buttocks. Philippa gasped. She felt that she should be revolted by this vulgar display – by another woman being forced to expose herself for her benefit during a humiliating beating – and yet she was not. Admittedly, she was shocked in one sense – she was finding it very hard to follow the plot, as it were, in this strange house. But she was also unable to take her eyes off what was going on before her.

The redness of Jenny's bottom dissipated towards its

very centre, where Jack's hand would not have struck her skin. Her twin globes were not far enough apart for her anus to be visible, although a few of the wispy hairs which must have surrounded that most secret place were now in view. Below that, however, the lips of Jenny's vagina were clearly visible. Smooth and symmetrical, the generous, fleshy lobes were glistening wet and swollen with arousal. The spanking had apparently done her a power of good.

Jack now ran the end of the tawse down the very insides of Jenny's cheeks, only just outside her labia, causing her to wriggle involuntarily. For one brief moment he smiled, but then he returned to his role of stony-faced disciplinarian. Taking a step back, he lined up the strap along his target.

Philippa watched Jenny flinch as the broad leather was laid across her skin. Her legs twitched and she whimpered softly, but soon brought herself back under control. How on earth could she bear this dreadful anticipation so stoically, Philippa wondered, then realised, to her horror, that she was actually wondering what it would be like to receive a dose of the strap or the cane. Not that she would ever actually want to, she told herself. But she could not stop trying to imagine how it would be, if only for a stroke or two . . .

Jack drew the tawse back. He did not take it very far, only about two or three feet. He waited a few more seconds, adding to the tension which already hung like a mist in the room, then flicked the instrument down. It made a whooshing sound as it cut through the air on its short journey to Jenny's bottom, and then a wicked 'thwack!' as it connected with her buttocks. Jenny jumped slightly forward again, as she had done during her spanking, but this time she could not stop a grunt of pain from escaping through her clenched teeth. The blow had obviously hurt.

Jack raised the strap again. As he waited to deliver

the second stroke, Philippa stared at the wide white track across Jenny's bottom. It was quickly becoming red. It had landed across the centre of her buttocks, though it was not quite evenly spaced over both, being more to the left than to the right. The second stroke landed, this time causing Jenny to open her mouth fully and give vent to her feelings more forcefully, although it was by no means a full-scale scream. As the strap was lifted again, it became clear that Jack had compensated for the slight misalignment of his first attempt, by leaning more towards the right side, and, as Philippa watched this second line redden, she wondered how hard he was having to hit Jenny to make the weals stand out against her already crimson bottom.

A third stroke landed just below the first, although the impressions left by the strap were so wide that they were already beginning to merge into one big patch of red pain on Jenny's bottom. She took this one a little more quietly, but not so the fourth. Her bottom was small and pert, which meant that sooner or later a stroke had to cross one previously landed. This the fourth one did, causing Jenny to squeal louder than she had done all night, and Philippa to wonder how painful it must be at the point where the two broad lines met.

Showing no mercy, Jack laid on the fifth, again crossing existing weals, and another strangled yell from Jenny showed just how effective this tactic was. He waited a little longer before allowing the sixth to land, this time right across the centre of her bottom. It must have connected with at least three others, and this time, not only did Jenny squeal, but unlike before she actually moved, shifting her weight from foot to foot and wiggling her bottom in an effort to dull the pain. But she did not dare to stand up or reach around to protect herself. And she was still only halfway through her sentence.

Jack looked down at Jenny's reddened bottom, obviously pleased with the results of his work. Philippa expected him to waste no more time in giving Jenny the second half of her strapping, according to the sentence he had imposed. But instead he turned and looked at Philippa.

'Philippa,' he said, now turning on the smooth charm she knew he possessed in abundance. 'Jennifer's wrongdoing was against you. It doesn't feel right for me to carry out all the punishment. Why don't you give her the rest of it?'

Philippa stared at him. Was he serious? Was he mad? Was she herself mad? He could not be expecting her to take that thing and hit another person with it – that sort of thing was for people like him! 'Certainly not,' she replied in the strongest tone she could muster.

'Oh, come along,' he said, moving closer to her. 'Surely we've got you just a little bit curious by now? Don't you want to know how it feels to swing this length of leather on to a soft, yielding, and – believe me – very willing bottom?' Philippa could do nothing but stare at him. She knew exactly what she wanted to say to him, but the words just would not come out. 'Surely you're still angry at her for what she did to you yesterday, even though the result was rather pleasant for you in the end?' he continued.

'None of that would have happened if you hadn't been such a bastard to me first,' she blurted out. 'So no way am I going to take it out on Jenny for your benefit!'

'Very well, then,' said Jack, returning to Jenny's side. 'I'll just have to finish the job myself. But I promise you these six are going to be hard ones. I was only getting loosened up before.'

Inspiration suddenly hit Philippa like a kick from a horse. 'Wait,' she called out. 'If you – if you really think I should give her the last six, then I'll do it,' she said, 'but on one condition.'

'Name it.'

'That I can make them as hard or soft as I like. Like you said, the crime was committed against me.'

Jack smiled at her wryly. 'Clever girl. Very well, then. As hard as you deem necessary. I promise I won't interfere. But,' he added, as she stood up, 'I will show you how to use the tawse. We don't want to cause Jenny any lasting damage, do we?'

Philippa approached the bending girl, and Jack put the leather into her hand. He made sure she was gripping it tightly, then lined it up against Jenny's buttocks. 'It's easier to use than a cane or a riding crop.' Philippa winced at the mere thought of these other two implements. 'Just keep an eye on where the tip lands – that's the part which causes the biggest sting when it catches you.' Philippa wondered how he knew this. Had he ever been on the receiving end? Now that would be a sight worth seeing!

Philippa was ready. Her thinking in volunteering had been clear – if Jack gave Jenny another six, they would no doubt be excruciating. She, however, could make them as gentle as she liked, keeping the poor girl's suffering to a minimum, but completing the punishment to the letter of the rules by which the pair appeared to play their games.

She looked down at the bottom she was about to strike. Jenny had not moved throughout the discourse between herself and Jack, and Philippa didn't doubt that she had to be getting awfully stiff as well as sore. At least the punishment would soon be over. She lifted the strap, not, by her reckoning, particularly high, although she had no previous experience by which to judge the impact it would have. Then, with a sweep of her arm, she landed it gently. At least she thought she had been gentle, but the flick of the heavy, supple leather caught her by surprise, and it wrapped itself around Jenny's curves with quite a crack. It also proved much more difficult to aim than Philippa had imagined after watching Jack. She had been aiming it high, as far away from Jenny's other weals as possible, but had missed to the extent of landing it just below the centre, where the skin was presumably at its most tender.

Jenny gave a little shriek and jumped. It had been nothing like as hard as the strokes she had been getting from Jack, but nevertheless it must have stung. 'Sorry,' bleated Philippa.

'I should bloody well think so,' moaned Jenny. Philippa was surprised to hear her flatmate swear, but even more thrown by her next outburst. 'If you're not going to use that thing properly, give it back to Jack so he can finish me off with a good six.' She turned her head to look back at Philippa. Her eyes were slightly tearful, and her eyeliner just beginning to smudge, but there could be no mistaking the glare on her face. She was serious. 'Start again,' she ordered. 'Six good ones. That one didn't count.'

Philippa stared down at Jenny and then up at Jack. 'I thought you said you wouldn't interfere,' she said.

'I said *I* wouldn't interfere,' he answered. 'I said nothing about the lady. If she wants six of the best she'd better have six of the best, don't you think? Would you like me to take over for you?'

Damn it, Philippa said to herself, they're not going to make me look stupid. I know they think I'm just a country mouse down here in the big city, but I'll show them how fast I can learn. I'll soon wipe the smile off his smarmy face, and as for missy here, well, if she wants six of the best, she can have six of the bloody best!

'No thank you,' she replied, haughtily. 'I'll just have to see what I can do.' She turned back to Jenny, who, she noticed, was now stretching and limbering her joints. 'Stop fidgeting!' Philippa barked. The tone of her voice took her by surprise as much as it did the others. Jenny froze, while Philippa heard Jack's intake of breath from across the room. 'As you wish,' Philippa continued. 'We'll start again. And since you'll probably complain about my maths, too, I think we'll have you counting them, just so there'll be no mistake.' This last touch she had picked up the day before from the text of one of Jack's magazines. It was obviously the sort of thing they expected of her, and she was not going to disappoint them.

Philippa brought the tawse up again. This time she took it higher. She concentrated on her target for a few moments, then allowed the leather to fall. Her aim was truer this time around, and the tawse landed almost where she had meant it to, right across the centre of Jenny's bottom. Jenny grunted, took a deep breath, then announced, 'One ... miss.' A nice touch, thought Philippa, I'm getting through. She raised the implement again and put a similar blow higher up on Jenny's bottom, slightly higher than she had actually intended. No matter, Jenny still let out a strangled gasp before counting off 'two, miss.'

'Try to use your wrist a little more.' It was Jack. 'You're using your whole arm in a sweeping motion, but if you flick your wrist as the strap lands, it'll create more of a sting.'

Philippa rounded on him. 'If I need your advice I'll ask for it,' she told him, coldly. 'You've had your chance to punish her, now it's my turn.' And she redirected her attention to the bending figure beneath her.

Raising her arm again, she gave Jenny – and herself – a few seconds to savour the moment before whipping the strap down. Despite her harsh words to Jack, she had taken notice and tried to follow his instructions. She found them surprisingly effective, the leather landing squarely across Jenny's seat with more force as she flicked it. 'Ow! Three, miss.' This was what she had asked for, and this was what she was getting.

Philippa was stunned to find herself actually revelling in what she was doing. Here she was, taking part in some wild, kinky sex game, using a strap to actually

84

hurt another person – and another woman at that – and if she was honest with herself, she was enjoying it. Why was that? Was it the fact that Jenny was so willingly offering herself up for this brutal treatment? Was it because she was doing something she knew society would deem to be 'wicked'? Or was it a way of working out the frustrations of yesterday, when she had felt so much of a victim herself? Yes, maybe that was it; she was relishing the opportunity to turn the tables on at least one of the people who had taken advantage of her. Once again she wondered if Jack, the real villain, could be persuaded to lower his trousers for a dose.

'Eeah! Three, miss.' The tawse had landed again, laying another fat red path across Jenny's buttocks, this one towards the bottom, just above where cheek met thigh, splitting the two tails and making a loud satisfying whack. Three more, thought Philippa, so they have to be good ones. She laid on an equally vicious fourth blow, then lifted the strap a little higher and brought it down with an extra flick. 'Struth! Aah! Five, miss. You're not messing around any more are you?' Jenny grunted, hoarsely.

'I thought that was exactly what you wanted,' Philippa replied sarcastically.

'Quite right. We just didn't expect you to pick it up quite so quickly. Eeeah! Six, miss.' The final stroke was delivered with still more venom than the others, a sign of Philippa's growing confidence.

'You may stand up now.' Philippa stepped back and watched as Jenny slowly uncurled herself from the chair. Her limbs were obviously quite stiff from holding the position for so long, but her main concern by far was her bottom, a map of angry red lines criss-crossing each other at several points, but mainly at the centre. She reached behind her with both hands and gently prodded the area with her fingers, gasping as she first made contact but becoming bolder as she gained relief. Her eyes were closed, her face lifted to the ceiling, and her mouth still gaping slightly. For the moment she was in a world of her own, and it did not look as if she was finding it such a bad place to be.

Philippa turned to Jack and handed him the tawse. 'Thank you,' she said. 'You know, you were right. I really do feel much better after that.' And she walked out and upstairs to her bedroom without a backward glance.

She could not help but congratulate herself on the way she had turned the tables on Jack and Jenny tonight, and allowed herself a smile as she climbed the stairs. She opened the bedroom door, switched on the light and walked in – then stopped in her tracks. There, on the wall, was the erotic print she had seen when Jack had first shown her the room. It had been replaced exactly where it had hung before.

Five

Despite the satisfaction she felt at what she considered to be something of a victory over Jack and Jenny, Philippa did not get a restful night's sleep. As she lay in bed, her mind was filled with images she could not shake. The sight of Jenny's bottom turning red under Jack's hand and then the strap. The strap in her hand; the marks appearing across the girl's defenceless skin; Jenny's submissive performance as the maid, contrasting so sharply with Jack's self-confident masterfulness. More than once she found her hand involuntarily stealing under her nightdress towards her sex, but she always stopped just short of touching herself, never allowing her fingers to do more than make contact with the first few strands of springy hair.

She had gone straight to bed, and not long afterwards, had heard the others following her upstairs. At first she had worried that they had decided to come and fetch her, in order to use her again in some way, but then she had heard the door of Jack's room shutting, and their voices coming from within. It was obvious that the scene had got them highly excited, and that they were determined to work off some of that tension. Muffled exclamations were soon reaching Philippa's ears. So they liked to fuck after playing one of these games? No big surprise. Of course, she was not interested in any of that – was she? She tried to shut out that particular image, but could not shake from her head the idea of what Jack and Jenny looked like at that exact moment, naked and copulating on the bed. It was the last thing she remembered before she fell asleep. That, and a sense of disappointment because she was lying in bed alone.

She expected some sort of move to be made on her during the following couple of days, and was therefore rather surprised when nothing happened. No more was said about her moving out, and she was quite happy to leave it at that. She had played along with their little game, they had had their fun so to speak, and so she decided that she would act as though none of this had happened. She was relieved to find that Jack and Jenny, too, appeared to take this attitude, and the atmosphere and conversation between them once again became as polite and run-of-the-mill as one could hope to get in any suburban household. It was indeed as if nothing had happened.

Then, about two weeks after the 'dinner incident', as Philippa had taken to thinking of it, Jenny had come into the living room as Philippa had sat in there watching TV. Jack was out, meeting some friends after work. Philippa was glad of the peace and solitude for one evening, although she did not feel disappointed to have the other girl's company. But Jenny had not come to watch the television.

She sat on the couch next to Philippa, and looked at her with an earnest but friendly expression. 'Philippa,' she said in her brightest tone, 'what are you doing on Saturday?'

The question caught her unawares. She searched for an answer. 'Er, nothing, not a thing, I think. Why?'

'Would you like to come to a party with us?'

'Do you mean with you and Jack?' she asked cautiously.

'Who else? Look, don't worry; I promise there's no catch. Jack's not going to try and put you across his knee again – at least, not unless you want him to.'

Philippa suddenly felt uneasy; it was the first time any of them had mentioned the events of that bizarre couple of days since it had all happened, and she was even more disturbed by the realisation that she was getting a strange thrill at the memory of how she had enjoyed strapping this lovely girl's bottom. Should she trust her? They had not tried anything on since then, so the invitation was probably innocent. And was there something inside telling her to accept it even if it was not? She took a deep breath.

'OK, then. You're on. Saturday it is. Whose party is it?'

'Oh, just some friends of ours. It's a very informal affair, and they told us to bring along anyone we liked, so we thought you might like to come.'

'Thanks for inviting me. I'll look forward to it.'

The weekend approached, and Philippa thought no more about it. She did ask Jenny for advice on what she should wear but the girl's answers were always vague and therefore rather unhelpful. 'Oh, I haven't even decided what I'm wearing yet – you just wear what you feel most comfortable in – you'll look fine, whatever you choose.'

Saturday evening finally arrived, and Philippa prepared herself, choosing a simple red velvet dress. The neckline was low, although not particularly daring, while the hem came to just above her knees. She completed the outfit with black hold-up stockings, black shoes and a matching handbag, and wore her hair loose around her shoulders.

She went downstairs to find Jack waiting in the living room. He had opted for a black roll-neck sweater and a blue linen suit. 'Just waiting for Jenny,' he told her, 'then we'll be off. You look terrific, by the way.'

'Where is this party?' Philippa asked. 'And whose is it?'

'It's in a village out in Surrey,' he told her, 'at the house of a friend of mine – a sort of business associate.'

'You mean someone you work with?'

'Not exactly. Well, not at all, really. I just have dealings with him from time to time. But he's a very nice chap, and so are the other people who'll be there tonight. You'll enjoy yourself. In fact, I think we all will. Ah, here she is.'

Jenny had appeared in the doorway, and Philippa turned to check what she was wearing. She was surprised to see that the girl had already put on her coat, a long black garment which completely covered whichever outfit she had finally chosen. It was not exactly warm outside, but it was also not that chilly, and it certainly was not cold in the house. Jenny must be particularly susceptible to chills, Philippa thought.

They got into Jack's BMW, and he drove out of the suburbs and into the countryside. Philippa tried to follow their route, but lost herself when they got into open country, as it was already dark, and she did not know the area. So she gave up, and just settled down in the plush back seat. She found she was actually looking forward to this evening; the incidents with Jack and Jenny aside, work had been taking over her life lately, and she relished the opportunity to widen her social circle in her new home.

After driving for about three-quarters of an hour, they reached a small village. Philippa saw the name, and it vaguely registered with her as a place she had heard of, but had had no inclination to visit up until now. Like many places in Surrey, it was just a hideaway for wealthy stockbrokers and commodities dealers; a place to escape from the city. If Jack had friends out here, they must be fairly well-to-do friends.

They drove down the single main street, then turned up a side road. It was lined with trees, and had no street lights. The houses were all well set back from the road, and had long, impressive-looking drives and neatly tended gardens. Expensive cars, sometimes a pair of them, sat outside, as if waiting for their well-heeled owners' journey to work on Monday.

Then, in the distance, Philippa spotted a house with a large number of such cars parked on either side of the street outside. This must be the place. Jack guided his saloon into a space about twenty yards from the house, and they all got out.

The two girls waited for him to lock the doors, then followed him up the gravel drive. As he knocked on the oak front door, they could hear music and voices coming from within. Obviously, the party was already in full swing. The door was opened by a middle-aged man, his full head of wavy grey hair and thick moustache giving him something of a distinguished look. He recognised Jack immediately. 'Jack, dear boy, how wonderful to see you! Come in, come in!' he enthused. The girls followed their housemate into the hallway. Philippa could see a throng of people through a door to the left, and to the right was another open door, this one leading to a kitchen loaded with food and drink. 'And I see you've brought the lovely Jenny with you. How good to see you, my dear,' their host continued. 'And who is this?' he said, turning to Philippa.

'My name's Philippa,' she said, accepting a gentle peck on her cheek in the same way Jenny had. 'I live with Jack and Jenny, and they invited me this evening. I hope that's okay.'

'Okay? It's more than okay for my friends to bring along such a beautiful woman!' Philippa blushed at the unexpected compliment, feeling a little uneasy but also a tiny bit proud. 'Oh, but I'm being rude. Allow me to take your coats.' Philippa slipped her jacket from her shoulders, and was handing it to their host when she caught sight of Jenny's outfit for the first time.

Attention-seeking would have been one way of

describing it. And, had Jenny not had the poise, elegance and confidence to carry it off, downright tarty would have been another. A slinky black number, it was cut both low at the front and high at the hem, and the two straps holding it in place at the shoulders indicated that Jenny had chosen to emphasise the effect by going braless. Whether she had also decided to go knickerless could not be seen – at least not quite. A provocative slit in her already short skirt almost reached the top of her right thigh, and as she moved to join the main body of the party, a flash of black stocking top was revealed. Philippa was still staring after her when Jack whispered in her ear, 'Stunning eh? She'll certainly be the life and soul of the party this evening.' Then in a louder voice he went on, 'This is my friend, Guy. I did some work for his company some time ago, and we got on well so we stayed in touch. Now he invites me along whenever he has a little soirée like this. Come on, I'll introduce you to the rest of the gang.'

Philippa followed him into the living room, where Jenny was already at the centre of a small circle of men, all apparently eager to welcome her. But as Philippa looked around, she saw Jenny was not alone in underdressing. Most of the women seemed to have made a conscious effort to look as sensual as possible. The partygoers seemed to range in age from people in their early twenties to those in their mid forties, and there was a remarkable display not only of outfits, but also of naked cleavages and thighs. It made Philippa feel a little uncomfortable and out of place, although she knew she would never have had the nerve to have turned up in a dress like Jenny's.

Jack provided her with a glass of wine, and began to introduce her to some of the other guests. After a couple of drinks she relaxed and began to enjoy herself. All the people she met were friendly and attractive, good at making conversation, and apparently genuinely interested in what she had to say about herself. Gradually she lost the feeling of unease about the other women's choice of evening wear.

She had just finished speaking to a couple in their thirties, who had said they were from the coast, when she noticed her glass was empty. Excusing herself, she turned to find a refill, and was met by a man carrying a glass of chilled white wine, the very thing she sought. 'Medium dry – that's right isn't it?' he asked, holding it out to her.

'Er, yes, that's fine,' she replied, taking the glass from him, a puzzled look on her face.

'I'm sorry,' he went on, 'an appalling chat-up line, I'll admit, but I've been watching you since you arrived, and I couldn't think of any other way of starting a conversation. I asked Guy what you'd been drinking, and I've been poised with that glass ever since.'

'Oh, I'm – well, flattered, I suppose.' Philippa was actually completely taken aback by the man's behaviour. He looked to be in his thirties, and around six feet tall, with thick blond-brown hair which reached his collar. He was smartly dressed in a blazer and slacks, worn with a white shirt and a paisley tie.

'My name's Steve, by the way,' he added.

'Philippa,' she said, holding out her hand for it to be shaken gently.

'Yes, I know,' he said. 'Guy told me that too.' Despite the apparent shyness of his approach, there was something about the tone of his voice which made her think this might be an act. She could imagine him being in control in any situation. And he was what most women would call good-looking. There were certainly worse ways to pass an evening, she decided.

They stood and chatted for some time, discovering that they had much in common. He too had come to London from a small provincial town, and had not been sure as to how he should go about meeting people. But that had been over five years ago, and now he said he had as wide a circle of friends as he could wish for. Like Jack, he also knew Guy through business, and knew Jack himself because they were in the same line of work. Philippa wondered whether he knew exactly how Jack liked to spend his evenings, and to her amazement, she suddenly found herself musing on what it would be like to be disciplined by this man – how he would want her to stand, and what he would do to her. She tried to put these ideas to the back of her mind. She was attracted to him, for sure, but did she now equate attraction with punishment? No, she was not going to let herself be spanked again, of that she was certain.

Another thing of which she was certain, was her need to visit the bathroom. Explaining this as delicately as she could to her new friend, and also asking where she might find the room, she put down her glass and set off upstairs, following the directions he had given. On the way, she saw Jack talking with some of the other men – and telling one of his dubious jokes, going by the reaction he was getting. She could not see Jenny anywhere, but assumed that she was either in the kitchen, or at the other end of the room, probably obscured by the crowd of men who had not seemed to leave her side all evening.

She locked the bathroom door and turned her back to the lavatory. Sliding her skirt up and her knickers down, she lowered herself on to the seat and let herself go, revelling in the relief as the stream of liquid left her bladder and hit the water. As the last drops trickled into the pan, she reached for a sheet of toilet paper, which she used to wipe away the final drops. She found herself lingering a little longer than was necessary over this task, and was not sure if all the moisture she mopped away was the result of the evening's drinking. Steve's face flashed into her consciousness and she felt herself shiver, then, as she stood up and rearranged her clothing, she subconsciously ran her palms over her buttocks, lingering for few seconds as she smoothed her panties across her taut flesh. Snapping out of her daydream, she pulled her dress back down, washed her hands, and went to rejoin the party.

She was walking along the landing when she heard sounds coming from one of the bedrooms. Ordinarily this would not have surprised her, and she would have passed by without stopping, but this was the sound of raised voices, and enough to pique anybody's curiosity. So, despite it being someone else's house and the argument, or whatever it was, being nothing to do with her, Philippa stole closer to the door.

It was slightly ajar, and, by crouching and angling herself properly, she could see most of what was happening inside. And it was not something she had prepared herself to see, at least not this evening and not in this house.

It was Jenny. But it had not been Jenny's voice she had heard. That had been male, and she now saw it belonged to another of the guests – one of the men she had glimpsed Jenny talking and laughing with downstairs. Now Jenny stood passively before him. Her head was bowed, and her hands were clasped in front of her. And the mood was certainly different to that of the party room. 'You're a disgrace young lady, an absolute disgrace!' the man was saying. 'Parading around in front of all these people dressed like that! Have you no shame?'

'No, sir. I mean, yes, sir, sorry, sir,' Jenny mumbled, meekly. Once again she appeared the scared little submissive she had been when she had served dinner to Jack and Philippa.

'I've a good mind to put you over my knee and smack your bottom for this,' the man went on. 'Yes, I think that's exactly what I'll do!'

'Oh, sir, please, no, sir!' But Jenny made no attempt

to escape as the middle-aged and balding man pulled her by the wrist to the edge of the bed and hauled her over his lap.

'This is the only language girls like you understand,' he told her, as he tugged what there was of her dress up over her bottom. It seemed she had at least chosen to wear knickers, and very flattering black lacy ones at that. They were cut high, leaving most of her cheeks exposed, and soon those cheeks were on the receiving end of a spanking, the man's big hand slapping down resolutely. Jenny's only response came in the form of little cries of 'Ooh!' and 'Aah!' as she was punished, but otherwise she just lay limply across her tormentor's lap.

Philippa stood up and reeled backward in shock. She could not believe what she had seen. She had just about got used to the idea of her flatmates acting out their kinky little scenes in their own home, but to carry on like this in someone else's house? It was beyond belief! She turned to flee downstairs, deciding to leave Jenny and the strange man to take whatever consequences their actions led to – and found herself face to face with Steve.

He did not say a word but looked at her with a bemused and quizzical expression. She opened her mouth in an attempt to say something – anything – which might preclude her having to explain exactly what she was doing and why, but he placed a finger on his lips, then took her hand in a firm grip. She did not resist as he drew her back along the landing and into a smaller bedroom. Once inside, he turned on the light and closed the door. Only then did he speak.

'Philippa, why were you looking around the door like that?'

'I – well, that is, I, er . . .' she began, not really able to think of an explanation that she felt this gorgeous new man in her life would find convincing.

'Why didn't you just walk in and ask if you could watch?'

'I – I'm sorry?' Now she was confused.

'You do know exactly what kind of party this is, don't you?' She would have said yes, but the look on her face would have made it pointless. Instead, she just shrugged and shook her head. 'Oh my God,' he moaned. 'You didn't realise this is a spanking party. Just terrific!' Steve put his hands on his hips and rolled his eyes skyward. 'What was Jack thinking of when he asked you to come?'

'I think I know,' said Philippa – an answer she could tell he was not really expecting. He looked down at her, another unspoken question in his eyes. 'Jack and Jenny didn't tell me it was a spanking party, whatever that is, but I do know they're into that kind of thing. In fact, Jack has spanked me, and I've strapped Jenny, too. But they knew I wouldn't have come if they'd told me straight out, so I guess they were hoping I'd find out the way I did and go along with it.'

'Instead of demanding to be taken home straight away. Well, not to worry; if you get your coat I'll drive you there,' he said, and as she stared up at him she knew he really meant it. But he was not getting away from her that easily. Her experiences with Jack and Jenny had given her an idea as to what she had to do. Now she just had to do it.

'And why should I want to go home when things are just getting interesting?' she said. 'Come on, let's talk.' And she led him by the hand over to the small bed, and they sat down.

She gave him a potted history of her adventures in the house so far. He listened patiently, a wry smile or the raising of an eyebrow his only occasional indicator of emotion. Then she asked him exactly what kind of gathering she had found herself in the middle of tonight.

'Like I said, it's a spanking party,' he told her. 'Everyone downstairs, without exception, is a devotee of corporal punishment. Usually, of course, we just indulge our little whims in twos or sometimes threes, but every now and again we get together for one of these bashes – or, should I say, thrashes!' Philippa giggled, and squeezed his hand at the joke. He was making her feel very much at ease in what should have seemed like a threatening situation.

'People bring their partners, of course, but during the evening they may pair off with each other's, then head upstairs to indulge a particular fantasy that either may have. Sometimes these are arranged before the party, but a lot are just spur of the moment things. One important rule is that we don't talk about what we do until we get upstairs.'

'Because you never know who might be listening?'

'No, it just makes it more exciting when you get there – the thought of all those people downstairs acting like it was an ordinary party, while you're upstairs smacking a woman's lovely bottom. Oh, I'm sorry, I didn't mean to offend, it's just I'm used to speaking frankly when I'm with these people.'

'Who's offended?' asked Philippa. I could get up and walk away from this right now, she thought, or I could ask this man to take me home, and he would do so, without a second's hesitation. How can such a gentleman really be into this sort of thing? He's not like Jack at all, yet they obviously have a great deal in common. And suddenly she got the urge to find out exactly how much.

Gripping his hand even more firmly, she stared straight into his eyes, took a deep breath and said, 'Would you like to spank me, Steve?'

At this, his expression lost a little of its confidence – in fact he seemed genuinely surprised by this turn of events. But he soon recovered his composure. 'Yes, of course I would; I've wanted to since I saw you downstairs. Is that what you want me to do?'

Philippa did not answer. Instead, she stretched herself out and lay across his lap, with her buttocks thrust into the air. He did not move for a moment, but then she felt his left arm snake across her back and encircle her trim waist. She shivered and closed her eyes as his right hand slowly stroked her covered bottom, and then she felt her dress being lifted. She sensed that Steve was struggling to get the tight garment up past her hips, and so she raised them a little to allow him to do so more easily. Then she relaxed as she felt its hem being tucked up around her waist, leaving her with her lower half covered by only her black lacy briefs and stockings.

Steve smoothed his hand over her knickers for a couple of minutes, seemingly transfixed by the sight before him. Philippa felt she was being stretched like piano wire, so great was the sexual tension in the room. Eventually, he hooked his fingers and thumbs into each side of her briefs and slowly drew them down. Philippa exhaled deeply as they slid down over her cheeks and then her thighs, stopping just above her knees. Now her bottom was naked – naked and defenceless. Steve could do just as he wished with it, and there was nothing she could, or would, do to stop him.

She expected him to begin stroking her again now her cheeks were bare, and was therefore surprised to suddenly receive the first slap. It was not too hard, more of a tap, landing on the crown of her left buttock. She gasped, more in shock than in pain, and quickly felt a second spank on her other cheek. As Steve continued smacking her, she was conscious of the vibrations rippling through her bottom, and of a growing heat down there. Gradually, he increased the tempo of the spanking and the strength of the blows, but it felt nothing like that first time with Jack had done. Then, she had been consumed with shame and anger, both with herself for allowing him to manipulate her into the situation, and with him for taking advantage of her. But now she was over Steve's lap on her own terms, and in many ways, he was dancing to her tune.

The stinging sensation increased, and slowly became a deep, fiery ache. Philippa began to groan through clenched teeth. She arched her spine and threw her head back, her hair flying around her head. Steve would have had to have been blind not to notice her excitement. A final flurry of spanks assailed her bottom, and then he stopped. Instantly, his hand was put to a different use. Reaching between her legs, he quickly found her clitoris. It did not take much to push her over the edge, and Steve obviously knew exactly what he was doing. In a matter of seconds she was stretching, twitching, and rolling on his lap, as a wave of ecstasy overcame her.

Then it was gone, and she lay limply on the bed. His hand had left her sex and was now resting on her inflamed bottom. She was aware now not of the pain, but of a warm glow which seemed to cover her whole body, though it was centred in her bottom. 'Did you enjoy that?' Steve's question was rhetorical, but she still murmured a barely audible positive reply. 'So,' he said, 'let's try something else,' and she found herself being gently rolled over and lifted in his arms.

She realised that this must have exposed her pubic area to his view, but after the experience he had just given her, she did not think this mattered. Sitting her up in his lap, he held her with his left arm around her shoulder, and they kissed, slowly at first, but gradually with more passion. Her hands explored his chest, and she began to assume that the encounter was moving towards a more conventionally sexy conclusion. But she had not seen where his right hand had gone, at least not until it had reappeared in front of her face. In it, he brandished a large carpet slipper. 'A pair like this is stored under every bed in this house,' he told her, 'just for occasions such as these.'

She stared at the slipper. It was large, probably a size eleven or twelve, and looked well worn and very flexible. It had a red tartan upper, and a thick rubber sole.

Philippa knew exactly why it had been left in the room, but she did not know if she could go through with it, so early on in the proceedings. The spanking had been nice, and the orgasm even better, but this – well, she was just not sure.

Steve must have read the doubt in her eyes. 'Look, if you'd rather we didn't, I'll understand. But I promise it won't be too hard. And judging by the way you reacted to having your bottom smacked, I think you're a natural anyway.'

Philippa looked from the slipper to his face and back again. If it had been Jack, there would have been no way she would have trusted him, but Steve seemed different. She had no doubt that if it all got too much she could just get up and walk out. But had that not been the problem all her life? Every time a situation had got difficult, she had just turned her back on it and left. She was only in London because that had been her solution to Paul's unfaithfulness. Walking out now meant she would risk missing the most exciting moment of her life so far. But what would she be risking by staying?

Her mind made up, she leant forward and put her arms around Steve's neck. She kissed him full on the lips, then glared into his eyes. 'Come on, then,' she said, 'if you think you're man enough to use that on me, then give it your best shot.'

Steve's eyes narrowed and a thin smile played across his lips. She had let him know that she wanted to go on with the game, and he did not intend to disappoint her. Taking her right wrist in his left hand, he pulled her off his lap and into a standing position by the bed. 'Right,' he said gruffly. 'If that's the way you want it, that's the way we're going to play it.' He released her wrist and pointed to the bed. 'Over you go,' he ordered.

'Steve, I –' she began.

'No arguments. Get yourself bent over it now.' It

seemed there was no arguing with him. Submissively, she stretched her upper body out over the coverlet, with her hips resting on the edge of the bed. Her dress had slipped back down when she had stood up, but Steve reached down and pulled it back up around her waist. Her panties had stayed down around her knees, and once her buttocks had been fully exposed, he took hold of the flimsy garment and pulled it down then off altogether. He clearly meant business.

Then Philippa felt the cold rubber sole being laid across her skin. She trembled, anticipating what she knew would be a far greater pain than anything she had already experienced. Then it left her bottom, and she tensed in anticipation.

Steve waited a few seconds, deliberately taunting her she felt, before it landed across both of her cheeks with a resounding slap. A sharp pain cut into her already-tender cheeks, and she let out a loud yell. The blow had felt like the impact of a palm, but much stronger, and spread over a far wider area. Philippa clutched the coverlet, seeking relief from the smarting impact of the second blow, which landed about five seconds later. This time it fell a little higher, just above the crown of her buttocks, and again she called out, but this time not just in pain. As the slippering continued, she could feel the pent-up tension inside herself being released in much the same way as her recent orgasm had done. She could deny it to herself no longer – this was what she wanted.

Steve went on slippering her for some time – she was not sure for exactly how long – but, by the time he had finished, her cries had become long, low moans, each of them practically indistinguishable from the previous one. Her bottom hurt so much that she hardly noticed when he stopped, only becoming aware that he had done so when she heard the slipper drop to the floor next to her, and felt him take her by the shoulders. He turned her over and eased her further up the bed, and she winced as her sore cheeks made contact with the coverlet. Then she saw the bulge in his trousers.

He stood back, a look of sheer lust on his face as he regarded her. Then he pulled off his jacket and tie, and practically tore off his trousers and briefs, revealing a large and swollen erection. Philippa gulped and breathed more heavily. What should she do? Call a halt now before it was too late? No way – she wanted this man too much.

By now, Steve had rolled on a condom which he had apparently been carrying in his jacket. Advancing on her, he put an arm around each of her thighs, parted them and rested his knees on the edge of the bed. 'Oh!' she yelped, as the tender skin of her bottom pressed against the tops of his thighs. But the pain only served to heighten her need for him to do what he obviously planned next. The head of his penis brushed the lips of her vagina four or five times, bringing little gasps from her. She was moist, open and ready for him, and he knew it. With a sudden lunge he entered her, and they both called out their pleasure.

Philippa had, quite simply, never experienced anything like this. Steve waited a few seconds, as he savoured the initial penetration, and then began, slowly, to work in and out of her. Philippa moved her hips in response, feeling the hot sensation in her bottom as part of a kaleidoscope of impressions. She looked down between her breasts, still covered by the crumped velvet dress, to see their union, and gasped as she saw how her pussy lips seemed spontaneously to be sucking on Steve's rubber-clad organ.

Then she looked back up at his face, and it was clear he did not have much further to go. His eyes were closed, and his mouth gaped open. Then she felt him begin to throb inside her, and his lunges become deeper but less frequent, and at the same time he growled and gripped her legs even tighter. It was all too much for

Philippa, and she felt herself starting to orgasm for the second time that night. She flung her arms out and thrashed her head from side to side as the wild, primitive sensation reduced her to a shaking mass.

After a few moments, she felt Steve gently withdrawing from her, and looked up to see him sinking back on to his knees. His face was flushed, and his chest still heaved slightly. Suddenly she was very conscious of her own semi-nakedness, and of the soreness in her bottom. Rolling over on to her right side, she reached down with her left hand and started to rub her abused cheeks. But she felt her hand being brushed away, to be replaced by a strange, moist smoothness. Looking back over her shoulder, she was amazed to see Steve's face up close to her bottom; he was busily using his tongue on the crimson flesh, soothing and cooling it for her. With a contented sigh Philippa relaxed, and rested her head on the bed to enjoy his attentions.

After another fifteen minutes they had dressed, tidied themselves up and remade the bed, and were ready to rejoin the party. Steve opened the door, and Philippa stepped out on to the landing – and nearly jumped out of her skin when she came face to face with a broadly smiling Jack. Behind him stood an attractive redhead in a revealing cocktail dress. Had he been there all the time, or had he only just appeared? Whatever the case, he and the lady were clearly waiting to use the room and, with a knowing nod to Steve as he came out after Philippa, he ushered the blushing woman in. 'Relax,' said Steve as they walked down the stairs. 'Nothing's written on your face, and this crowd wouldn't care if it was.' Whether or not his words reassured her, there was no way she could deny the power and intensity of the experience she had just had.

She spent the rest of the evening with Steve. She was aware that the rules of the party allowed them both to seek liaisons with any of the others, and so she was flattered that he chose not to do so. For herself, she did not care to try any other man at the moment, and besides, she was too sore to take another spanking.

The same did not seem to apply to Jenny, though; Philippa saw her disappear with at least two more men besides the one she had been with earlier. Jack, too, seemed to be taking full advantage of what was on offer, as, shortly after he and the redhead had returned, Philippa had spied him talking earnestly to, and then slipping away with, a voluptuous brunette.

Soon enough the party came to an end, and Philippa found herself being collected by Jack, who told her it was time to go. As he did so he winked and then looked over at Steve, who was chatting to the host. She did her best to ignore Jack, but still felt a pang of embarrassment.

As she parted from Steve he kissed her gently on the cheek. 'Thanks for this evening,' he said, 'you made it for me. And I will be in touch.' As she drove home with the others she wondered if he ever would.

They arrived at around one, and Jack announced that he was going straight to bed, as 'the exertions of the evening,' had left him exhausted. As he disappeared up the stairs, Jenny gave Philippa a sardonic smile.

'If he thinks *he* exerted himself, then how the hell should *we* feel?' she asked, rhetorically. Philippa just smiled. She did not want to let on that she had been spying on Jenny. 'Jack told me you cottoned on to what kind of party if was,' the blonde girl went on. 'Are you angry with us?'

'No, I guess I'm not really, although I don't think I would have gone if you'd been upfront with me.'

'Don't think?' repeated Jenny. 'Is that all? Looks like you're more into this sort of thing than you thought you were. Did you get any action?'

'Well, er, yes, I –'

'It's OK, you don't need to tell me who it was with

or what they did to you. But I did notice you spending a lot of time with that rather attractive acquaintance of Jack's, you lucky girl. Tell you what – my arse is killing me. How about returning that favour I did you with the cold cream?'

'Well, if you really want me to.' What Philippa really wanted was to go to bed and dream of Steve, and replay what he had done to her in her mind, but she also welcomed the chance to talk to Jenny while Jack wasn't around to eavesdrop.

'Of course I want you to,' Jenny told her, 'and I'll do the same for you again if you want me to. Did you get a good seeing-to?'

'Yes, I suppose you could say I did,' replied Philippa reluctantly.

'Well, what are we waiting for? You get the cold cream, and I'll make myself comfortable.'

Jenny began to collect cushions from around the living room, and to arrange them on the sofa. Philippa decided that there was no way out other than to go along with her, and so she walked upstairs to the bathroom, slipping off her heels so as not to attract Jack's attention, and to give her feet a much-needed rest. She found the tub of cream in the medicine cabinet, and quickly returned to the living room. Jenny was already lying face-down on the couch, her dress discarded in a crumpled heap on the floor. She was almost completely naked, her bottom framed by her black stockings and suspenders. She had removed her panties, and when Philippa looked hard she saw them lying camouflaged on top of the dress. But what really held her attention was the state of Jenny's bottom. The girl's normally pale skin was angry and red, with clear blotches and hand prints. 'Oh, Jenny!' she exclaimed. 'That looks terrible! What on earth happened to you?'

'I got my bottom smacked. Quite hard and quite often. If you look closely, you can probably see the tram

lines where my last session ended with a caning.'
Philippa crouched next to the prostrate girl and peered
at her punished flesh. She could indeed see the long
straight marks, already a slightly deeper red.

'That's terrible,' she muttered. 'How do you put up
with it?'

'If you do it often enough, and you really want to,
you soon get the head to cope with it. And besides,' she
added, 'don't tell me you didn't get a thrill out of Steve
spanking you, if that's what he did.'

'And slippering me,' Philippa added softly, feeling
Jenny's candour deserved her own in return.

'He slippered you too? Well, he'll soon have you
bending over for the cane, my dear, now you've let him
go that far.'

'Oh, I don't think so. Steve doesn't seem that sort of
bloke.'

'They all are, believe me, babe. But are you going to
admire my trophies all night, or are you going to use
that cream?'

'Oh sorry.' Philippa had forgotten about the tub in
her hand. Now she unscrewed the lid, and scooped out
a generous handful of the unguent. Its coldness felt
good on her fingers, and she anticipated its soothing
properties being applied to her own warm bottom. But
first she had to attend to Jenny. Flipping her hand over,
she gently slapped it on to the blonde girl's buttocks.

'Ooh! Aah!' Jenny moaned. 'That's terrific, just terrific!' Philippa gently applied the cream in ever-widening
circles, taking care to massage it well into the reddest
parts of Jenny's skin, from the centre of her bottom
onwards.

'Their aim was certainly good,' she commented, and
gave a little giggle in spite of herself.

'Wasn't it just! I've been attended to by some real
experts tonight.' And Jenny plumped up the cushion
under her head and hugged it tighter. Her thighs began

to move slowly apart, so slowly that Philippa did not notice at first. Then suddenly, she found her fingers brushing the short, curly hairs around Jenny's vagina. She instantly slid her hand back up to the top of the girl's bottom, but it was too late – Jenny had registered the contact. 'Go on, you can touch me there if you like,' she urged. 'In fact I'd really appreciate it if you did. A good spanking always leaves me horny, and I've had no other way of relieving myself tonight.'

'But, Jenny, I've – I've never – not with another woman, not like you did to me.' Philippa's head was spinning. Was this all part of the evening's plan, or a genuinely spontaneous development? And what did it matter which it was? At that moment, she was not able to say for sure that she really did not want to touch Jenny down there.

'Please, Philippa – you'll be doing me a favour, and it's no big deal, I promise you. All you have to do is touch me in the way, I guess, you touch yourself – no, don't be shocked, we all do it – and keep on doing it, nice and gently, until I look like I've had enough, or I ask you to stop. Please, Philippa?'

This was outrageous, Philippa told herself. How could she have let herself be dragged into such a situation? But here she was, and it was by no means the first time. Then the thought of Jack sleeping soundly upstairs occurred to her. Would he not love to be down here with them, watching what she was doing to Jenny, getting hard and just itching to join in? Instead, he was safely tucked up in bed, missing the whole event. This was just her and Jenny sharing a moment of feminine intimacy, and that was exactly the way she wanted it to stay. Dipping her fingers back into the jar, she made sure they were well covered with the ointment, and then began to massage it into Jenny's inner thighs. Jenny began to let out little moans of pleasure, which grew louder as Philippa's slender fingers moved closer to her most intimate spot. Then they brushed her sensitive lips, which were already beginning to pout, and a groan came from within the depths of the cushion where Jenny's head rested. Philippa took a deep breath, then slipped the tips of her fingers between the labia and stroked the moist groove from top to bottom for a few seconds before pulling her hand away.

'Ooh, yes!' cooed Jenny. 'Do that again!' Encouraged, Philippa obliged, and was rewarded with a longer, drawn-out, deeper moan of pleasure as she let her fingers delve further and more lovingly, right into the entrance of Jenny's pussy. She could see it swell and open now, in much the same way as her own did when she touched herself. Now she had a different viewpoint, looking down between Jenny's cheeks. She compared the colour to that of her own vagina, which she had inspected, on a couple of occasions, using a mirror, and found the other girl to have darker lips, but an interior which was just as moist and red.

Jenny continued to make inspiring noises, and Philippa became bolder, pushing her first two fingers even further into Jenny's pouting hole, whilst using her thumb for leverage against the soft cushion of her buttocks. She began to work her hand in and out, feeling the tempo of Jenny's breathing increase as she speeded up her own rhythm. Jenny's excitement was obviously growing. She squeezed the pillow as if she were trying to burst it, and threw back her head, opening her mouth to draw in as much air as possible.

Philippa pushed her fingers in as hard and deep as she could. There was no way she could explain the feeling that doing this to the other girl was giving her. She was powerful, she was totally in control. It was she who would decide how soon Jenny would climax. This, she mused, as she stroked in and out, must be what it feels like to be a man, deciding how and when your partner was going to reach orgasm.

'Aah!' Jenny breathed, as her whole body stiffened and stretched. Philippa continued rubbing her, but gradually reduced the speed and depth of her strokes until she was doing little more than tickling the girl's entrance. Jenny's head sank on to the cushion. For a long moment she was silent, save for her breathing, which gradually became more regular. Her eyes were closed, and Philippa, crouched on the floor beside her, wondered if she had gone to sleep and whether she should wake her. But she finally stirred, opening her eyes and looking dreamily at Philippa. 'Mmm, that was incredible! My head's still on the ceiling somewhere! Are you sure you haven't done that before?'

'Never,' whispered Philippa. 'Well, not to anyone else, anyway.'

Jenny put out a hand and languidly stroked Philippa's hair away from her face. 'Well, you should do it more often – you're a natural.'

Philippa looked at Jenny's lovely face, her naked body, and the vivid red marks on her cheeks, shiny now with their coating of cream. At the same time, pictures of herself and Steve together in the bedroom at the party ran through her mind, as if she were watching another person performing those lewd acts. She knew it now. She had been denying her true self all her young life, but now she realised that this was what she wanted. And Jenny had shown her how she could get it. But there was so much more to discover. Who would guide her? There seemed to her to be only one choice.

'Jenny?' she said, in a soft pleading tone. Jenny raised her eyebrows in response, her expression urging Philippa to go on. 'Teach me, please. I want to know more.'

Six

All day long Philippa's insides had been churning at the thought of what might lie in store for her this evening. She had felt this way since the Monday morning after the party. She had been preparing to leave for work as usual, when Jenny had walked down the stairs and passed her on her own way to the front door. As she had been halfway out of the door she had turned and spoken to Philippa. 'Wednesday,' she had said. 'Keep Wednesday night free. We're going to have a little fun.'

She had said nothing more since then, but Philippa had been in no doubt as to what she had meant. Her request to be taken further into this mysterious world was to be granted.

Now the day had come, and she was just counting the hours. Nothing more had even been hinted about what was to happen, but by now she was sure she could trust Jenny to arrange everything perfectly. Time had lain heavy on her that afternoon. The journey home had seemed interminable, with the stops at the underground and railway stations seeming to take twice as long as usual, and once or twice, as she had crossed or un-crossed her legs or stood up, she had been aware of a slight dampness between her thighs.

Her feet had carried her home from the station far more quickly than ever before, and at last, she found herself at the front door of the house. Her fingers fumbled with the key, and she eventually got it into the lock. Why was she this nervous? Was it apprehension at the pain? Or excitement at the prospect of the ecstasy she now knew would come in its wake?

As she closed the door, the smell of Chinese food wafted in from the kitchen. Jenny appeared in the hallway. 'Welcome home,' she smiled, genially. 'Had a good day?'

'Er, yes – fine, thanks,' Philippa responded, unsure as to what atmosphere to expect.

'I didn't feel like wasting any time on cooking, so I just got a takeaway,' the blonde girl went on. 'There's plenty of it, so let's tuck in, and then we can get going. And don't worry about Jack,' she went on, as she saw Philippa casting a nervous and involuntary glance up the stairs, 'he's been told in no uncertain terms to stay out of our way this evening. He's booked a squash court with a friend from work, then after all that exercise they'll undo it with a few pints, so we won't be seeing him until much later on.'

'Oh, well, I expect he'll enjoy himself just as much as we will,' said Philippa, trying to be tactful in not saying how relieved she actually was that she and Jenny would be alone that evening.

'No,' said Jenny, emphatically. 'He won't enjoy himself anything like as much as we're going to.' And with a smile, she turned and led the way into the kitchen.

She served the food from its foil containers on to two plates, which they took into the living room. They sat and watched the evening news while they ate, with Jenny passing the occasional comment about world events, and how crazy the rest of the planet was. Philippa, though, was too wound-up to talk or to eat much. She could feel the mental and physical tension stretching inside her, and just wanted to hear Jenny say that it was time.

Finally, Jenny set her fork and empty plate down at her feet, but instead of standing up, she just sat back and dabbed at her mouth with her paper napkin. 'Is that all you're going to eat?' she asked, looking at Philippa's plate, which was still half full.

'I'm sorry, Jenny. It was very nice, but I just don't seem to be hungry. I don't know – nerves, I guess.'

'Oh, surely you're not afraid of little me, are you? I'm your friend – Jack and I both are. We wouldn't lead you into something we didn't think you could handle. And this evening was your idea; I think that shows how involved you've become.'

'Yes, Jenny, and don't think I'm not grateful. It's just – well, I'm not sure I belong in your world. You and Jack both seem so confident and self-assured, and so did all the other people I met at the party. It was purely by accident that I found this house, and if I hadn't then I know I would never even have thought about doing . . . what it is you do.'

'We do, my dear, what we do, and we're going to do it tonight,' said Jenny softly, reaching out and laying a hand on Philippa's wrist. 'Do you want to start?'

'Oh, yes please – I'd love to!' Philippa felt the emotional dam burst, and relief washed all over her.

Jenny took the plates and crockery back through to the kitchen, and then Philippa heard her leave it by the other door which led to the stairs. Her light footsteps disappeared up them and, from one of the bedrooms, there then came the sound of boxes or cases being moved around, opened and shut again. Then she heard the girl descending the stairs again.

'Here we are.' Jenny reappeared, carrying a large cardboard box. Kneeling down, she tipped its contents out on to the rug in front of Philippa, who stared at the pile of implements. 'Help yourself,' said Jenny. 'Take your time and have a good look.'

Philippa slipped off the sofa and knelt by the pile. Reaching out, she picked up a thick leather strap, similar to the one she had used on Jenny but a little heavier. This one was about a foot long with a loop of cord through a hole at one end, and the other end split in two. The leather felt cool as she ran it through her fingers, and as she weighed it in her hands, she found it surprisingly heavy.

'That's a tawse,' Jenny told her. 'You know all about that, of course, and I can vouch for you being able to use it.'

'It looks pretty fierce,' said Philippa.

'Oh, it is,' Jenny assured her. 'I'm sure you remember how effective it was on me. But it's not as sharp as the cane or riding crop.'

'Riding crop?'

'Like this one.' Jenny pulled a long black whip from the collection. She swished it through the air a couple of times, making Philippa flinch.

'Jenny, I – I don't think I . . .'

'Oh, don't worry, sweetie.' Jenny touched her arm lightly. 'I've only brought this lot down to show to you. I wouldn't use all of them, or even any of them if you're having second thoughts.'

'No, Jenny,' she answered resolutely. 'I want to do this, and I need you to show me how. Just – just remember how little I know.'

'No problem. You just choose something you think you'll like, and I'll make sure I don't go over the top. But we can't use any of them on you as you are.'

'As I am?' Philippa was mystified.

'Cold. Have you any idea how painful it would be to use one of these on you without warming you up first?'

'Warming me up?' Philippa had an awful idea as to what Jenny meant, but was not sure she liked the prospect.

'Your bottom needs a gentle start – we can't go straight in at the deep end. I'll have to give you a little spanking first.'

'Oh,' said Philippa, with resignation. This was not

114

something she had anticipated, but Jenny seemed determined that the rest of the evening would not go ahead until the spanking had taken place. 'So how do you want me?'

'Across my lap, of course – how else? Come on, young lady, let's get on with it!' And Jenny jumped athletically to her feet, before sinking back down on to the sofa. The change in her voice to a brisk commanding tone stunned Philippa for a second, but she soon clambered to her feet to obey.

Jenny had placed herself on the edge of the sofa, drawing her knees together. She smoothed the material of her tight, knee-length blue skirt down over her thighs, then looked up at Philippa and patted them. Philippa realised she had created the perfect platform for her, and so taking a deep breath, she bent forward and stretched herself across her flatmate's legs.

After a few seconds of wriggling and shuffling, she was positioned to Jenny's satisfaction. She soon realised that this felt slightly different again to the other spanking she had been given. There was no sense of the fear or anger she had felt with Jack, nor of the lust she had felt towards Steve. Instead, she now felt something akin to the excitement she remembered from her late adolescence, when she had done grown-up things for the first time – her first visit to a pub, or when she had been about to have her ears pierced. She tried to keep her breathing steady, and waited for Jenny to begin.

Jenny used her right palm to caress Philippa's bottom, smoothing the creases from her business skirt in just the same way as she had done with her own. Philippa found it intensely exciting for some reason, and fought to contain herself as she anticipated what was to come. When Jenny's hand left her bottom, she expected her buttocks to be bared as they had been when each of the men had punished her, and so she let out a surprised gasp as the first smack landed over the material.

'Oh, Jenny! Through my skirt? Jack and Steve didn't do that!'

'Men!' snorted Jenny, as the second slap and then the third landed on the tight material. 'They always want to get our knickers down straight away. No self-control at all. Don't worry, your bottom will be bare before long, but I do like to work up to things properly.'

The spanking continued through Philippa's skirt for some minutes. It was fairly thick, and along with her panties, it offered quite a degree of protection. She also noticed how different the spanks sounded – muffled thumps instead of the crisp slap of a hand on naked flesh.

Then Jenny stopped, and Philippa knew that her period of grace was over. Sure enough, up went the hem of her skirt, and she blushed as she felt the cool air on her thighs and bottom cheeks. She had worn her most daring panties – red lacy briefs which barely covered her bottom – wanting to impress Jenny with her ability to be sexy. It seemed to work, as Jenny whistled admiringly. 'Beautiful, Philippa. I've got a pair just like them, only in black. Next time you see Steve you should wear these – you can't go far wrong with a few frills.' And as if to emphasise her point, she rained down a few spanks over the thin gossamer. Philippa sucked in her breath as the sharp pain replaced the almost painless spanking over her skirt.

Of course, Jenny's agenda did not include allowing Philippa the dignity of keeping her knickers on for long. After about a dozen hand-spanks, Philippa felt fingers being slid inside her waist band, and then the wispy garment was hauled down to her knees. Her bottom was now bare, naked and vulnerable, as she stretched out across the other girl's knees. A thrill ran through Philippa as she closed her eyes and imagined what Jenny must be seeing from her dominant position.

The next flurry of smacks was soon landing, and they

116

were strong enough to make Philippa cry out in pain, even though she could tell her friend was not spanking her as hard as she could have done. Taking a deep breath, she tried to bring herself under control, determined that Jenny would not think of her as a cry-baby.

Nevertheless, it became increasingly difficult for her to keep a cool head. Jenny's technique was very different from Jack's or Steve's. Where the men had used the entire widths of their big palms, deliberately pausing for a few seconds between each stroke, Jenny made up for having much smaller hands by landing her blows in rapid succession, covering all of Philippa's bottom, then quickly working back to the same spot. The cumulative effect of this was too much for her and she began to squirm and moan, wondering if she was going to have to suffer the humiliation of asking Jenny to stop.

But just as this prospect was about to become a reality, Jenny stopped of her own accord and Philippa breathed a sigh of relief. 'A nice, rosy red,' she heard Jenny say. 'I think that should set you up nicely.' Philippa felt her knickers being pulled further down, then gasped as they were slipped over her feet and removed completely. 'Well, you're not going to be needing them again this evening, are you?' Jenny replied to the unasked question. 'No matter how pretty they are. And I think you can take that skirt off, too, as soon as you're up.' And Philippa felt herself being pushed off Jenny's lap. Instinctively, she put her knees down and slid on to the soft carpet. Jenny stood up and moved to the pile of implements. Philippa watched her for a few seconds, then remembered the order she had been given to remove her skirt. Standing up so that it fell back down across her stinging cheeks, she fumbled with the catch and then the zipper, before finally letting it drop to the floor and stepping out of it.

She reached down to pick it up, and was folding it carefully over the arm of the sofa when she saw that

Jenny was back in front of her. In her hand she held the tawse. 'I think it's only fair that we should start with this,' she said. 'After all, you did get to use it on me.' Philippa gulped at the memory of strapping this lovely girl's bottom, and silently prayed that Jenny would be gentler with it than she herself had been.

'How would you like me?' she asked, her hands clasped in front of her pubic area, more to give them something to do than to hide her nudity from Jenny. She knew they had passed the time for modesty long ago.

'Let's see. You've laid your skirt out nicely on the arm of the sofa – why don't you put yourself on top of it?' Philippa moved to obey, carefully lowering herself on to the arm, feeling the soft material of her skirt against her thighs. Resting her forearms on the seat and her head on her forearms, she wiggled her hips and stretched out her legs until they were completely straight and her toes dug into the shagpile. She was ready.

With her head turned to the left, she saw Jenny's lower half come into view, and shuddered as she saw the strap clutched in the girl's hands. 'Now Philippa,' she said, 'prepare yourself for retribution. I'll give you six strokes with the tawse and I want you to count off each one, thanking me nicely for it. Do you understand?'

Philippa was a little uncertain as to what Jenny actually wanted, but she still mumbled, 'Yes, Jenny.'

'That's "Yes, miss"!' Jenny barked. 'And don't you forget it!'

'Yes, miss,' said Philippa in a weak voice. She had not expected this, but then she *had* asked Jenny to show her more of this strange and wonderful world. If this was what it took, then this was what she would do.

The strap was lined up against her already sore bottom, making her flinch. Jenny seemed to wait until she had got herself under control again, and then it was drawn back. Philippa closed her eyes and gritted her teeth. The wait was bad enough, but not as bad as the stroke which ignited her bottom a few seconds later. 'Aah!' she cried, as the red hot stripe landed squarely across the middle of her cheeks. She took a deep breath and tried to steady herself for the next stroke, but it did not come. Instead, she heard Jenny's commanding voice. 'Haven't you forgotten something young lady?'

Philippa suddenly remembered Jenny's instructions about counting off the blows. 'Yes, miss. One, thank you, miss. Sorry, miss,' she said contritely. Just saying the words gave her an odd thrill. She was totally powerless. Jenny was in control for the moment. Whatever happened this evening, she had no need to feel any guilt.

'That's better,' Jenny said. 'Normally, I'd just start again, but I'll let this one go since you're new to this – but not again, so be warned!'

'Thank you, miss,' said Philippa, grateful for her leniency, and for the excitement that this situation was generating within her. It soon turned to pain once again as the second blow landed, but this time she kept a cooler head. 'Ooh! Two, thank you, miss!'

'Very good, Philippa. You see, you do learn quickly.'

'I have a good teacher, miss – Oww! Three, thank you, miss!' Jenny was laying the strokes on carefully, so they did not all land on the same place. For this at least, Philippa was grateful, although the sting of the strap was such that it was only a minor relief, as the punishment went on relentlessly. 'Four, thank you, miss – oh, five, thank you, miss – ow! Six, thank you, miss!' The last stroke Philippa counted off with relish, knowing it meant the strapping was at an end.

'Well done, sweetheart,' said Jenny, as she helped the trembling girl to her feet, and Philippa noted with interest how suddenly Jenny could switch from being a heartless virago to being her good-natured friend again. 'Now take a seat – if you can – and we'll see where you want to go now.'

Philippa followed her instructions, wincing as her stinging bottom connected with the soft material of the sofa. The pain, however, was already becoming more of a glow, just as it had done when Steve had slippered her, and she was also getting the same warm feeling in the pit of her stomach. She wondered if Jenny intended to bring her to orgasm again tonight, and if so, how soon.

Jenny dropped the strap into the box, as if pleased with the job it had done. 'One off the list,' she said cheerfully. 'Hey, I've got an idea. Don't go away.' And she darted out the room and up the stairs, leaving Philippa alone in the living room. She got up to stretch her legs, which were a little stiff after being held in the awkward position on the sofa even for a brief time. She massaged her bottom, revelling in how good this felt, and then saw the mirror over the fireplace, and could not resist manoeuvring herself around to take a look at the damage. Holding up the tail of her blouse, she gasped when she saw her bottom.

Its redness contrasted sharply with her pale legs and thighs, but most vivid of all, were the wide, dark stripes which crossed her cheeks. She was able to count every one of the six Jenny had given her. She poked one of them with her finger, drawing in a sharp little breath as she felt the sting. But it was not sharp enough to stop her doing it again. She stretched the skin of her left buttock with one hand and began to trace the outline of the marks with her other fingers, reliving the strapping blow by blow.

She must have enjoyed doing this very much, for she lost track of how long she stood in front of the mirror, and did not even hear Jenny come back into the room. 'Jack was right,' she said, 'they always want to examine their marks.' Philippa looked up, surprised by Jenny's voice, and was then shocked beyond words by her appearance.

Gone was the sensible office outfit; the beautiful

120

blonde had replaced it with tight black leather jeans and a matching biker jacket. This was zipped up, but Philippa guessed that underneath it, Jenny wore nothing else. She stood up straight, looking all the more imposing for the extra height added by the stiletto-heeled black knee-boots she had chosen to complete the outfit. Her long hair had been drawn back into a tight ponytail. The overall effect was one of total severity.

'Do you like it?' Jenny asked, after allowing Philippa a few seconds to take the new situation in.

'Jenny, I – you look – well . . .'

'Dominant is the word I hope you're looking for, Philippa. There's something about leather. I find I can never really be submissive while wearing it, which of course makes it the ideal choice for moments such as this. Are you ready for some more, then?' And she strode across the room, her new clothes creaking softly as she went. She stopped by the pile of implements on the floor, and crouched beside it. Taking her time, she very carefully selected a large black paddle, which looked rather like a table-tennis bat, but which was actually made of a thicker black leather than her jacket and trousers. Twice she slapped it none too gently against her palm, then stood up and stared at Philippa with something approaching menace.

Philippa hoped that this was still just an act, but she knew that even if things had moved beyond that, there was no way she could go back. The excitement was growing for her all the time. Still clutching her abused bottom with both hands, she signalled her assent to Jenny by lowering her eyes. 'How would you like me to prepare myself this time, miss?' she murmured.

'I think you're ready for something a little more challenging. Just stay where you are, but turn around, bend over and grasp your ankles. But before you do that, take off your blouse.'

Philippa blushed as her fingers fumbled to obey these

most explicit instructions. Was this the same woman who had, in this very room, dressed as a French maid and submissively offered herself to her housemates for a humiliating punishment?

Philippa was soon holding the white cotton shirt in her hand, and Jenny strode briskly up and took it from her. She carried it back to the sofa, where it joined Philippa's skirt on the arm. Meanwhile, their owner stood shivering in embarrassment, stripped down to her bra, stockings and suspenders. Philippa crossed her arms defensively in front of her chest, until Jenny spoke. 'Come on, girl, you have your instructions. Turn around and let's see those cheeks properly presented!'

Philippa turned and bent over. Taking hold of each of her ankles, she shuffled about to find the most comfortable way of achieving the position that Jenny wanted her in. It was not easy, and it was most certainly humiliating. She had to open her legs quite wide in order to maintain her balance, and could feel the lips of her sex being forced open by this manoeuvre. She was wet and getting wetter, she was in no doubt about that, but Jenny was not yet happy with the result. Taking her place beside Philippa, she put her free hand on her back and pushed her yet further down. This forced Philippa to open her legs even wider, which was apparently Jenny's objective, as the blonde girl tapped the insides of Philippa's thighs with the blade of the paddle to make sure she got the idea. By the time Jenny was happy, Philippa was completely helpless, and both of her holes were fully exposed to the woman she knew was about to chastise her. In this position, she was not able to see Jenny, but she could still smell her, the unmistakable odour of leather mixing with the familiar fragrance of her perfume.

Jenny's hand remained on Philippa's back. Then she spoke. 'The paddle can be a cruel implement when wielded properly.' Philippa's breath stuck in her throat, and she prayed that Jenny had been pleased with the

122

way she had got into position without arguing. 'But since you are a novice I will be gentle – well, fairly gentle. The main objective of this particular punishment is for you to enjoy the humiliatory aspect of your position. You have nothing I cannot see and touch, Philippa, so brace yourself – twelve coming up.'

There was a gap of a few seconds, and then the blade of the paddle landed right in the centre of Philippa's cheeks. She gasped at the shock and pain of it, but this time there was another sensation. The blow had fallen squarely on top of her exposed anus, and it sent a weird thrill right up her back passage. 'One, thank you, miss,' she hissed through her teeth.

'Very good,' said Jenny. 'You remembered the procedure without being told.'

'Yes, of course I – ow! Two, thank you, miss!' The second blow landed a little lower, sending a similar jolt of pleasure through Philippa's vagina. The third fell wholly on her right cheek and the fourth on her left, and then Jenny returned to her first choice of target area.

Eventually, Philippa had gasped and choked her way through the full twelve. Jenny removed her hand from her back and stepped away. Very slowly Philippa straightened up, kneading her bottom enthusiastically as she did so. As she stretched upright she felt a tear trickle down her right cheek, and yet she had not even been aware that she had been crying. She turned to look at Jenny – and found herself looking straight at the other girl's naked breasts.

Jenny had dropped the paddle on to the floor and then unzipped her jacket. As Philippa had suspected, she was naked beneath it. Now she held the leather garment open, exposing a perfectly formed, mid-sized pair of orbs, vanilla-white, and each one topped by a perfect cherry of a nipple. Philippa was by now well acquainted with Jenny's lovely bottom, but she had to admit that the girl's breasts were equally as impressive.

123

'Jenny, what are you doing?' she mumbled.

'Your reward, Philippa. For being such a good girl.'

'Reward?' Philippa was puzzled, and did not want to offend Jenny by saying or doing the wrong thing again.

'Oh, Philippa, you are sweetly naïve sometimes. I'd like you to kiss my breasts. Go on – I'm told they taste delicious.'

Philippa stared at Jenny, as the full impact of her audacious suggestion hit her just as hard as had any of the strokes from the tawse or paddle. She had never in her life contemplated doing anything like this. But then she and Jenny had already got up to some pretty wild stuff. Jenny's breasts were beautiful, and she was in charge for this evening. Philippa stepped towards her and lowered her head.

Placing her hands on Jenny's ribcage just inside the folds of her jacket, she fixed her lips gently on to Jenny's left nipple. It felt strange in her mouth, hard and rubbery, almost as if it were not real. Above her, she heard Jenny sigh. Encouraged, she tightened her lips and began to suck harder. She moved her hands further around until they almost met behind Jenny's back. She could feel Jenny's breathing getting heavier as her breast rose and fell in her mouth. 'Don't you have a tongue in there?'

Jenny was being nothing if not frank about what she wanted. Philippa turned her head to look up and saw her gazing down with a look of supreme affection. She felt Jenny's hands on her back, unhooking her bra. As it fell forward, she pulled her arms out of Jenny's jacket to allow the lacy garment to fall away and land on the floor next to the paddle, and then she encircled Jenny's waist again, tighter this time. She felt Jenny's hands cupping her own breasts, and her nipples swelled with excitement. Looking Jenny straight in the eye, she opened her mouth and released her breast, then ran her tongue over her lips. Then, as slowly as she could, she poked it out and placed the tip on the end of Jenny's nipple.

The effect was electric. Jenny threw her head back and gasped, 'Oh yes – *yes*! That's it! That's *it*!' Encouraged, Philippa ran her tongue over the whole of Jenny's nipple, and then her areola, in ever widening circles, until she came to the breast-flesh itself. This she savoured, tasting the sweet, smooth dryness, and eventually opening her mouth wide to take the whole nipple and as much of the tip of Jenny's breast as was possible into it.

She became ever bolder, nipping gently with her teeth, and biting down a little harder when Jenny groaned her assent. Without even being aware she was doing it, Philippa trailed her right hand up Jenny's body, until she held her right breast in her fingers. The yielding softness was much like that of her own, and she revelled in its beauty.

Suddenly, she felt Jenny's hands leave her body to clasp her gently on either side of her head. Reluctantly, Philippa allowed herself to be pulled away from Jenny's nipple, but was then delighted to find her mouth being guided to Jenny's other breast. Eagerly, she started sucking once again, this time using both hands to squeeze the other, blood-engorged nipple into prominence for her hard-working lips and tongue.

She lost track of all time while she was doing this. Jenny's hands flitted over as much of Philippa's upper body as she could reach – through her hair, around her shoulders, down over her arms and back up to her breasts again. After driving her to the limits of pain with the whipping, she was now taking her to the heights of ecstasy.

Finally, she pulled Philippa away once again. Helping her upright, she looked at her deeply and lovingly. 'That was beautiful, Philippa. You were born to this. Now let me repay you.' Standing straight, Philippa pushed forward her own chest, expecting Jenny to repay the favour directly in kind, and was surprised to find herself being led over to the sofa once again. More spanking? She was not sure she could take any more! But she breathed a sigh of relief when she realised that Jenny had other ideas.

Jenny pushed her down on to the couch and told her to lie back with her bottom on the edge of the seat. Then the blonde girl parted Philippa's legs and knelt between them. It was a strange sensation as the leather of her jacket and trousers brushed against Philippa's naked thighs, and she shivered pleasurably.

Jenny rested her hands on the tops of Philippa's thighs, and looked up at her. Then, leaning forward, she placed a kiss directly on the lips of Philippa's sex.

Philippa bucked at the contact, but made an effort to pull herself together. For all their intimacy up to now, this was strange territory for Jenny to be taking her into, but it was also highly erotic territory, into which Philippa could not imagine any man leading her, so she tried to relax as Jenny kissed her again.

This time, Jenny's mouth made contact with Philippa's mound for a little longer. She felt a tingle as the blonde head worked between her legs and knew she was too highly aroused to be able to hold back from coming for too long. She closed her eyes again, as she sucked in as much air as her lungs would hold, then she looked down again as a new sensation invaded her. She saw that Jenny was now poking her tongue in between her pussy lips, and swathing it up and down her labia. Then Jenny moved her left hand, and used her fingers to gently open up her entrance. Philippa just watched in fascination, then gave a little cry as Jenny licked her clitoris.

Instinctively, Philippa lifted her legs and hooked them over Jenny's leather-clad shoulders, the smooth material cold against her calves. In doing so, she pushed her crotch further into Jenny's face, an act which seemed to please the more experienced girl, for she licked and sucked even more enthusiastically. A few more seconds of this was all it took to send Philippa over the edge. Throwing her arms out to grasp fistfuls of the cushions, she came with an almighty shout, grinding her pubis so hard into Jenny's mouth that she had to wrap her arms around Jenny's thighs to maintain her hold. But maintain it she did, and Philippa was not released until Jenny had brought her to two more climaxes.

Eventually, though, she disengaged and leant back, gently taking hold of Philippa's legs and unwinding them, one at a time, from her shoulders. 'You enjoyed that, I can tell,' she said, needlessly. Philippa heard her as if in a far-away dream. 'Hey, come on, don't pass out on me now.' And she felt herself being tugged slowly up and on to her feet. She embraced Jenny fondly, although she also needed her for physical support. 'Tell you what, why don't we go to my room and you can have a little nap, and then we'll play it by ear.' Philippa did not have the strength to answer, and so she allowed herself to be led from the living room and up the stairs, and then along the landing to Jenny's room. Without turning the light on, Jenny guided her to the bed, and laid her down. Jenny's bed was a little bigger than Philippa's and she revelled in the comfort of having more room to curl up. Moonlight was creeping through a gap in the curtains, and she saw Jenny's silhouette as she sat down on a chair to remove her boots. Philippa had assumed that Jenny would leave her now, and so she was surprised to see her slip off her jacket, and then undo the tight leather trousers. With some effort, she skinned them down to her ankles and then stepped out of them. They joined the jacket on the chair, and Jenny stepped over to the bed, drew back the duvet and joined Philippa underneath it. Evidently, she had also been naked under the jeans, as Philippa felt her pubic hair brush against the front of her thigh as the blonde girl embraced her again. Feeling more satisfied than she had ever done before in her life, she difted off to sleep in Jenny's arms.

She had no idea how long she slept, but she woke to find Jenny still cradling her in one arm, and gently stroking her hair with the other hand. 'Welcome back, sleeping beauty,' she whispered softly, before kissing Philippa gently on the lips. Philippa returned the kiss with interest, feeling her own tongue meet Jenny's, and she trembled with pleasure as she remembered where that tongue had taken her.

They made love again, this time with Philippa doing her best to return the compliment. She lay on her back as Jenny crouched over her, her arms looped, once again, around her thighs, and her head buried deep between them. Jenny's own legs and bottom were spread out over Philippa's face, and she took one of the girl's buttocks in each hand and used her thumbs to prise them apart. To begin with she just gazed in fascination at the pouting red lips and tight little anus she had discovered, but then a wiggle of Jenny's hips told her the blonde girl wanted attention.

Moistening her own lips with her tongue, she lifted her head and placed them squarely on Jenny's opening. She had not been sure what to expect from the taste, and was surprised to find that it was not unpleasant. The little hairs above Jenny's slit tickled the tip of her nose, making it twitch, but undeterred by this, she set about her task in earnest, pulling the lips wider apart and gingerly poking her tongue in between them.

Encouraged by Jenny's response – which was to let out a muffled sigh, and eat Philippa even deeper – Philippa began to roll her tongue up and down the labia. As it went deeper, she was able to use her lips to stimulate the outer edges, something which seemed to give Jenny a great deal of pleasure. And it was not long before she found what she knew she had been looking for all along – Jenny's clitoris.

The touch of Philippa's tongue on this most sensitive little organ had an electric effect on Jenny. She bucked and cried out, but not once did she take her mouth from Philippa's crotch, and a few seconds later, her tongue found Philippa's clitoris once again, and she reciprocated, measure for measure.

The two girls sucked in harmony, as if they were racing to bring each other to the peak of pleasure. Occasionally, Philippa's bottom would rub a little harder against the sheets, reminding her of the scorching pain from the strap and paddle, but this only served to heighten her excitement. It could not go on for much longer. Jenny's more experienced ministrations brought Philippa to a climax first, but her own orgasm was not far behind. Her hips began to jerk spasmodically forcing Philippa to dig her fingernails deeper into the soft pillows of her bottom cheeks. The sharp pain this must have caused Jenny did not seem to bother her – on the contrary, it only seemed to increase the power of her orgasm. Both girls came with a series of shuddering gasps, which seemed to Philippa to go on forever.

Of course, they had to land sooner or later; Jenny rolled sideways, and they lay head to toe for some time before the blonde girl stretched and made the effort to pull herself around to face the right way on the bed. She pulled the duvet back up from the floor where it had been kicked by a thrashing foot, and covered herself and Philippa with it. She trailed a hand down the side of Philippa's face and over her neck, eventually letting it come to rest on her left breast. Then she kissed her ear, before nibbling the lobe affectionately. 'Know what?' Philippa heard her whisper as she drifted off to sleep. 'I think you're ready to take a look down our cellar.'

Seven

Philippa sat nervously drinking coffee. Jack and Jenny had told her to wait in the kitchen while they prepared themselves in the cellar, so she had made herself a cup as much to pass the time as out of a genuine desire for caffeine stimulation. Not that she needed that – she was feeling intense enough as it was.

Three days had passed since her evening with Jenny. She had woken up alone in Jenny's bed the following morning, although Jenny had thoughtfully set the alarm clock so that she would not oversleep and miss work. Maybe just as thoughtfully, Jenny herself had left the house early. Philippa knew it would not have been easy waking up in the other girl's arms or having breakfast with her. The lust brought on by the corporal punishment session could explain the enthusiasm with which she had entered into sex with her. The girl was very beautiful, and Philippa was flattered by her attentions, but, she kept telling herself, she was not a lesbian. All day at work, moreover, she was reassured to find herself thinking about Steve when her mind flashed back to the previous night's events, and as her bottom shifted sorely on her seat.

Both Jack and Jenny had been at home when she had arrived there, and for this she was grateful, as she knew that Jenny would not discuss in detail what had happened between them – not with Jack there. But she had obviously told him at least one part of it – her belief that

Philippa was ready to see what was kept down in the cellar.

Of course, she did not let on that she had known all along that it was not just a dark room, and neither had she confessed what she had actually seen on that fateful night. But they still did not let her completely into their confidence; all they did was ask her to wait until the weekend, and to keep the Saturday night free.

And now it was finally Saturday night. After tea they had appeared in the living room, dressed, so far as she could tell, perfectly normally in jeans and sweaters. Each had, however, been carrying a large black plastic bag, and had given her the instruction about waiting in the kitchen. Then Jack had unlocked the cellar door and they had disappeared down the steps into the gloom, shutting and locking the door behind them.

There followed muffled noises from below, but nothing Philippa could put a positive identity to. Once she thought she heard the clank of chains, but the sound was too brief for her to be sure. There was also what could have been described as the moving of furniture, but again it was difficult to pin down exactly what she was hearing. She paced about anxiously, checking her watch more often than was strictly necessary for her to know it would be twenty minutes or so before the key turned and the door was reopened by Jack.

But he did not look like the same Jack who had disappeared down those steps. Evidently the bag had contained a change of clothing, for his casual weekend attire had been replaced by tight jodhpurs, knee-high riding boots, and a loose white shirt. In his hand he carried a black riding crop – the same one she had seen with all the other implements a few days earlier, Philippa assumed. Was it just for effect? Philippa doubted that very much, and wondered which of them he was thinking of using it on.

'Oh, very Mr Darcy.' She could not resist the

wisecrack, but Jack's face showed not a flicker of emotion.

'Don't mock, young lady – you don't know what fate awaits you down here.' Philippa knew deep down that she could actually trust Jack, despite her misgivings about his motives, but she still felt her blood run cold. She was taking a big risk following him down there. But still she followed, as he turned and led the way.

It was dark. The only light came from a dim bulb at the far end of the cellar. The centre of the room, where she had seen Jenny chained to the chair as Jack had caned her, was now empty. And this time she could see no sign of Jenny.

Once she had reached the foot of the steps, and when her eyes had grown more accustomed to the gloom, Philippa saw that the cellar was actually constructed in a 'T' shape, with a large central section and a similarly sized annexe. This was shut off from the rest of the room with a curtain, which had been drawn. Philippa assumed that this part served as a changing room, in which Jenny was refining whichever costume she had chosen for the event.

She looked around and realised how strange her surroundings were. At first glance it had seemed just like an ordinary cellar, probably identical to those underneath every house in this street. But now she saw that its fittings were not of the everyday toolbox variety. Looking to her left, she saw a black chain set into the stone wall by a rivet hammered into its middle link. This had reduced it to two equal halves of about a foot in length. From the ends dangled leather cuffs, open but obviously capable of being closed by two sturdy-looking buckles on each. A few feet along the wall, and set at the same height, was another pair of cuffs, this time attached to two separate chains fixed to the wall at about two feet apart. The two sets of shackles looked ominous to Philippa. They could have been purely ornamental, but somehow she doubted it.

She peered further into the long, dark space, and saw the caning stool tucked away in the corner, obviously not needed for the time being. Looking up, she noticed a large wooden post running from the ceiling to the floor at the back of the room. A pair of heavy black rings had been set into the wood, one on either side of the post, at about a foot below the roof. Her eyes then found a series of metal hooks, screwed into the ceiling at intervals of about two or three feet, stretching all the way to the back of the cellar. There were six in all, and they looked very sturdy. The rack of canes she had seen before, but it was no less frightening for that reason, loaded as it was with rods of different lengths and thicknesses. Lying on the floor and against the wall under the rack, was a pile of chains – or maybe it was just one long chain coiled up – with at least three large padlocks resting on top of it.

Philippa wondered how long Jenny was going to be. She had heard no sounds and had detected no movement from behind the curtain, and so she assumed that the girl was already dressed – or undressed – and waiting to be instructed by Jack to make her entrance. Jack, however, now spoke to Philippa, having allowed her time to take in what she saw.

'Pretty impressive, eh? It took me a long time to get everything just the way I wanted it – and even longer to find the right people to share it with. Special people, like you and Jenny.' Philippa glanced at the curtain, expecting the other girl to come marching out on cue. Nothing. But Jack had seen to where she had switched her attention. 'Oh – you want to know what Jenny's up to? Of course – but first, I must insist on one little precaution.' He walked up to the pile of chains on the floor, delved in and rattled them about, and then came out with a pair of silver handcuffs. 'These,' he said, brandishing them in the air.

Philippa looked at him, nonplussed. What was he

talking about? 'Not with me?' he said, in a slightly sarcastic tone. 'Come here and I'll show you.' Against her better judgement, she stepped across the floor, her sandals tapping against the stones. As she reached him, he suddenly dropped the riding crop and his right hand flashed out. He caught her by her left wrist and she felt the bracelet click into place. She guessed what his next action would be and tried to escape it, but he was far too quick and strong for her. Her right arm was dragged forward and her wrists were locked together.

She protested throughout. 'No! Get off me, you bastard! Let me go! No!' The idea occurred to her that she should kick out at his shins, but for some reason she did not. She told herself it was because she knew he would not feel a thing through his boots. But how much of a fight did she really want to put up this time?

Jack let go of her once she was handcuffed. Ignoring her protests and pleas to be released, he walked to the corner and picked up the stool, then came back to where Philippa stood alternately jangling and examining the cuffs. Placing it on the floor in front of her, he stepped up on to it, quickly taking hold of the chain again. Philippa felt her arms being raised, then heard a clinking noise as one of the links was slipped over a hook. As quickly as he had got up on to it, Jack stepped down from the stool, just as the idea of kicking it away came to her. But in a few seconds he was out of her reach, casually putting the stool back out of the way. Philippa was trapped.

For the moment, her position was not uncomfortable. The ceiling was low enough for her to be able to rest her feet on the floor, but her arms were at full stretch above her. She could gather up a fair length of the chain in her hands, but the hook was just out of reach, making it impossible for her to release herself – and anyway, even if she were to succeed in doing that, she would still be shackled.

At least, thought Philippa, she had dressed sensibly for the occasion, in a mid-length grey pleated skirt and thick tights, and a blue pullover on top of a T-shirt. Now, obviously, she had to resign herself to the fact that Jack could easily pull her lower clothes down to her ankles, and this was what she expected him to do, so she was more than surprised when he finally spoke.

'Sorry about that, Philippa, but I just don't think you'd have gone willingly into bondage. Don't worry – you're not my target for tonight – well, not unless you ask me very nicely. No, I just wanted to make sure that you had a ringside seat for the performance, and that I would have your undivided attention. Oh, and we both wanted to be certain that you wouldn't try to intervene. Please remember, we are experts. Don't try this at home, as they say – well, not just yet anyway.'

By 'we' she guessed he meant himself and Jenny, but she still had no idea where the girl was. She was, however, confident that she would not be kept in the dark for very much longer. Picking up the crop again, Jack walked over to the curtain across the annexe. 'You were wondering where our little flatmate is. Well, I'm afraid she's been a bad girl again, showing you all those naughty things you can do together, and not letting me in on the action. And that is why she finds herself like this.' And with a theatrical flourish he drew back the curtain, and Philippa saw how comfortable her own position was by comparison.

Jenny's hands, too, were fixed to a ceiling hook and raised right up above her head. But unlike Philippa's, her legs were not free. Or together. Similar hooks had been placed in the opposite walls of the annexe, and her legs had been drawn as far apart as they could go. Then short chains had been attached to the leather cuffs she wore on her ankles – she was effectively spread out as an inverted human 'Y'.

And she had definitely changed her outfit before Jack

had trussed her up; her sensible house clothes were nowhere to be seen. Instead, she wore a black basque from her bust to her waist. The cups had been lowered, and her full breasts pulled out. Despite her predicament, Philippa could see that her nipples were swollen and red. Her legs were encased in sheer black stockings, clipped to the suspenders of her corset, and she wore high-heeled black pumps on her feet. She wore no knickers, and her vaginal lips, parted by the manner in which she had been bound, looked rather moist.

But what shocked Philippa the most was Jenny's silent acceptance of her situation. Not because she was being a well-behaved, meek little slave, but because she had no choice. Her mouth was open, and yet she was unable to speak, due to the red plastic ball she held clenched in between her teeth. Philippa peered more closely at the gag, and saw the brown straps which extended from either side of the ball. She imagined it must be buckled fast behind the girl's head.

'Do you like her, Philippa?' Jack's voice reminded her that there was a third person in the room. 'As you will no doubt have gathered, it took some time to get her sufficiently restrained, but it was worth it. Look at her – she can't move an arm or leg in any direction. Her tits and cunny are completely exposed, and she can't do a thing to stop me doing whatever I want to do to her. And neither, for that matter, can you.'

'What – what are you going to do to her?' Philippa finally found her voice.

'Whatever I wish. She knows that. And that is what she's getting so excited about.' He strolled over to the blonde girl and gently rubbed the lips of her vagina, then raised his fingers to his nose and sniffed them appreciatively. Philippa saw Jenny's eyes follow his hand as he did this, and she squirmed as he touched her, but it was clearly with pleasure and not with revulsion. Then she closed her eyes and exhaled as best she could through her gag.

Jack stepped back and took up the riding crop from where it had fallen on the floor. He flexed it threateningly as he smiled at the restrained girl. 'Yes, Jenny's been very wicked with you, and she knows it. She was only supposed to show you how the implements work, not seduce you into bed – and for that, she knows the penalty only too well. In fact, I do believe that's why she did it.' And without any more warning he raised the crop, and brought it down on Jenny's behind. The girl groaned as it landed, and Philippa herself let out a little cry and jerked against her own chains. She remembered what Jenny had taught her about how important it was to be warmed up before anything serious was used on your bottom, and as far as she could tell Jack had not allowed Jenny that luxury this time around.

The crop landed again and again, and Jenny's muffled cries grew louder. She was clearly in some degree of discomfort, and Philippa saw tears begin to brim in her beautiful eyes. But Jack showed her no mercy, and swiped relentlessly at her bottom with the long black crop, ignoring even Philippa's pleas on her behalf. He only ceased after about two dozen strokes, and Philippa could only imagine what Jenny's rear looked like. Tears were rolling down the girl's cheeks, and she breathed heavily through the gag.

Having tossed the riding crop into the corner, Jack took up the plastic bag and reached inside. He pulled out something cylindrical and pink, and approached Philippa. 'Remind you of anything?' he asked, as he brandished the dildo in front of her. It was large, at least ten inches long, but otherwise a perfect reproduction of the male organ. 'Now, you may feel I've been a little hard on Jenny,' he went on, 'but I intend to show you that the exact opposite is true. Watch and learn.' And he walked over to the suspended girl, whose eyes followed his every movement. They widened considerably as he traced the end of the phallus over her breasts, concentrating firstly on her erect nipples, and then on the valley between them. Next he moved it down over her lace-clad belly, then finally, deliberately, brought it down to touch the lips of her sex. He ran the head over the engorged flesh for a few seconds, then plunged the object inside her with one clean motion, making her gasp and throw her head back. Jack took his hand away and stepped back. 'You see, Philippa,' he said to the shocked observer, 'could I really have done that so easily if she hadn't been as hot as hell down there after the whipping?' Returning to Jenny's side, he placed his right hand over her left breast and began to massage it gently, while his left hand went back to the dildo and began to ease it in and out.

Jenny started moaning again, but this time with obvious pleasure rather than pain. Most of the time her eyes were closed, but when she did open the lids, Philippa could see that they were rolling in ecstasy as the pressure built. Jack seemed to be pushing the object in deeper with every stroke, and Philippa watched as it rolled in and out, parting the flesh with each movement.

It did not take long. Within a couple of minutes, Jenny was making the little squeaks Philippa had heard her make the other night as she had built up to orgasm, albeit muffled this time by the obstruction in her mouth. Jack speeded up his tempo accordingly, and moments later, Jenny shrieked and seemed to bite down hard on the plastic ball. After a few final and particularly hard lunges, Jack slowed to a halt and then stopped his movement of the dildo, but he did not remove it as Philippa had thought he would. Instead he pushed it in as far as it would comfortably go, and then let go of it altogether.

Once again, he stood back and surveyed the sobbing, ecstatic wreckage to which he had reduced Jenny. Philippa guessed that were it not for the chains, her friend would have been unable to stand. As it was, she was literally hanging by her wrists, and her head had drooped against her chest, which heaved with the effort of breathing. Her eyes were closed, and Philippa wondered if she had passed out altogether. The large dildo protruded obscenely from her vagina, its lips now crimson and swollen with excitement.

'Normally I would have provided that service for her myself,' Jack's voice cut in from the side. Philippa turned in her own bonds to look at him, the picture of composure. 'So much more fun for everyone. But I feel I may need to preserve as much of my strength as is possible for later on – we so rarely get to entertain visitors down here. And of course, I wouldn't normally allow Jenny release so soon, but I felt it was important to show both sides of the pain and pleasure equation to you as quickly and simply as was possible.'

'So, what are you going to do with her now?' Philippa finally found her voice again after the shock of what she had just witnessed. 'And with me for that matter? You can't leave us hanging here all night.'

'Not true, Philippa. I could if I wanted to, couldn't I?' By now, Jenny seemed to have recovered a little, and she opened her eyes at these words. Then she looked down at her crotch as if she were seeing and feeling the dildo inside her for the first time. She stared back at Jack, obviously expecting him to remove it, but unable to ask him to in the conventional way. Philippa wondered if it was becoming uncomfortable by now.

'I haven't quite decided what I shall do with you next, Philippa, but rest assured it will be fun for all of us. Now there's a very good bottle of white chilling in the fridge upstairs, and whipping deserving female bottoms is very thirsty work, so if you'll excuse me, I'm going to put my feet up for a bit and plan the rest of the evening. Don't go away, you two.' And with that he turned, and headed up the cellar steps.

'Wait! Jack, come back! You can't just leave us here

like this! *Come back!*' But Philippa's calls were ignored as his footsteps disappeared up the wooden steps and the door closed behind him. She heard him walking about in the kitchen above them, and then disappearing into the hall.

Philippa looked desperately at Jenny, who simply stared back. A half-smile seemed to play across her face, lighting up her red-rimmed eyes. Philippa opened her mouth to ask her a question, but it died in her throat as Jenny gently shook her head to tell her that any more complaints would be futile.

And so they hung together in silence, Jenny's enforced, and Philippa's for lack of anything to say. From time to time, one of them would flex her limbs to try to get a little more comfortable in the creaking chains. Jenny would also move her thighs as much as she could, making the dildo bob up and down. Was she trying to expel it, or could she have another objective? Perhaps she was trying to stimulate herself again? It must be touching her clitoris – it would not be impossible for Jenny to bring herself to another orgasm. Philippa wondered what she would do were Jenny to bring herself to a climax here in front of her, and realised that she would have no choice but to watch. And for some reason the idea excited her, even though she knew she should be horribly embarrassed by the thought. She even found herself hoping it would happen, just so she could find out for sure how she felt about the other girl.

But if that was Jenny's plan, it was thwarted by Jack's return. There was no clock in the cellar, but by twisting her left hand around and leaning back as far as she could, Philippa was able to see her watch, and she estimated that they had been left to stew for at least half an hour. Jenny's eyes widened as she heard Jack's footsteps above them, then the cellar door opening, and finally his approach down the steps, and Philippa looked around to regard him as he reappeared. 'Enjoy your wine?' she asked sarcastically.

'Come now, Philippa, that tone of voice doesn't suit such a pleasant, polite young lady as yourself. If you're going to take that attitude, I may have to gag you in the same way as I have gagged Jenny.' Philippa looked at the ball gag in Jenny's mouth, and froze at the thought. She realised that following Jack's instructions was the best course open to her. This, after all, was his territory, and she had asked to be initiated this far.

'Sorry, I'll try to be more respectful from now on,' she muttered, humbly.

'Glad to hear it. Now I believe it's time for the next stage of Jenny's punishment, and that calls for a change of scene.' He approached the muted girl and stroked her face gently, seeming to look lovingly in her eyes. Then his hand travelled down to her crotch, where it seized the plastic rod. Jenny gasped as he manipulated it, and Philippa thought she might have another climax. But it seemed Jack was not going to allow her that, for he slowly drew the dildo out from her vagina. He held it up before Jenny's face in a way which seemed to mock the state of sheer lust to which she had been brought, and then he stepped away from her and dropped the object back into the plastic bag. Reaching into his pocket he pulled out a set of keys and approached Jenny once more, then, dropping to one knee behind her, he unlocked each of the shackles which held her ankles. Gratefully, she moved her legs together, and flexed them to get the circulation moving again. Jack stood up again and reached up to release her wrists, and Jenny was finally free, but, Philippa noted, she made no attempt to remove her gag, even though it appeared to be a simple enough operation. Instead she reached around and rubbed her buttocks, a feeling of intense relief registering on her face.

Leaving the shackles dangling from the ceiling, Jack now addressed Jenny directly 'To the post,' he ordered, reinforcing the instruction with a finger pointed straight at the wooden beam. Jenny looked up at him as if she were trying to make some silent protest, but even Philippa could tell by his expression that there would be no arguing with him. She watched, intrigued, as Jenny walked to the wooden pole at the far end of the cellar. In the meantime Jack had gone to the opposite corner, where he flicked a switch in the wall, and a small spotlight suddenly illuminated the post. He had, it seemed, thought of everything when he had furnished this cellar. As Jenny approached the post, Philippa could see why she had not even bothered to try removing the ball in her mouth; where the straps met behind her head, a small padlock held them in place. Even her gag was secured.

Her movements seemed well rehearsed – something Philippa had come to expect, as she learned more of the rituals of this strange house. Setting her feet carefully on each side of the post, Jenny reached up and grasped the rings which were set into it just above the height of her head. Then she leant forward, and rested her lovely face on one side of the rough wood and waited.

Only when she was positioned thus did Jack approach her. On the way, he paused to remove two sets of handcuffs from the bag. Methodically, he clipped one to each ring and then to Jenny's corresponding wrist. Although she was now manacled to them, she continued to grip the rings, as though she needed the support. Her posture seemed to confirm this, as she leant the front of her body against the wood.

Her legs were left free, but chained as she was, there was little she could have done to change her position anyway. Her bottom was thrust out and exposed, and Philippa regarded the weals which covered it – thin red tram lines contrasting sharply with the pale flesh of her bottom. On seeing them, Philippa's heart went out in sympathy to Jenny, and she wished that there were something she could do to help. Jack took up the riding crop again, and suddenly it occurred to her there might, after all, be some way for her to intervene.

Jack placed himself to Jenny's left, and lined up the crop against his target. Jenny twitched as the whip rested on her sore cheeks, and Philippa saw her brace herself. Jenny's head was turned towards Philippa, which meant that Philippa was able to see her screw her eyes up tightly in preparation for the stroke they all knew was about to fall. The crop was drawn back, held in the air for a few seconds, and then whistled down. The sound of its impact was almost drowned out by Jenny's muffled scream, but Jack showed her no mercy, and another blow followed a few seconds later, to the same vocal accompaniment. As the third blow fell, Philippa felt she had to try to do something to save Jenny from this terrible beating. 'Wait! Stop!' she called.

Jack paused, the crop poised in mid-air. He stared quizzically at her. Even Jenny opened her eyes and looked at her, her breath heavy through the obstruction in her mouth.

'Can I help you?' Jack asked, returning the note of sarcasm she had used on him on his return to the cellar.

'Please – don't whip her any more. If you're punishing her for making love to me, then there's no need to. I'm as much to blame as she is, so if you must whip someone, whip me instead. But please, leave her alone – she's had enough.'

Jack lowered the riding crop and looked at her, then gave her one of his most enigmatic smiles. It was impossible for Philippa to tell if he was actually considering the idea, or if he just found the concept amusing. Then, after what seemed a very long pause, he finally spoke. 'You do realise that such a whipping would be extremely painful?'

'Yes, yes, of course. I know exactly how much it would hurt – Jenny showed me.'

'I don't believe she went as far as using the riding

crop on you. This is not for the faint-hearted, you know.'

'But – you've already whipped her so severely. I can't just hang here and watch you do it to her again. Please, whip me instead.' Deep down, Philippa knew she would probably regret saying these words, but she felt she had no choice other than to try to save the girl who had given her so much friendship and pleasure since she had arrived at the house.

'Very well,' said Jack, after another lengthy pause. 'But don't expect me to be gentle with you just because you volunteered.'

'I won't – just don't whip Jenny any more.'

'So, let's prepare you then,' he said and, theatrically tucking the crop into his right boot, he strode to where Philippa hung from the ceiling. Was he going to whip her right there? Or would he move her to the whipping post so she could take Jenny's place? What she did not expect, was for his hands to disappear up her skirt.

She shrieked in surprise, and demanded to know what he thought he was doing, but he paid no attention to her. She twisted and turned as she felt his hands grasping the waist bands of both her tights and her knickers, but his grip was firm, and in her vulnerable position there was nothing she could do to stop him. She felt her underwear being pulled down, and as the cool air blew around her exposed legs, she caught sight of Jenny, still chained to the post and watching developments with a fascinated look on her face. Her expression seemed to be a mixture of intense desire and love, and it was directed solely at Philippa.

Philippa's tights and briefs were now right down around her ankles, and it came as no surprise to her when Jack seized first her right foot and then her left, and removed each of her shoes in turn. Tossing them aside, he was then able to take the other garments completely off, and these joined her shoes in a heap on the floor. He stood up again, and Philippa felt his hands on the back of her skirt, feeling for the fastener. All she could do was wriggle ineffectively, which in no way prevented him from finding the catch and zip. She felt first one being undone and then the other, and then her skirt fell open at the back. Its journey downward was inevitable, and it soon joined the rest of the pile.

She now hung naked from the waist down. Jack stepped in front of her and surveyed her with some satisfaction. She fumed silently at him, too angry to be embarrassed by the idea of him seeing her half-naked again, and as if in answer to her unvoiced thoughts, he spoke.

'Well, you didn't think I was going to whip you through all that padding, did you? Jenny should have explained to you that all whippings in this house are on the bare. Please accept my apologies for manhandling you just then, but somehow I didn't think you were quite at the stage where you would happily have undressed at my command, so it seemed logical and much quicker to carry out the operation while you couldn't fight back. Now, all I need to do is get you in place.'

Fetching the stool from the far corner of the cellar, he placed it behind Philippa and stepped up on to it so that he could unhook the chain of her handcuffs from the ceiling. It seemed he was going to be chaining her to the whipping post after all, and she wondered why he had not yet released Jenny to make room for her. It also appeared that Jack did not yet trust her enough to take the handcuffs off before chaining her to the post, as he had done with Jenny, and instead, he took the chain and led her to her fate. She shivered as her bare feet touched the freezing stone floor; they would be filthy by the time she left the cellar, she thought. But she also knew that was the least of her worries at the moment.

Jack led her around the post, and right past Jenny, who seemed to be finding this new development curious, if not downright amusing. It soon became clear why Jack had left her there – he had no intention of removing her at all. Instead, he placed Philippa against the post on the opposite side to his blonde captive. Fishing out his keys once again, he unlocked the cuff on Philippa's right wrist, and then brought it up to the ring above her left hand and clicked it shut. He then returned to the bag and pulled another set of handcuffs from it, and returned to fasten her left wrist to the opposite ring. 'It always pays to have plenty of handcuffs down here,' he said, cheerfully. 'You never know when you're going to need them.' Philippa looked over to where Jenny was shackled, only inches away. Their eyes met, and Philippa thought she read sympathy and compassion in Jenny's beautiful green pools. Only then did the reality of what she had volunteered for hit home. She knew this was going to hurt like nothing she had experienced so far.

Jack took his place to her left. With what she would have described as an exaggerated swagger, he reached for the riding crop in his boot and pulled it out, brandishing it like a rapier. She watched in horror as he lined it up against her naked bottom. Instinctively, she pushed her loins forward to escape it, and felt the rough wood press against her belly and crotch, which gave her a strange and unexpected thrill. Suddenly, she was aware of having butterflies in her stomach – the same kind she had experienced when she had lost her virginity to Paul all those years ago – only now they were much more intense. And she did not know why, but she could swear she was getting wet.

She closed her eyes and laid her head against the post, bracing herself for the impact. She did not have long to wait. The crop was lifted from her bottom, and in her mind's eye she saw it being raised above her in Jack's hand. There was a whistle, and a rush of wind, and then a line of fire was drawn across her cheeks.

'Aah!' she wailed, as the agony shot through her. It

146

hurt more than anything else she could possibly imagine. Even the slipper and strap had not prepared her for how painful it was. And Jenny had been absolutely right – no warm-up beforehand made an almighty difference to its intensity. The stroke had not added to an already burning ache; it was a searing pain all of its own.

Jack slashed at her again with the crop, a little higher this time. She screamed again. Her entire being seemed to be focused on the suffering in her bottom. A third blow made her open her eyes, and once again she found herself looking straight into the lovely face of Jenny. And even though the other girl was unable to speak, she still seemed to be able to get her message across, through her pleading, compassionate expression 'Hold on Philippa. Please, just for me, stay with it.'

A fourth stripe, lower than the rest, almost where her bottom ended and her thighs began, forced a piercing shriek from her. The fifth, thankfully, landed somewhat higher, but it crossed a couple of previous weals, demonstrating to Philippa just how effective that particular technique could be. Then a sixth stroke landed, right across the middle of her cheeks, eliciting an almost inhuman groan from her. She could not take much more of this kind of treatment.

Fortunately Jack must have realised this. He lowered the crop and left her side. Philippa opened her eyes and blinked through the tears she now found she was crying, her breath coming in short sobbing gasps. As her vision became clearer, she saw that Jack had moved back around the post and was now aiming the crop at Jenny's bottom once again. 'Wait!' Philippa yelled. 'I thought we'd agreed – you'd whip me in return for not whipping Jenny any more!'

'We did not agree, you suggested it. I never agreed that it would be the case. All I did was take you up on your offering yourself for a dose of the riding crop. Jenny gets the rest of her share just the same.'

'But that's not fair!' Philippa wailed.

'And who told you life was fair? It isn't, Jenny knows it isn't, and you're going to have to learn that too.' And the crop rose, then flashed down.

Philippa saw Jenny's face screw up in pain as it landed. She groaned through the gag, and her hands clasped the rings tighter than ever. Jack allowed her just enough time to relax before the next stroke, which made her hug the post as if it were a lover, her head thrown back as she lost herself in the turbulent emotions she must have been experiencing. Four more times he brought the riding crop down across her bottom, and all Philippa could do was watch as the pain registered on Jenny's beautiful but distorted face.

Then Jack seemed to decide she had had enough; he obviously had the capacity to show mercy eventually, Philippa thought to herself. But what he did next took her completely by surprise.

Casting the riding whip into a corner of the cellar, he began to unbutton his jodhpurs. He opened them completely and pulled his shirt free, then reached into his underwear to free his penis. It was large, maybe a little more so than Steve's – Philippa was shocked to find herself instinctively comparing him to her lover – and ready for action. Despite its threatening appearance Philippa felt reasonably safe, since he made no move towards her. Indeed, he did not even look at her, keeping his eyes firmly fixed on Jenny's punished behind. Reaching into the pocket of the tight trousers, he pulled out a condom, tore open the packet and slid the sheath on as quickly as he could.

He placed his hands on Jenny's waist. She let out a soft sigh and wriggled her bottom closer to him. From where she was chained she was unable to see him, but she had obviously heard the rustle of his clothing being removed. And had she had any doubt about his state of dress, it would have disappeared the second his engorged member touched her between her cheeks.

Philippa saw her eyes open and light up at the contact; there was a gleam there which was certainly new. Wiggling a little more, Jenny did everything she could to encourage further union with Jack, but he was not to be hurried. He ran his hands lasciviously up and down the front of her body, once again enjoying the fullness of her breasts, and pausing to tweak her nipples whilst kissing her neck and nibbling at the lobe of her right ear.

Jenny's lust had obviously reached a peak beyond which she would not have been prepared to wait, had she had any choice in the matter. However, as she was chained to the whipping post, the situation could only develop as quickly – or as slowly – as Jack wished it to.

Fortunately, his own desire must have been strong by this stage, and he prolonged the foreplay for only a few more seconds. His right hand left Jenny's breast and disappeared under her bottom. He fiddled about momentarily, then lunged forward with his hips, a look of pure lust written all over his face. Jenny's eyes bulged, and her hands dragged at the chains holding her in place. She spread her legs wide and they tensed and stretched, forcing her up to her full height. From her mouth came a strangled groan – Jack had penetrated her.

They stayed still for a few seconds, seemingly to savour the moment for as long as possible. Then, slowly, Jack began to move back and forth, gently at first, then quickening the tempo as Jenny's grunts became wilder and louder. Both his hands were again on Jenny's waist, his fingers digging deeply into the soft white flesh.

Philippa knew that such lovemaking could not go on for long. Jenny's squeals rose to become a high-pitched, continuous moan, the gag making any other kind of verbal communication impossible. But even if it had not been there, she would not have needed to have told anyone else in the room that she had reached a most spectacular orgasm. Jack seemed to find this the very spur he needed, and slammed home even harder with about half a dozen more lunges, then stopped at the deepest in-stroke and let out a long, low moan of animal gratification. His loins twitched, and he pumped gently into Jenny once or twice, but it seemed he was soon spent, having reached his own climax just after Jenny had attained hers.

All this had taken place only a matter of inches from where Philippa was helplessly bound. The only way she could have avoided it would have been to have closed her eyes. But she had not. In fact she had kept them wide open all the time, watching every little detail of Jack and Jenny's copulation, or as much of it as she could see from her position on the other side of the post. A few weeks ago she would have found this situation abhorrent, unbearable – a disgusting violation of her liberty and modesty. But now she had to admit to herself that it was fascinating. Her own backside still stung like hell where Jack had whipped her – now that the show was over, her mind was able to return to her own pain – but, despite the severity of her whipping, she was beginning to feel that warm glow she had known would arrive eventually, if her experiences so far were anything to go by.

She watched as Jack pulled out of Jenny, leaving her hanging helplessly in her bonds, apparently exhausted by her experience. He did not bother to close his jodhpurs or even to put his organ away, letting it hang limply from the front of his trousers. Philippa reflected how a penis looked so much less fearsome in that state.

The game was obviously nearing an end, as Jack eventually produced the keys to Jenny's cuffs, and unlocked her. He supported her as she almost fell away from the whipping post, and guided her to a convenient chair. He walked across the cellar and climbed halfway up the stairs to where, Philippa now saw, he had left the bottle of wine of which he had boasted before leaving earlier on. Evidently he had enough consideration for the girls to have left some of it for them, as three glasses sat beside it. Bringing one back with the bottle, he filled it and offered it to Jenny. She took it, even though she could have had no use for it at that moment because of her gag. Jack pulled out the keys once more and remedied the situation, reaching up behind her head and unlocking the strap which held the ball in place. Unclipping it, he brought the two ends forward, then gently eased the object out of her mouth, enabling her to relax her jaw properly for the first time in what had doubtless been a couple of hours. After throwing her head back and taking a deep breath in through her mouth, Jenny then turned her attention to the wine. She took a short gulp to lubricate her throat, and then a large one to quench her thirst. Only then did she speak.

'My God! What did you do to me? I don't think I can walk!' she exclaimed, and emptied her wine glass in another long draught before looking up and seeing Philippa still chained to the post. Naturally enough Philippa had expected to be released as soon as Jenny was, and she blushed at the thought of the girl, now free, being able to see her still bound and captive. 'And what about Philippa?' Jenny asked. 'How do you intend to see to her needs?'

Philippa stared at her. At first she had assumed that the girl was telling Jack to release her, but her last sentence implied that she had something else in mind entirely. Surely Jenny would not do that to her?

Jack was looking down at his limp member. 'There's no way I can do anything for her at the moment,' he said, 'even though she is lovely. But I'm sure you can summon up the strength. After all, you've had all the fun so far.'

'Wait!' called Philippa, 'I – I'm not sure I want any

151

. . . fun! Just unchain me, then we can all go upstairs! I know I asked you to show me what you do down here, but I think I've seen enough for now! Please, let me go!'

'Nonsense, sweetheart,' said Jenny, getting up on her feet, which were still unsteady, 'I wouldn't dream of it. It would be rude to let you go without coming.' She giggled at her own humour. 'Let me see what I can do.'

Despite Philippa's further entreaties that it really didn't matter, Jenny put down her wine glass and returned to the bag in which Jack had put the dildo. Picking it up, she looked at it with something approaching awe. The she turned to Philippa, the familiar, wicked glint back in her eye. 'Just relax, Philippa, this won't hurt a bit – quite the opposite, actually.' And she approached the helpless girl with a look of firm resolution.

Philippa had instinctively struggled against her chains at first, but now she realised that doing so was a futile waste of energy. And pleading with Jenny was also pointless, it seemed, so what could she do? She searched her mind and, to her own surprise, could only come up with one suggestion: be grateful that she picked up the sex toy and not the whip, and enjoy whatever she does to you, because she's going to do it, whatever you say.

Philippa's first wave of panic disappeared. Jenny was not going to hurt her. Indeed, she probably genuinely wanted to give her pleasure, and this was her way of doing it. Philippa became calmer, and her breathing steadied. By now the blonde girl was right beside her, the phallus held by its root in her right hand.

Philippa winced as Jenny ran her left hand down over her bottom. It really was sore this time. Despite Philippa's reaction, Jenny did not take her hand away, but stroked her skin lightly, murmuring soothing words in her ear. Philippa began to relax again. Then she felt it – the head of the dildo being inserted slowly but surely into the lips of her vagina. She bucked at first, but Jenny

152

was ready for this, and pushed a little harder so that the insistent invasion continued. She was pushing from behind, up from beneath the curve of Philippa's cheeks, and in between her parted thighs. Philippa noted that despite the shock and indecency of what Jenny was doing, her thighs remained apart.

The plastic rod travelled on relentlessly. It felt nothing like the real, flesh-and-blood cocks that Philippa had experienced so far – first Paul's and then Steve's. There was no give in this inanimate object, no warmth or softness, and yet that in itself made it even more exciting – this was going to be nothing but pure, self-centred pleasure.

Jenny seemed to sense when Philippa was full, and stopped pushing. She let things rest for a few seconds so Philippa could get used to the idea of the dildo being inside her, then began to reverse the action, pulling it out as slowly as it had gone in. Philippa moaned and tugged on the chains, knowing full well that she was still utterly helpless. Good, she thought, no guilt about this afterwards for me. When the dildo was almost out of her vagina, Jenny changed tack and began to push it in again. This time it slid in a little faster and deeper, drawing an appropriate vocal response from Philippa. The process was repeated: the dildo was pulled out then pushed back in. Philippa felt herself getting wetter and more welcoming with every stroke, and an insistent, and by now familiar heat began to build inside her. Jenny was unmistakably masturbating her to orgasm.

She could not help herself. She began to encourage the girl, vocally. 'Oh yes – yes, Jenny, let me have it! Oh God, fill me up! Yes, shove it in, Jenny – please let me have it!'

From a few feet away, and as if in a dream, she heard Jack's voice. 'Just as well we didn't gag her too – we'd have missed all this. She's really throwing herself into the spirit of things.' But even this ribald comment was not enough to distract her. As Jenny's strokes into her became harder and shorter, Philippa felt the fire smoulder, ignite, and finally explode within her belly. She came with a loud wail which she heard echo around the old stone walls, even as the tension flooded from her body and her muscles relaxed, letting her wilt against the post in the same way she had seen Jenny do a few minutes before.

In a daze, she felt Jenny kiss her lightly on the side of her face and stroke her tousled hair away from her eyes. Then she was left alone for some minutes to compose herself.

Eventually, she felt hands lifting hers and unlocking the cuffs around her wrists; once again it was Jenny, and she was grateful for the support of the other girl's shoulder as she was led from the post. She expected to be offered the chair, and was therefore rather surprised to find Jack using it. She was, however, less surprised to find him perched on the edge of it, using his fingers to put the finishing touches to another large erection. She looked at him, a question forming on her lips. He seemed to have a very expectant and greedy look upon his face. The she turned to Jenny, and saw a half-serene, half-encouraging smile on hers.

'What –' Philippa began, 'what do you expect me to do now?'

'Well, you don't have to –' Jenny began, as though she were ashamed to be answering the question.

'It's just that we thought it would be rather nice – and good for your education, as it were – if you were to, er –'

'Suck my prick,' Jack said, bluntly.

'Suck your – your prick?' Philippa could not believe he had just said that, after all he had put the two women through tonight. What did he think they were – his concubines?

'You don't have to do it all the way,' Jenny assured

154

her, hastily. 'Just until he says he's ready, then I'll dive in and take over.'

'Oh yes, and I'm sure he'll tell me exactly when he's ready,' said Philippa. She remembered one occasion on which Paul had, without warning, come in her mouth. It had been a most unpleasant surprise.

'On my honour,' promised Jack. 'And if I don't, then you can chain me to the whipping post and get your own back for everything that's happened this evening.'

An opportunity almost too good to miss, Philippa told herself. It may even be worth the risk of him having an accident. And after all, she had asked Jack and Jenny to take her further into their world – it seemed that she was trusted implicitly. Besides, Steve would want this done to him sooner or later and, as it had been a long time since she had tried it, she probably needed the practice. 'OK,' she announced. 'You're on.'

'Good girl,' said Jenny, hugging her warmly. 'I'll be right beside you all the way.'

Taking Jenny's hand, Philippa knelt next to her on the floor in front of Jack, who looked down on them with obvious pleasure. Perhaps we are his concubines after all, thought Philippa. But she had little time for reflection as he moved forward to the very edge of his seat, his fingers encircling the base of his penis, the whole intimidating length of which was now being offered to Philippa's mouth. For a second she looked at it as if hypnotised, then pulled herself together. Jenny gave her hand a reassuring squeeze, then released it. Philippa reached out with both hands and took hold of Jack's cock.

The organ twitched and Jack gasped as she wrapped her fingers around its thickness. Then she ran them gently up and down its length, feeling the blood pumping through his veins, so much more vibrant and – literally – alive than the dildo. And she realised right now it did not matter that it was Jack's cock she was handling. It might just as well have been Steve's or even Paul's – she was aroused, and all she needed was a solid male member.

Inexperienced though she was, she knew enough about sex to realise that Jack's earlier exertions with Jenny would make it possible for him to go on longer this time, so she rubbed him a little harder. She wanted to get him good and ready before putting him in her mouth. She was rewarded by the sound of his breathing becoming even more laboured, and guessing he was nearing the point of losing it once again, she decided the time had come. Opening her mouth, she extended her tongue and ran it over the purple tip of his penis. Jack shuddered, and she felt his hand run through her hair, although he made no attempt to force her mouth down, as she might have expected him to. Instead, he left her to flick her tongue over his glans a few more times, and then, when she was ready, she formed her lips into a small 'o' and slid them down over the head of his cock.

The thick pole filled the inside of her mouth, and she had to struggle to breathe through her nose at first. But then she found her breathing rhythm, and was able to begin a slow sucking motion with her mouth.

She was surprised at how much she remembered from the handful of times she had performed this particular love act on Paul. Jack's musky body scent was similar to Paul's but there was no question that he was bigger than her ex. And he also had a lot more self-control, it seemed. Sucking Paul had included contending with his continual attempts to shove himself deeper into her mouth. She had almost choked the last time they had done it – indeed, that had been the reason why it had been the last time. Jack was different; he was allowing her to find her own pace, and not forcing her to take in any more than she wanted to.

Gradually, she began to draw more of his length into her mouth, although the furtive memory she had of spying on Jenny while she had done the same thing to him in almost the same spot seemed to include a picture of the girl taking almost all of his eight or so inches down. Philippa knew she was only halfway there. Not bad for a beginner, though, she told herself.

Instinctively, she spread her hands out over the insides of Jack's thighs, and as she did this she felt Jenny stroking her back through her remaining clothes and running her fingers down her spine. She shuddered when the girl lightly touched her bottom, tracing the outline of one of the weals across her cheeks. But now the sting was more than just pain; it was another element to heighten her arousal, to make her realise how turned on she was by everything which had happened this evening. In short, she welcomed the whipping she had been given, and now she was enjoying herself in giving Jack the best blow job she had ever given.

She grew bolder, and started to move her head faster, trying to take more of his penis into her mouth. To her great surprise she succeeded, and this emboldened her to use her cheeks even harder, even pressing her tongue against the underside of Jack's cock as it was encased in the warm softness of her mouth. Jenny's hand continued its downward journey, and suddenly Philippa felt her fingers intruding hard into her sex. Jenny leant forward again and kissed Philippa on the neck once more, harder this time, as she found the little button of her clitoris and manipulated it skilfully.

All this could not fail to have an effect on Philippa, or indeed on Jack, who seemed to benefit second-hand from Jenny's new involvement. He raised his hand and clenched it in what could have been a victory salute, but was clearly meant as the signal for the girls to change over as agreed. He tried to communicate using words, but seemed to find that a little difficult, managing only a vague 'N – now, Jenny . . . y – yes, now.'

Philippa felt Jenny's hot breath in her ear, then heard

her whisper, 'I think it's time, darling. Quick, let me in before he comes!' But – and she could not explain this even to herself long after that night – Philippa suddenly decided that she was going to finish what she had started. She had worked on this erection, she had got Jack this far, and no one, not even Jenny who had been so kind and supportive towards her, was going to take it away from her. Casting her eyes sideways, she shook her head as vigorously as she could without dislodging Jack's cock. Jenny seemed to understand, even if Jack did not. He looked down at the two girls, mystified as to why they had ignored his clear signal. Jenny looked back at him and said, quietly, 'I think Philippa wants to do you more of a favour than you ever dreamed she would,' and then returned her attentions to masturbating the other girl.

Jack's upper body rocked back in the chair, thrusting his tool further into Philippa's mouth. There was no way he was going to pull out now, and for a second Philippa wondered if she was going to be able to do this. But then she readjusted to the extra length, and sucked even harder. She could feel the tip against the roof of her mouth, and the whole organ pulsing between her lips. Then, a second later, it jumped and jerked, and her mouth was filled with Jack's seed.

The harsh, salty taste was overwhelming at first. She was so full of him she had no choice but to swallow, and he had shot so far into her mouth that most of his semen slipped easily down her throat. But it just kept coming, even as she tried to disengage herself, and she actually thought that she might drown in the stuff if it did not stop soon. At the same time, she felt another orgasm welling up in her own sex, from Jenny's ministrations. When it eventually overtook her it was not as strong as the one she had experienced at the whipping post, but added to the sensation of having a dripping penis in her mouth, she felt it was mind-blowing enough.

Eventually Jack withdrew his prick from Philippa's mouth. She felt some of his seed fall from her lips as he did so, landing on her sweater. Jenny immediately put her tongue to work on Jack, cleaning the residue from him as if she felt a little disappointed at missing out on what she had been promised.

Philippa sat back in a daze. Had she really just done that? Had this evening been real, or just a wonderful dream? No, it had all been real; the evidence was all around her – the taste in her mouth, Jack's wet prick dangling before her, the dull ache in her wrists and bottom, even the cold stone floor beneath her knees. All bore testament to the fact that she had just gone through the most intense erotic experience of her life.

Jack looked down at the two women, his face flushed and his chest still heaving a little. 'I hope,' he said cautiously, 'you're not thinking of taking me up on my offer of being chained to the whipping post. It certainly wasn't my fault that you didn't pull away, Philippa. I gave you enough warning.'

'That's OK, lover,' Jenny answered, cheerily. 'We'll let you off for tonight. But I don't think it'll be too long before we have you up there. I think Philippa's learning faster than we can teach her.'

Eight

Philippa stood in her room and looked in the mirror. She barely recognised the woman who stared back at her. Gone was the naïve and timid country girl, replaced by a vamp with only one thing on her mind tonight – sex.

It was a week since Jack and Jenny had shown her the cellar, the event she now thought of as her full inauguration. After she had performed oral sex on Jack the trio had left the basement, finished another bottle of wine in the living room, and had then adjourned to Jack's large bedroom where they had spent the night. Having revived his flagging penis with her mouth, Jenny had gently coaxed Philippa into having full sex with Jack. Reclining on the Victorian-style double bed, her head cradled in Jenny's soft, warm lap, she had opened her thighs to allow him in. It had been a slow, languorous session, as Jack had been nearing the end of his staying power by then, but Philippa had enjoyed it, orgasming once again as Jenny had reached over her shoulders to stimulate her nipples.

As she had lain between them, only half awake, and only just aware of Jack's hand on her right thigh and Jenny's arm across her breasts, she had wondered aloud, 'How many more are there like us?' And over a large breakfast, cooked surprisingly well by Jack the next morning, she had been reminded of her question by Jenny.

'You're really curious about our scene, now, aren't you?' the blonde girl had smiled, over her bacon and eggs.

'Was it that obvious last night?' replied Philippa, with mock innocence.

'I got a feeling. No, really – there's far more to it than what we did last night, or even what you saw at the party. If you want to – and *only* if you want to, because it's a big step – we can go to a club next weekend.'

'A club? As in music? Raves? That sort of thing?'

'Well, they do play music, yes,' said Jack, joining them at the table with his own plate. 'But that's more of a sideline. There's not much dancing going on – well, not of the regular variety, anyway.'

'We're talking about a fetish club,' said Jenny, in answer to Philippa's puzzled expression. 'There are a few in London, some better than others, but Jack's a member of most of them.'

'Now, why doesn't that surprise me?' laughed Philippa.

'Careful, young lady – you're not too old to go back over my knee again!'

She could tell this time that he was only joking, and she was pleased that the atmosphere between them seemed to have improved dramatically. It's amazing what a bit of serious sex can achieve, she thought.

'Anyway,' continued Jack. 'About these clubs. They're open most weekends, and some of them on weekdays, and getting in wouldn't be a problem. Except –'

'There always has to be an "except",' said Philippa. 'How many people do I have to have sex with when I get there?' She meant this as a joke, but the leap in her stomach made her realise how appealing she might find having to do it.

'You don't actually have to have sex with anyone, in fact, you don't have to do anything to anyone, or with

161

anyone at all; you can just sit and watch. A lot of people get off on just doing that. The "except" is that there's a dress code – strict fetishwear only.'

'I don't have any,' said Philippa. 'Or do I? I don't even know what fetishwear is.'

'Don't worry,' Jenny cut in, 'I'll help you. Mr Macho here will probably just put his leathers on, and assume he's ready for anything. We girls have to put a bit more thought into our outfits. Don't panic, I won't go over the top,' she said, seeing the worried look on Philippa's face. 'Although that does help sometimes.'

'So that's settled, then,' declared Jack, pushing a forkful of bacon into his mouth and rudely speaking through it. 'I'll get us on the guest list for somewhere good on Saturday, and Jenny will kit you out so you turn all the heads which aren't wearing blindfolds.'

They had all chuckled at this last remark, but Philippa had wondered how true it might be – and she had found that thought just a little exciting.

And now it was Saturday, and she was ready to go. She stared at her reflection. It was fortunate that she and Jenny were roughly the same size, as she had been able to borrow one of her dresses rather than having to buy an expensive outfit of her own. Looking at it, she did not doubt that this kind of dress would be expensive – and it certainly wasn't the kind of thing that would be found on sale in the average high-street shop.

From bosom to mid-thigh, she was encased in tight black rubber. The dress itself was a simple design, cut a little lower at the front and higher in the leg than she would normally have chosen, and with shoulder straps and a tapered waist. Only a slim girl such as Philippa or Jenny would have been able to get into it, and Philippa was pleased with the unusual way in which it showed off her figure. Her legs were not bare, despite the garment's brevity; they were encased in four-inch stiletto-heeled thigh boots, which bared no more than a couple of inches of leg just below her hemline. Similarly, long PVC gloves covered her hands, forearms and elbows, and the tightness of the dress meant that her usual layer of underwear had been replaced by a simple sprinkling of talcum powder.

As she viewed herself, she sensed the power her appearance would give her over any man she encountered. She did not look like a woman to be crossed tonight. But how far was she prepared to go? She could not say yet. She had no idea what she would find at the club or how she would react to it. She had certainly come a long way, but she was nevertheless acutely aware of how far she still had to go.

Choosing the outfit had been fun. Jenny had laid every suitable item of clothing in her wardrobe out on her bed and, like any two women getting ready for a party, she and Philippa had spent over an hour going through them, before Philippa had settled on the clothes she was now squeezed into. She had been amazed at the amount of fetish clothing in her friend's collection, which included some impossibly short and revealing outfits, and others which seemed to perform no useful function at all. She was particularly taken aback by one leather girdle, which had all the support necessary for a plump pair of breasts but no actual cups to cover them. Philippa passed on the offer of trying on that one, but was quite thrilled when Jenny offered to model it for her anyway. She showed how it made her breasts seem far more pert and inviting, and asked Philippa to bestow a kiss upon each nipple by way of demonstration. The situation might have developed from there, had Philippa not at that moment been anxious to find an ensemble that she herself would be prepared to wear.

Now, as she stood before the mirror, she felt apprehensive, but also exhilarated. If this was not a case of going out into the big wide world and taking it by storm, then nothing was. A sudden knock at the door made her jump. 'Only me,' called Jenny, from outside it. 'Are you decent?'

'In this get-up? You must be joking! Come on in, Jenny.'

The door opened to admit the beautiful blonde, and Philippa had to stop herself staring too hard as she entered. Jenny had not told her which clothes she was going to wear, and her choice was certainly radical. She was kitted out from throat to toe in black PVC, but rather than opting for a skirt as Philippa had done, Jenny had chosen a tight-fitting catsuit, the clinging shape of which outlined every curve of her gorgeous form. Her hair had been back-combed and teased to give it a suitably wild appearance, and high-heeled ankle boots added a couple of inches to her height. The zip of the catsuit ran all the way up to the top of the collar, but Jenny had only pulled it up far enough to cover her nipples, and a generous amount of her creamy cleavage was on display. In her right hand she held a pair of short black leather gloves, while her left clutched what appeared to be a short strap with a buckle at one end.

Jenny, too, had been taking in Philippa's appearance, and seemed genuinely pleased with it. 'Perfect,' she purred. 'What a team we'll make. And I have just the thing to set off your ensemble right here,' she added, holding up the strap.

'What is it?' asked Philippa, bemused.

'It's your collar.'

'Collar? You mean as in a dog collar?' It certainly resembled one.

'Well, sort of, but no pooch will ever wear one as lovingly made as this. In fact, it's the very collar Jack had me wear the first time he took me to a club. Here, let me help you on with it.' And she stepped up to Philippa, fastened it quickly around her throat, and rotated it gently so that the buckle was at the back. The two girls' heels elevated them to an equal height, and

Philippa could smell Jenny's perfume mingled with her own scent as she attached the thick band. 'Perfect. Now we know you won't get into any trouble tonight.'

'What do you mean?' asked Philippa, a little alarmed by Jenny's last remark. Was she being put under control before they had even left the house?

'It's called a slave collar. Don't worry, it doesn't mean we'll be ordering you about all night,' Jenny said, reassuringly, when she saw the effect the word 'slave' had had on Philippa. 'It'll just mark you out as being with us, which means no one will ask you to play without checking with us first, and then you can say yes or no through us. Besides,' she added with a wicked grin, 'if you walk into this place without one of those, everyone will assume you're a mistress, and you'll spend the night being pestered by submissives who want you to whip them.'

'Is that how you plan to spend your evening?' asked Philippa, regarding Jenny's bare neck.

'Only part of it. I'll be chaperoning you, remember.' And she leant forward and kissed Philippa on the lips, holding it for just a second or two longer than would have been strictly necessary had it just been a gesture of friendship. 'Grab your coat. Jack's ready, and he doesn't like to be kept waiting when he's planning a night of fun.'

When Philippa had asked how they were going to get to the club venue whilst wearing such risqué outfits, Jenny had explained that they would be taking Jack's car, and that they would be wearing their longest overcoats. With these buttoned to the chin, all that could really be seen of their attire was their boots, and the night was chilly enough for them to justify the thick jackets. Jack, whom they found waiting for them in the lounge, was wearing a black leather biker jacket and matching jeans tucked into the same riding boots he had worn for Philippa's inauguration in the cellar. A black

T-shirt under the jacket completed the outfit, and seen driving the car, he would not look at all out of place.

The girls sat together in the roomy back seat as Jack steered them through the suburbs and then the city itself. They enjoyed the feeling of being chauffeured, even though they were only sitting together in the back because Philippa wanted to find out as much as she could about the club from Jenny before they arrived. What exactly went on there? What would she be expected to do? What if someone asked her to do something she really did not want to do? What if she saw someone she liked and wanted to do something with him – or her? Jenny answered all her questions but was vague on exact details, because, she told Philippa, she wanted her to discover everything for herself and make it her own experience, and not have it mapped out for her by anyone else.

They drove out of the city heading north, until they reached an area which Philippa felt looked a little run down and insalubrious. She said as much to her housemates, but Jenny reassured her that the club itself was as secure and safe on the inside as it was possible to be. 'It's got a great name too,' she said. 'It's called Canes and Chains.'

Eventually, Jack turned down a small side street. By now, they were deep in the heart of North London, as Philippa was able to tell by the name of the borough on the street signs. Most of the buildings along the street seemed to be shops, and all were closed up for the night. Indeed, she was able to see very few residential buildings, and those that she did see, seemed quiet and unlit inside. The only exception was a big, detached three-storey Victorian house halfway down the road. Dim lights burned out from behind heavily shuttered windows on all three levels, but other than that, there was nothing to set the grey stone building apart from any other that might have been found in the capital. The car pulled to a halt at the nearest available parking space, and Jack slowly reversed into it. 'Here we are, then,' he announced as he pulled up the handbrake and switched off the engine. 'It's now or never, Philippa. Are you ready for the experience of your life?'

She did not answer him, but pulled her coat protectively around herself. Jenny reached over and took her hand. 'It's OK, darling, we'll be right there with you if you need us. Come on, let's go.'

They climbed out of the BMW, Philippa tottering a little on her heels, unused to their height. Jack hit a button on his key fob to activate the central locking and alarm, and then turned to the girls, who were huddled together against the cold night, although Philippa was also drawing moral support from Jenny's closeness. Jack turned and led the way across the deserted street, then strode up the stone steps to the big front door of the dimly-lit house. Philippa and Jenny followed a few feet behind him, Philippa clutching Jenny's hand tighter than ever. They stood on the step below Jack as he rang the doorbell, and eventually the intercom beneath it buzzed with words the girls could not hear properly, but that he evidently did. He said his name into the speaker, adding '– and guests', with a knowing look over his shoulder. Then there was a click, and the door opened a fraction. He pushed it and stepped inside.

For a few seconds, Philippa felt as though her feet were rooted to the spot. She could see nothing beyond the door, though she was able to hear the vague throb of music coming from somewhere within the building. Her stomach was turning cartwheels and her heart was pounding. Then she felt Jenny move forward beside her and give her arm a little tug. She looked up and saw the blonde girl's reassuring smile once more. 'Trust me,' Jenny whispered, 'I know you want to come in with us. Give in to yourself and find out – you owe yourself that much at least.' Suddenly, Philippa seemed to get a hold of herself. Taking a deep breath – difficult in itself in the restrictive clothing under her coat – she stepped forward with Jenny and allowed the girl to lead her through the door, which closed behind her with an ominous click.

She found herself in a dark entrance hall, the only illumination coming from a single, low-wattage bulb burning further down the corridor. Ahead of her, she could see Jack standing with his back to them. He was talking to someone. Philippa let go of Jenny's hand and shuffled around to see if she could make out who it was, curiosity beginning to replace the fear she had felt. It was a woman – and evidently some kind of doorkeeper, since she was examining a small card which she then handed back to Jack with an approving nod. But she was not dressed in the manner of a conventional night-club bouncer. Thigh boots, similar to those Philippa herself was wearing, encased her legs, and the gap between the tops of these, and the several inches of naked thigh she was showing, was filled by the sheen of a pair of black stockings. The stockings were connected to a suspender belt, which itself ran above a pair of briefs. These shone as they caught what light there was in the passageway, and Philippa realised that they were actually made of leather. But the most striking feature of the woman's appearance was above her waist, for she wore a black leather corset of the same style as that which Philippa had seen in Jenny's collection. Her midriff was covered by the shiny material, but her full breasts were exposed, and thrust provocatively forward and upward by three straps, one running on either side and the third travelling straight up through her cleavage. All three were then attached to a small collar around her neck. Her nipples were large and appeared to be swollen and erect. It could have been make-up, or the natural consequence of standing in the draughty passageway. Or, of course, it could have been that the woman found that having her body so crudely exposed actually turned her on. Unlike Philippa and Jenny, the doorkeeper wore no gloves, but her authoritative appearance was reinforced by a pair of studded wristbands made of thick leather.

By now, Jack had finished the job of signing himself and his guests in. He turned to Philippa and Jenny and crooked his head, indicating that it was time to go in. Jenny slipped off her overcoat and handed it to the woman, who took it just as any cloakroom attendant at any mainstream club might do. Not wanting to appear naïve or out of her depth Philippa did the same, and felt a chill run over her body as her arms were exposed to the air. At least she assumed it was a chill – it could have been excitement at what lay before her tonight. The woman took her coat too, and turned to open a large steel wardrobe. The garments joined a rackful of similarly innocuous-looking jackets; clearly everyone had to come here in disguise. As the women hung up their coats, Philippa found herself looking at her bottom, little of which was hidden by her leather knickers. The flesh was firm and pale, and Philippa thought she could just about make out a couple of red tracks peeking out from either side of the black material. Had the woman been the subject of recent discipline? It was a tantalising question, but not one she had time to dwell on, as Jenny was holding the inner door open for her, Jack having gone already into the gloom beyond.

'Stop ogling the hired help,' Jenny whispered to her as she followed her through the door.

'I wasn't!' Philippa shot back, a little flustered at being caught out. 'I was – I was just – curious, you know.'

'I know, sweetie,' Jenny laughed. 'I was only joking. I was just the same when Jack brought me here for the first time. But believe me, she's about the most conservatively dressed person you're likely to see all night.' Philippa felt herself colour at these words, but fought to regain her composure.

They had begun to climb a long flight of stairs now, the distant music growing louder as they ascended. 'It used to be a photographic studio, I think,' Jenny said, conversationally. 'When it went bust, the club owner snapped it up because it was already purpose built – all those big, wide rooms on three different levels.'

'Who *is* the owner?'

'Good question. I've never met him – well, at least I assume it's a him. Jack knows him but won't tell me who he is. He says it's for security reasons, because he's quite a big noise in the city, some kind of property developer. Apparently he does come to the club, but he always wears a mask. Not that that would make him stand out in this place – oh, look what we have here!'

They had rounded a corner on the stairs, and had reached a small landing. On a wooden chair in a corner sat a figure, dressed in the regulation black clothing. Wearing it, in fact, from head to toe, and not having much choice but to use the chair.

The figure's head was almost completely covered in a tight leather hood. A hole exposed the nose and mouth, although the prisoner was obliged to breathe through her nose, as a large ball-gag, similar to the one that Jenny had worn in the cellar, was jammed into her mouth and strapped to the sides of the hood. Zipped panels covered her eyes, and these had been fastened shut, leaving the wearer in the dark. Her body – for the curves of her breasts and the feminine lips stretched around the red ball told the three friends this was indeed a woman – was encased from neck to toe in a close-fitting PVC body suit. Her ankles were secured to the feet of the chair by heavy straps, and her arms pinned to her sides by a chain padlocked around each wrist and obviously passed under the seat. She could neither move nor speak.

'Is she all right?' asked Philippa, anxiously.

'Probably not,' said Jack, who had stopped to admire

the sight. 'I don't know how long she's been here, but if it's since opening time, then she'll be approaching a state of ecstasy with no way of relieving herself.'

'Why is she here? What has she done?'

'What has she done? Oh, Philippa – you do ask the silliest questions sometimes,' Jenny chided her. 'This is Caroline. She asks to be left here like this. It's her thing – she really gets off on being left bound and helpless for us all to see as we pass by.'

'And do they always leave her here?'

'Not always. A couple of times, I've come across her in the ladies', Jack even claims he found her in the gents' once, chained to one of the bowls. If she's in, you'll always find her lying around somewhere in the club.'

'What on earth does she get out of it?'

'She gets one almighty orgasm at the end of the night, when she's released and allowed to touch herself. You might even see for yourself later on. But we'll have to leave her for now – more interesting things await us inside.' Jack and Jenny continued up the stairs, and after taking one last look at the masked and helpless woman, Philippa followed them.

Another flight of steps took them to a large fire door. The music was obviously coming from behind it, and lights played on the window, set at head-height. Jack pulled the door open and turned to make sure the girls were following him. 'This is it, Philippa – a pervert's Shangri-La,' he said, and then disappeared inside.

Jenny pulled the door open, and put her arm around Philippa's shoulders. 'Come on, precious, don't be afraid. Auntie Jenny's with you. Welcome to Canes and Chains. Let's go.' And Philippa found herself being propelled gently but firmly through the door and into the gloom inside.

The music was loud, but not as noisy as she would have expected it to be in a more mainstream nightclub. It rolled out from a set of small and unobtrusive speakers – background music rather than music for dancing. She peered around, unable to see in the dark room for a few seconds. Then, as her eyes grew accustomed to what light there was, they widened with amazement.

There were about a dozen people in the room, which was large and almost devoid of furniture. They were in various stages of undress, and some were more free to move about than others. In the centre stood two women, both naked and apparently in an emotional embrace. A man in an outfit almost identical to Jack's watched them, a riding crop flexed between his hands. Suddenly, he lashed at one of the women. Both jerked simultaneously as it landed, and Philippa realised that their embrace was due to their hands being cuffed together, one behind the other's head, and her partner's behind her back. The man overseeing the bizarre dance walked slowly around so he could whip the other girl, producing much the same effect.

Turning her shocked gaze to a far corner of the room, Philippa saw a rectangular wooden frame. It was occupied by another girl – one with long blonde hair which hung halfway down her back, which she had turned towards Philippa. She too was quite naked. Her arms were stretched up above her head and shackled to the crossbar, and her feet had been drawn apart and secured to the posts. A woman stood beside this captive, and in her hand, which rested on her hip, was a nasty-looking whip consisting of several tails hanging from a short handle. She leant against the wall with her other hand, chatting to a man in leather trousers and a PVC T-shirt, and both were apparently oblivious to the girl stretched out before them. Or were they discussing her? Philippa was not close enough to hear them, but she felt sure that if she approached the captive, she would find that her bottom and back had been marked by the whip.

Philippa turned back to Jenny, who was still by her

side, but then caught sight of Jack, a few feet away. He was talking to a woman of striking appearance. She had bucked the trend and had chosen to wear a red rubber dress, similar in design to Philippa's but longer, so that it reached to just below her knees. Her arms were encased to above her elbows in matching gloves, though her shapely calves were bare, and red stilettos added a few elegant inches to her height. Her make-up was perfect, even down to her lipstick being the same shade as her dress, gloves and shoes. Her neck was long and slender, and her nose aquiline and aristocratic. Her jet black hair was gathered up in a severe-looking bun, and her whole appearance was one of haughtiness and superiority – and that, presumably, was what the man kneeling at her heels found so irresistible about her.

He was on all fours, and seemed to be wearing a male version of the harness Philippa had seen on the woman at the door. His neat brown hair and clean-shaven face would not have looked out of place in a business suit or in a bank. He too wore a gag – not a ball this time, but a strip of leather passed between his teeth like a horse's bit, and securely fastened behind his head. A lead ran from the collar of his harness up to the woman's hand, and she held it as idly as she would have held that of a pet dog, as she talked with Jack.

Philippa's suspicion that they knew each other well was confirmed when Jenny whispered into her ear, 'That's Christine. She's one of London's top dominatrices. I didn't expect to see her here tonight. I wouldn't get mixed up with her for the moment if I were you. She's a real bitch – I found myself alone with her once, and it took a week for the marks on my bum and back to fade. I screamed like a banshee when I came, but she's definitely not for beginners. Uh-oh, here she comes.' Philippa looked at Jenny, alarmed at what she had just heard, and also by the fact that Jack was leading this woman towards them. 'Don't worry – even

173

Jack wouldn't throw you in with her yet,' Jenny tried to reassure her. Philippa was not so sure.

'Philippa, meet an old friend of mine – Christine,' said Jack, as if it were a garden party.

'How do you do, my dear?' said the elegant woman, holding out a gloved hand. Philippa took it, and wondered at the weird sensation of her own hand slipping about in her glove as they shook. And she could not help but glance down at the man at Christine's feet, who had crawled over on his hands and knees, following his mistress. He knelt silently, looking at the floor. 'Do you like my slave? His name's Clive. I've borrowed him from another mistress for the evening. It's his first time here, too. Would you like to give him a few welcoming strokes, Philippa?' Philippa just stared at the self-confident woman, not sure what to say or even if she could speak at all.

'Christine, don't tease,' Jack rebuked her mildly. 'Philippa's still very new to this. I'm sure she'd like to whip your slave later tonight, but I was going to show her around first.'

'I'd like to whip him.' Jenny's voice took the others by surprise. Even Clive looked up from his place on the floor.

'Ah, yes, it's Jenny, isn't it?' said Christine, a slightly condescending note in her voice. 'I remember, we had such fun that time. We must do it again.' Jenny seemed to prickle at the way she was being spoken to, but said nothing more. 'Well,' continued Christine, 'if you really want to whip him, then I don't see any reason why you shouldn't, although I must say, I feel you're more suited to getting than giving. But he's all yours.'

Jenny took a deep breath and seemed to steel herself for the job ahead. Philippa sensed that for her to back down now would be seen as the ultimate submission to this dominant bitch, even worse than allowing the woman to whip her again. Jenny turned and walked

174

over to a wall. For the first time, Philippa saw that there were what looked like umbrella stands placed at various points around the room. She guessed that none of them contained umbrellas, and was proved right when Jenny pulled a short riding crop from one of them. Returning to the little group, she brandished it menacingly in front of them. Christine held the lead up to her delicately and Jenny took it, being careful not to snatch it from her hand.

Christine stood back. Jack and Philippa had already taken a step away from the action, instinctively giving Jenny more room to work. Winding the lead around her left hand, Jenny pulled it tight, making Clive raise his head slightly. His back arched, and his whole body tensed. 'Now, my boy,' said Jenny, menacingly, 'your mistress has told me that you need a good whipping. And that is exactly what you are going to get.' Without warning, the crop sliced through the air in a short arc and landed squarely across his exposed buttocks. Clive grunted through his gag, no other vocal outlet being available to him. Jenny swiped again, getting much the same result. The third stroke she angled differently, aiming it completely across his left cheek. The fourth was similar to this, but aimed at his right side. Then she went back to laying them straight across both cheeks.

Philippa moved in closer behind him, fascinated by Jenny's methodical approach. She watched as the crop landed again and again, leaving dark red lines across Clive's bottom. It was the first time she had seen a male bottom being beaten, and she noticed the different way it moved, in comparison with a female example, the firmer muscles twitching and jerking as Jenny laid into Clive with gusto.

Clive's muffled cries became louder as Jenny continued to whip him, and suddenly he began to jerk his hips, moaning continuously instead of just as the crop landed. At first, Philippa assumed that he was trying to escape, having had enough, but when his groans tailed off and his jerking slowed down into little spasms, she realised what had happened. The very act of being whipped by Jenny had made him orgasm inside his harness.

Jenny was well aware of what she had done, and began to wind down the strokes, making them less and less severe, until she stopped altogether. Breathing a little more heavily she turned to Christine, and handed the lead back to her. 'I don't think he'll give you any more trouble for the moment,' she said cattily. 'I rather think he enjoyed my attentions.'

'So it seems,' sniffed Christine. 'A remarkable achievement, given that I've brought him off myself three times this evening. Well, I must give him some exercise and find a quiet corner where he can pleasure me. Nice to see you again, Jenny, and I really must get to know you a little better sometime, Philippa. Cheerio for now.' And then she was gone, her last words leaving a chill in Philippa's heart. Clive scurried after her, not quite as easy on his hands and knees as he had been when Philippa had first seen him.

'You girls,' said Jack in mock despair. 'Will you ever stop trying to score points off each other?'

'Probably not,' Jenny replied, 'but then Clive seemed to enjoy it, whoever he is. Come on, I'm parched after all that exercise. Let's get a drink.'

Philippa looked about, but could see nowhere serving refreshments. Then she saw her friends heading across the room. She followed, looking around all the time. The blonde in the frame was now being whipped by the woman as her companion looked on, while the two girls who had been cuffed together were still being cruelly taunted by the man with the riding crop.

By now Jack and Jenny had reached the far corner of the room, and Philippa saw that there was a door, hidden because it had been painted the same black as

176

the wall. Jack pulled it open and ushered the girls through it. Philippa followed Jenny, and found herself in a better-lit room furnished with tables and chairs. About half-a-dozen more customers sat in various places around it, each wearing some form of bondage gear. At one table two men sat talking while a naked girl, her wrists shackled together with heavy leather cuffs, knelt beside one of them, a chain leading from his hand to a collar around her neck. The sight shocked Philippa at first, but when she looked more closely, she saw that the girl was regarding her master with an expression conveying something between awe and love. More to the point, she seemed blissfully happy being exactly where she was.

'You two get us a table and I'll organise some drinks,' Jack told the girls.

'Yes master,' said Jenny jokingly. Jack gave her a reproachful stare which was only half-humorous. 'Looks like I'd better watch my step,' she went on, as she and Philippa took their places at an empty table, 'or I'll end up in that whipping frame you were admiring back there.' Philippa blushed at being caught. 'Don't know if I'd fancy that tonight, with Mistress Christine loose about the place.'

'Did you whip that guy just to show her you weren't afraid of her?'

'Yes and no. It was the perfect opportunity to tell her where to get off, and to stop her sizing you up – oh yes she *was*, you know.'

Philippa's face went from red to white very quickly at the thought of Christine getting her hands on her. 'You won't let her get hold of me, will you? I mean, you won't leave me alone? She might come back.'

'Don't panic – if she comes anywhere near us tonight, I'll beat her off myself. You just relax and enjoy yourself. What do you think of Canes and Chains?'

'It's like nothing I've ever seen before. Do you come here very often?'

'Is that supposed to be some corny chat-up line? No, seriously, we don't need to visit too often because of Jack's ingenuity in kitting out the cellar, but we probably come here, or somewhere like here, once every couple of months.'

'You mean there are other places like this?'

'Oh, for sure; there are about half a dozen in London altogether. There are only two or three really big ones, the rest are all small to medium like this one. Most of them cater for some kind of specialist taste, like really heavy bondage or S and M. There's one place where everywhere you look there are tattoos and pierced body parts. Not really my scene – I only went there once. This one does a little bit of everything, and nothing over the top, that's why we chose it as the first one to bring you to.'

'Well, thank you,' Philippa said softly, and then added, 'No, I really mean it,' when she saw Jenny break into a wide grin. 'I don't know if this is quite my scene yet, but at least I'll know for sure if it is or if it isn't because I tried it.'

'I'm not sure about your logic, but I admire your sentiments,' replied Jenny. 'Ah, here he is at last.' Jack had returned to the table with a tray containing three large glasses. They were filled to the brim with an orange liquid, and topped off with umbrellas and straws in true Caribbean style. He handed one to Jenny, pushed a second over to Philippa, and took the third one for himself.

'Are you sure we should drink this evening?' said Philippa, tentatively. 'I mean, I don't want to end up getting drunk and losing my judgement.'

'Just taste it,' said Jack. A thirsty Jenny had already drained half of hers. Philippa took a sip, and found a mixture of neat fruit juices hitting her palate. 'Alcohol free cocktails,' Jack told her. 'No booze on the premises, so no need for a licence. Frankly, it's not worth the owner's trouble applying for one. After all, who comes to a club like this to drink?'

The cold juice was refreshing after the excitement of what had happened in the main room, and they finished their drinks in silence, as Philippa could think of no further questions she wanted answered. Eventually Jenny spoke. 'So, did you see anyone who took your fancy?'

'Sorry – where?' The question took Philippa by surprise.

'In the club. Anyone you want to play games with. If there is, we'll see what we can arrange. Most people here are fairly agreeable.'

'I didn't – I mean, no, not really.'

'Oh, come on – you must have seen something you want to try. You were looking at that whipping frame for some time. I'm sure they've let that poor girl down by now – we can have another look if you like.'

'No, really – surely there must be something you two want to do?'

'Well, there are a couple of smaller rooms upstairs,' said Jack. 'We can go and see what's occurring up there.'

'OK,' said Philippa, glad that the evening wasn't going to depend on her for its impetus. They went back through the main room, with Philippa noting, much to Jenny's amusement, that the frame was indeed still occupied by the blonde and that the woman who had been whipping her had now handed over her implement to the man who had been admiring her handiwork. 'She's going to be sore tomorrow,' Jenny murmured. 'Still, she knows the safe word to make them stop.' Back out on the landing, Jenny herself could not resist a peek over the banister to make sure that Caroline was still *in situ* on the flight below. Having satisfied herself that she was, Jenny steered Philippa, in Jack's wake, up the next set of steps and to another door.

This time, as he opened it there was no music from within, but another equally distinctive sound. Even Philippa now recognised the crack of an implement on bare flesh, and the accompanying cry of distress.

She followed Jack hesitantly, as Jenny, who was behind her, gave her a tiny shove to keep her moving, and she found herself in a room lit only by two small bulbs at either end of the ceiling. There was no furniture in there, but there would not have been any room for it, in any case. A wooden bar had been permanently fixed to span the width of the room, each end of it secured to an opposite wall, and over this bar were hanging, at present, six women, each in a state of undress. One wore a harness, another a dress like Philippa's, a third had leather jeans rucked down around her calves, and the other three appeared to be completely naked. The one thing they all had in common was a bare bottom, upturned and prominently displayed over the bar.

Above them stood two men and a woman. The woman was wearing a catsuit similar to Jenny's, but in a shinier silver-coloured material, while both men had leather trousers, one matching his with a simple T-shirt, while the second was wearing what looked to be a very expensive leather jacket. This second man was standing back and talking to the woman. He held a tawse, while she was running a school cane absent-mindedly through her hands. The other man was occupied at the bar, using a shorter strap to good effect on the line-up of naked and semi-naked women. He struck at random, never landing on the same bottom twice in succession.

'Now, that looks like fun!' exclaimed Jenny. 'Shall we join in, Philippa?' Philippa just shook her head, speechless at the sight in front of her. 'Well, I'm going to,' said Jenny, and quickly unzipped her catsuit. Without a shred of embarrassment, she peeled it back off her shoulders and exposed her breasts, and as she wriggled it down over her hips her naked bottom half came into view. Obviously, she too had decided against wearing underwear beneath her tight outfit.

With the top half of the catsuit bunched down around her thighs, she shuffled across to the bar. She nudged the girl on the end, who shifted a few inches to the left, making room for Jenny to bend over next to her. Again Jenny wriggled a little, until she was comfortable and balanced, and then she simply waited.

Her arrival had caught the attention of the man and woman who had been watching the proceedings and once she was in place, the woman strode forward and placed a gloved hand on Jenny's bare behind. Philippa saw her friend shiver. Then the woman drew back her hand and slapped it down on to Jenny's right cheek, which wobbled with the impact. The left received similar treatment, and then she returned to the right. She gave Jenny about a dozen spanks, then stepped back and lined her cane against her cheeks. It was raised and then whipped down with some force. Small shock waves ran through Jenny's bottom and thighs, and she rolled forward on the bar giving a little squeal, but soon regained her balance. A second stroke followed, and then a third. The woman went on until six strokes of the cane had been administered. Then she stepped away from the bar. But Jenny did not stand up.

By now the two men had swapped places, and the one who had previously been a spectator was now meting out punishment to the row of defenceless bottoms. Seeing that Jenny was no longer occupied, he moved to the end of the line and delivered two blows with his strap in quick succession, one forehand to her right cheek, the other backhand to her left. Then he moved back down the line, skipping her neighbour but giving the next girl similar treatment. Philippa watched the bizarre spectacle as if she were in a dream. 'Still don't want to give it a try?' Jack whispered behind her. She shook her head again – she was sure that this would all be too much for her, and the girls seemed to be getting hit terribly hard. 'Well, we can leave Jenny here for a bit. Why don't we go next door and see what's happening there?'

She did not resist as he took her hand and led her through the room, past the row of naked and reddening bottoms and their tormentors, and through another door at the far side of the room. As with all the others, this room was badly lit, having just a single bulb burning in the centre of the ceiling. Also hanging from the ceiling was a pair of chains, with shackles at their ends. A large cardboard box sat in one corner. Besides that, the room was empty.

'This one doesn't look to be too popular,' said Philippa, trying to inject a little humour into the situation, though for the life of her she could not think why it needed it.

'On the contrary, this place is usually very popular. We're lucky to find it empty.'

'Really? What happens in here, then?'

'It's where people come for private games they don't feel like playing in front of the rest of the club.'

'Such as?'

'Oh, such as – well, it would be easier for me to show you, rather than to explain.'

'And what exactly do you mean by "show me"?' By now, Philippa had a good idea as to what she might be getting herself into, but she decided to make Jack work for it a bit this time.

'Put your hands into those cuffs and you'll find out.'

'That's what I thought you'd say. What exactly are you planning for me this evening?'

'Really, Philippa, I would have thought that by now you'd know better than to ask. And even if I told you, how do you know I'd keep my word once you were chained up?'

'I don't. So why should I let you?'

'Because you're dying to find out, and the only way that you can do that is by going along with me.' She looked at him doubtfully. He had proved to be a bundle of paradoxes so far, and she was really in two minds as to whether or not to trust him. Jenny had promised to keep an eye on her this evening, but her friend was otherwise engaged at the moment. What would happen to her this time? Then Jack's next words turned her ice-cold inside. 'In case you hadn't realised it yet, this is it. The moment we find out if you really belong here.'

'You mean you're testing me?'

'In a sense. This may seem like a game to you, and in some ways it is, but it's a game we take very seriously. And if you want to carry on playing it, with me and Jenny at least, you'll go and put your hands in those cuffs.'

Philippa hesitated, unsure as to whether Jack was just blustering or if he really meant what he said. But since when had she cared about his opinion? Surely, she told herself, what really mattered was what she wanted. And right now she wanted to be a part of this strange and wonderful world, just like Jenny, maybe even like Jack, but most of all like Steve. To get closer to Steve, she would do it.

'I think you'll find that I belong here just as much as you do,' she said, trying to sound noncommittal, but detecting a tell-tale shake in her own voice which she knew Jack would pick up on.

'Excellent,' he replied. 'Now go and do as you're told.'

Walking with as much poise as she could muster, she turned and approached the dangling chains. Reaching up, she took one and fitted her left wrist into the leather shackle, and found the familiar padlocks, along with a pair of thick straps and buckles. Jack had followed her, and he reached over her shoulder to take the cuff in his hand. 'You'll need help to get these on – and off,' he

183

said ominously. And as he tightened the second buckle, then snapped the little padlock shut through the two metal rings which now met, she realised there was no way she would be able to free herself once both her wrists were strapped in. Indeed, this was soon the case, as her right wrist was secured and Jack moved back to get a better look at her.

She was not suspended as she had been in the cellar, but she could not lower her arms to a comfortable height. She was grateful that her feet were flat on the linoleum-covered floor, even though her movement of them would be severely restricted. And so she stood, awaiting sentence from Jack.

'Excellent,' he announced after a moment's contemplation. 'But I think we need something more to finish the look off.' And she heard him move across the room to the cardboard box. Looking around, she saw him delve in and come out holding several objects, each of them too small for her to see what they were. He approached her, and stood behind her once again. 'One of the most remarkable experiences you can ever have,' he said, as if delivering a learned lecture, 'is to go through a scene and never know who it was taking you through it. I think you'll find it most stimulating.' And his hands moved up over her face. The next thing she knew, what light there was disappeared.

'Hey! What's going on? Where are you?' she shouted. But it was too late, and she felt the straps of the blindfold being secured around her head. 'What do you think you're doing, Jack? What's the big ide– ugh!' The words were choked back inside her as a ball gag was fitted between her teeth, and then she felt it being buckled at the back of her head. She moaned pointlessly for a few seconds then gave up, deciding to save her breath.

'Now then,' said Jack from somewhere behind her once she had been subdued. 'I think it's time for you to learn a little patience and humility. I'll leave you for the time being, and come back to release you eventually. In the meantime, who knows who's going to come along?'

She let out a muffled cry intended to tell him to stay, but before it had even escaped her mouth as best it could, she heard the door slam shut. She was alone.

To begin with, she was baffled by Jack's decision to leave her on her own and as time wore on she became more and more frightened. Where had he gone? Why had he done this? What if he forgot about her while he was out there having fun? And why had he blindfolded and gagged her? She did not know it then, but the answer to this last question was looming ever closer.

She had no way of knowing how long she had been left. When she had been left in the cellar, she had at least been able to see her watch. Now she was not wearing it, and even if she had been, the blindfold would have rendered it useless. It might have been half an hour, three quarters of an hour, a whole hour or just twenty minutes. But eventually the door did open again. Philippa thanked God Jack had come back, and that he had left her ears unplugged so she could hear him, even if she could not ask him where the hell he had been.

She expected some caustic remark from him, and was surprised when none came. She began to twist and turn in her bonds as he paced about the room. Then she heard the rustle of the cardboard box. He must be getting the key to release me, she thought. Then he stepped behind her again, and she expected to feel him reach up to undo the shackles. What she did not expect was to feel a latex-gloved hand stroking her cheek and trailing down across her neck.

She flinched at the contact – Jack had not been wearing gloves. Who was this? Her chains allowed her only a certain amount of movement, and not enough to escape the touch of whoever she was now sharing the room with. She toyed with the idea that it might be Jack playing one of his little games – he could easily have donned the gloves while he had been away from her, and not speaking could be one of his little tricks to make her think she was in the room with a perfect stranger.

Whoever it was became bolder. She felt the neckline of her dress being pulled down, and it slid across her skin where she had perspired inside the hot garment. Her breasts were eased out of it, despite her struggles and inarticulate protests. The neckline was tucked under the curve of her breasts and the hands made free with them for a few moments, feeling their fullness and teasing her nipples with thumbs and forefingers. She moaned, feeling her body betray her as her nipples swelled and rose. Then the hands were gone, but she soon felt them again, this time at the short hem of her dress. Taking a firm hold to counteract Philippa's frantic wriggling, they rolled the material as far up as it would go above her waist. She felt the cool air on her naked bottom and thighs, in sharp contrast to the damp warmth she had felt when they had been clad in the tight rubber. Then the hands left her, and she heard the figure move back to the other side of the room and start rummaging in the box.

Philippa could do nothing but stand and await whatever it was fate had in store for her. Tears began to well in her eyes beneath the blindfold.

Then she heard a sound which was, by now, becoming very familiar to her – the swish of a cane or riding crop being slashed repeatedly through the air. She stopped struggling for a second as the other person in the room tested the efficiency of whichever implement they had selected, and then she began to tug against the chains again, while vainly trying to beg for mercy through the ball gag.

She felt the thin rod being laid against her bottom. Instinctively she jerked her hips forward to escape it, but it merely followed her movement. Then it was removed from her cheeks, and she knew it was being drawn back ready to strike.

She heard the warning hiss of the implement a second before the line of fire sank into her bottom, and let out a muffled scream as it bit home. She practically swung forward on her chains before reverting to her original position. The second blow landed just above the first, and was laid on with equal vigour. The third was low, close to where her buttocks met her thighs, and caused Philippa to squeal in pain. She was, however, aware enough of her situation to notice a separate sensation, that of a small piece of leather curling round to touch her far right thigh. So it was a riding crop which was being used on her.

The fourth lash was laid diagonally across her bottom, crossing all the other weals. The fifth crossed back the other way, going up from left to right, and the sixth landed squarely across her cheeks again, close to where the first had been placed. Then the mysterious tormentor stopped.

Philippa hung in her chains, exhausted from her attempts to cry out, her arms sore from pulling on the wrist cuffs and her jaws aching from being forced open by the gag for so long. But all this seemed irrelevant compared to the heat in her bottom – six lines of scorching agony. She breathed heavily through her nose, trying to draw in as much air as possible through her small nostrils, to compensate for her enforced inability to breathe through her mouth.

She was just beginning to regain her composure when she felt the hands upon her again, and this time the stranger was in front of her. She flinched as the latex-clad fingers suddenly probed her vaginal lips. They began gently at first, the thumbs just easing her open. To Philippa's own surprise – and to the evident delight of whoever her tormentor was – her entrance was moist and slick. Her predicament and subsequent punishment had clearly aroused her. She tried to tell herself it must have resulted from something else – perhaps it was a side effect of the wild movements she had made as she had been whipped – but as a single finger, and then another, slipped up her vagina with no resistance, she could not deny it to herself any longer. A thumb brushed her clitoris, and she gasped again. The fingers moved in and out, arousing her further and comforting her at the same time. Then they were gone again, and she was overcome by a sense of loss, as if she had been left hanging sexually as well as literally.

But she was not left unfilled for long. She felt her lips being pushed apart once again, but this time by something much larger than the fingers. Big and hard, the phallus pushed insistently home, inch by inch. It was smooth and rock solid, unyielding and definitely not human. Philippa felt herself being relentlessly dildoed as she dangled in her chains.

Did this mean her companion was a woman? That would seem to be the most likely explanation. But who could it be? The possibility that it might be Jenny crossed her mind, but Philippa had been living with the girl for some time now, and could not imagine her friend being able to keep her mouth shut for this long. Was it the wicked Christine? If it was, then Philippa counted herself lucky to have got away with the whipping she had been given if what Jenny had said about her was to be believed. Of course, this could all be part of a double bluff by Jack – might he be using a dildo instead of his own penis to confuse her? The fact was, it could be absolutely anyone, and all she could do was to hang there as the dildo was slipped in and out without remorse.

She was thankful, though, that whoever was using it obviously did not intend to keep her on the brink of orgasm – a form of torture Philippa did not think she could bear right now. The slick pole was rammed into her and pumped progressively faster as she climbed to the peak of excitement, and she knew her body movements and delighted squeaks through the solid gag would clearly give the game away to her captor. Within moments she came, her long low groans echoing throughout the room, as she climaxed heavily around the wand between her legs. Its thrusts were gently slowed until, eventually, it was pulled from inside her with a soft plop, leaving her gasping and shaking, and wishing for all the world that she could lie down immediately. But her companion made no move to release her; his – or her – footsteps merely crossed back to the corner where she knew the box was kept. She heard the sound of the fake penis being wiped clean with some kind of cloth, and then it was placed back in the box. Finally, the person went over to the door, and then through it, leaving Philippa alone again.

Fifteen minutes later – though it seemed like an eternity to Philippa – Jack and Jenny returned together to rescue her. They asked if she had enjoyed herself and she told them that she had done, but that now, she just wanted to go home. She did not ask them if they knew who had been in the room with her, either on the way out of the club or on the way home, as she perched painfully on a cushion in the back of the car. She was not even sure that either of them would know, and besides, she did not want to spoil what had been a unique and ultimately fulfilling experience.

Nine

It was Wednesday, four days after the eventful night at Canes and Chains. A busy day at work for Philippa had been followed by a meal in a nearby wine bar with three of her colleagues. From time to time she had shifted uncomfortably on the hard wooden seat; the worst of the soreness from the whipping had faded by the Monday, but there had still been lines on her bottom when she had dressed that morning.

She arrived home late. The entire house seemed to be in darkness, and Philippa mused wryly that the weekend must have taken it out of Jack and Jenny too. Pouring herself a glass of mineral water from a bottle in the fridge, Philippa crept upstairs. She entered her bedroom and switched on the light, and then she noticed the message which Jack had stuck to her door: STEVE CALLED, 9.00 PM – WANTS YOU TO CALL BACK.

Her heart leapt. Despite all the sexual adventures she'd had since she arrived in London, it was still Steve she thought of when she lay in bed at night and imagined herself with a man, giving herself and surrendering to him completely. She looked at her watch; it was just after midnight. Was it too late to call? She decided to risk phoning him, convinced that if she left it until the next day he might not be there at all, and so she went back downstairs, and dialled the number that Jack had written underneath the message.

She held her breath as it rang twice. Then it was picked up, and she heard Steve's voice saying hello.

'Hi, it's – it's me,' she stammered.

'Philippa! Great to hear from you – I was hoping you'd call back. In fact, I was kind of waiting up for you, as it happens.' So that was why he had picked the phone up so quickly, thought Philippa. 'Listen,' he continued, 'I don't know how you feel about this – we did have rather a strange first date, you might say – but I'd love to see you again.'

'You mean at another party?'

'No, nothing like that – not this time, anyway.' She said nothing, but in her heart she felt a little disappointed. 'Just you and me for dinner one night. How about it?'

'Great, I'd love to.' She did not really have to think twice about accepting his offer.

'Marvellous! How about Friday?' She told him she had nothing planned for that night. Had she made any previous arrangements, then of course she would have cancelled them, but she did not tell him that. It wouldn't do to appear too willing, she told herself. It might smack of desperation. Then Steve said he'd call for her at eight, and they said goodbye.

She returned to her bedroom, almost too excited to sleep. She undressed and slipped into her nightdress, pausing for a moment to lift the hem and turn her back to the wardrobe mirror. The weals were still there, though they were not as clear as they had been that morning, and nowhere near as livid as when she had awoken stiff and sore on Sunday. She traced the line of one of them right across the centre of her bottom, wondering again who had done this to her, but it seemed less important now. She had participated, and ultimately it had felt good. Now she could honestly say that she was like Jack and Jenny.

Her hand went to her sex, and she stroked it softly through her light pubic hair. Then she started to probe in between her nether lips with her forefinger, letting out a little sigh as they parted to allow it in. Her legs began to buckle and tremble as she pushed in deeper, and then inserted a second finger. Her other hand found her left breast through the soft cotton of her nightdress, and she massaged it slowly in time with her masturbation of her pussy. Feeling decidedly shaky, though in the nicest possible way, Philippa staggered over to her bed and collapsed on to it. She continued to stimulate herself as she lay, supine, on top of the duvet, her left hand easing down the top of her nightdress in order to expose her erect nipples, which she then rolled, pinched and pulled. Biting down on her lower lip to stop herself crying out in ecstasy, she found her clitoris and rubbed it, becoming highly aroused as myriad erotic images filled her mind. Steve featured prominently, of course, and she visualised herself – and also Jenny – lying, buttocks upward, across his lap. Her mind wandered slightly, to a vision of Jenny bent over her lap, but then it focused on Steve again, his face screwed up in passion above hers as it had been on the night of the party. Her muscles tensed for a moment, and then she came with a deep sigh, her mind and body relaxing as the day's stresses and strains flooded out of them and away for good.

She was up before Jenny the next morning, and was finishing her breakfast when the other girl appeared. Philippa told her about her date, and was pleased to find that Jenny was delighted for her. 'Would you like to borrow one of my outfits?' she asked, helpfully.

'Thanks, but I think Steve's planning something a little more mainstream. He mentioned a restaurant in the city somewhere, so I don't think a PVC dress would be quite the thing.'

'Hey, he *is* serious about you. Well, don't you go

skimping on the menu, Philippa – I've heard Jack say he's seriously loaded.'

'Jenny! The very thought that I could be after him for his money! Although it does make him that little bit more attractive, I must admit.' And they giggled over their mugs of tea.

The following night, they found themselves back in the kitchen, but this time Jenny was helping Philippa to put the finishing touches to her outfit. She had opted to wear a classic little black dress, simple but stylish, and had decided that she would splash out on a new one. The dress she had finally bought was a little shorter and lower cut than any she would ordinarily have chosen, but the need to make a devastating impression on this man had overwhelmed her natural conservatism. The thin straps left her slender shoulders virtually bare, and a single pendant, strung on a thong, adorned her bosom. Her legs were flattered by sheer silk stockings, while her black stilettos increased her height by a good couple of inches. Jenny was helping put the final touches to her hair when the doorbell rang.

They heard Jack leave the living room where he was watching television, and go to the front door. As expected, it was Steve, and Philippa's heart gave another little leap. 'How do I look – honestly?' she asked Jenny.

'Honestly? Drop dead gorgeous,' Jenny replied. 'If you weren't so keen on Steve, I'd send Jack out for the evening and try to seduce you again myself.' The pair laughed, but there was more than a touch of anxiety about Philippa's giggle. Then the door opened and Jack appeared.

'Steve's here, Philippa – and is he in for a treat tonight!' he announced as he caught sight of her. 'Jenny, I don't think we should bother waiting up tonight. If I were Steve I certainly wouldn't be in a hurry to get this gorgeous creature home.' Philippa said nothing, but stuck her tongue out at him.

'Get him a drink and tell him we won't be long,' said Jenny. 'Just a couple of minor adjustments and we'll be there.' Jack retreated as ordered.

Ten minutes later – a respectable time to keep a man waiting for a date, Jenny informed her – Philippa made her entrance. Steve, who had also made an effort with a suit and an expensive-looking silk tie, greeted her with as much enthusiasm as Jack had done, although his comments were altogether more gentlemanly. Finishing his drink, he asked if she was ready. She was, and as soon as Jenny had fetched her coat for her, they went on their way.

They walked down the drive, and Philippa found herself standing in front of a red Porsche which had been parked in front of the house. 'A little flashy, I know,' Steve said, as he pointed his key fob at the car and pressed a button to release the central locking, 'but I can justify it by saying what a good, solid car it is. And anyway, this and my flat are the only indulgences I allow myself.'

'What about beautiful women?' Philippa asked, as she tried to slide elegantly through the low door he had opened for her.

'Oh, that goes without saying,' he said, 'but it's been a long time since anyone as beautiful as you sat in this car.' She smiled at the compliment, but wondered just how true it could be.

The engine fired, and Steve guided the car slowly away from the kerb. He headed for the A3 and soon they were driving into town. They crossed the river about half an hour after they had left, and Steve was soon cutting up and down the maze of streets which made up the capital. Philippa was impressed. She barely knew London yet, and so she always was amazed by those people who could faultlessly steer a car through its heart. So far, the conversation had been polite and run of the mill. No mention had been made of their first

194

encounter, and Philippa did not think it was a very good moment to tell Steve about her adventures at Canes and Chains.

They stopped in a large street just outside the city centre. Steve's luck was in, and he found a parking space very close to the Chinese restaurant he indicated to Philippa he had booked. Once inside, she realised he had chosen well, as the place was authentically and stylishly decorated, and had a discreet ambience. She also noticed that more than a few of the other customers were Chinese – a sign of a good restaurant, she had always been told.

Her food, when it arrived, was certainly not a disappointment, and with Steve's help, she experimented with dishes she would not normally have chosen, her previous experience of exotic foreign foods having been limited to the small number of takeaways in and around her village. And still they did not talk about the real reason that they were here together – the mutual attraction they felt towards each other.

They left the restaurant just before ten-thirty. 'So, where do we go from here?' Steve asked her.

'Well, the pubs are still open,' said Philippa, before adding quickly, 'although I don't really think we're dressed for it tonight.'

'Agree. So what about a club?'

'A club?' said Philippa, her mind racing back to the previous weekend before she realised he meant a mainstream nightclub. 'Oh, a club! We could do, if you feel like dancing the night away.' What she really wanted, though, was to be alone with this man, so that she could show him just what she had learned and what she could do now.

'Alternatively I have an excellent bottle of Chardonnay in the fridge at my flat, which is only fifteen minutes' drive from here. But stop me if you think I'm being too presumptuous.'

'Presumptuous? After the way we met? It sounds great – let me just go to the ladies' and we'll go.' By the time she returned Steve had dealt with the bill and collected her coat, which he helped her to drape around her shoulders before they headed out into the cold night.

The drive to Steve's flat actually took about ten minutes, rather than the fifteen he had estimated. Obviously he was in something of a hurry to get home, which Philippa took to be a good sign. He lived in a rather imposing block, with a security gate requiring a swipe card to get through. Once in, he drove into the underground car park and headed straight for his reserved bay.

He locked the car, and then led Philippa to a lift, which they got into after a brief wait. He pushed the button for the top floor, and it glided silently upward.

The interior of the block was no less impressive, and he guided her along a luxuriously carpeted corridor to his flat. As he opened the door, light and warmth came from within, and Philippa assumed they had been left on to create a welcoming atmosphere on their return – she also shivered with pleasure at the thought that Steve had been planning, all along, to bring her here. She stepped inside and he took her coat, hung it on a large stand in the hallway, and opened the living room door. She went in ahead of him – and stopped dead in her tracks.

Steve's flat was as large, impressive and well-appointed as she had expected it to be. She had not, however, expected to find other people there, and so she stared in disbelief as two men rose politely from the large armchairs in which they had been sitting. As she stood, dumbfounded, in the doorway, Steve sidled up to her, cleared his throat, and spoke: 'There's a simple explanation for this, and I expect you want to hear it.'

She turned to look at him for a brief instant, and then she turned her attention back to the other men. They were both older than Steve – in their mid-forties she would have guessed – and dressed in suits as stylish and expensive as his own. She looked hard at the one on the right, and realised that she recognised him from somewhere – and somewhere she had been recently, at that.

'Although I really did want to see you again,' continued Steve, 'this evening wasn't entirely about pleasure. Well, it is in a way, but not in the usual way.'

Steve's attempts at an explanation were beginning to make the situation even more confusing. Philippa turned to look at him again, and tried to get him to come to the point. 'Who are these people, and why are they in your flat?'

'Good question.' Steve was obviously more nervous than she was at the moment. 'Well, this is David,' he said pointing to the man on the left, who nodded in acknowledgement, 'and this is Tony. You may remember him from the party a few weeks ago.' Of course, the party – that was where she had seen him before. She had even been introduced to him, shortly before she had gone upstairs and discovered exactly what was going on. The events of the rest of the evening had reduced the first half of the night to something of a blur, but now she even remembered being told his name.

'Well, David and Tony here are actually a couple of the chaps behind the party. You could say they are on the organising committee of parties for people like us. It seems they originally approved Jack's bringing you along, although they weren't too happy with him for not explaining the whole deal to you beforehand. Still, at least it all worked out OK in the end – didn't it?' Steve cast a hopeful glance at her before continuing. 'Anyway, they liked you a lot, and the committee proposed that you be offered full membership. So that's what David and Tony are doing here tonight – offering you, er – well, full membership.' And Steve clapped his hands as if to emphasise the point again.

'Sorry to spring this on you in such a way, Philippa.' It was Tony who spoke now. 'Please don't blame Steve. It was our idea to have him take you out for a meal first, since he thinks rather a lot of you and we knew an evening with his charm would be a perfect ice-breaker. And don't feel obliged to take us up. If you're not interested, we'll go right away and leave the two of you alone. You'll never hear from us again, and that's a promise.'

'And if I ask you to stay?' asked Philippa, loading the question with as much meaning as possible. She noticed that David and Tony seemed perfectly relaxed in this unusual situation, while Steve was so tense that she could feel it, and hear it in his breathing.

'If you ask us to stay, we can enrol you in the club,' said Tony, 'once you've passed our little test, that is.'

Philippa had already begun to think something like this might be on the cards. She had a good idea of what their test would involve. Steve obviously knew, as he was suddenly showing a great deal of interest in his shoes. 'And this test would be . . .?' she asked, determined to spin the moment out for his maximum embarrassment. He had got her into this situation, after all.

'Oh, nothing much,' replied Tony reassuringly. 'And I'm sure you'll pass it with flying colours.'

'A spanking.' This was David, speaking for the first time since she and Steve had entered the room. He had a very deep voice, with a solid, measured tone, which gave an impression of total self-confidence, as if he were in charge here. 'We'd like you to reassure us that you're completely up to the demands our club would make on you.'

'By letting you spank me?'

'Of course. How else could we be sure?'

'I suppose you're right. Who'll be handing it out, then? You or Tony?'

198

'Actually, both of us.' This was Tony, who seemed even more at ease, now it was clear that Philippa was not going to run screaming from the flat. 'Well, I mean one after the other, of course.'

'And just a spanking? You're not going to use anything else?'

'Why, no, not this time. Unless you'd like us to, of course?'

'No – if you're happy with just using your hands, then I'm happy with it too.' After what she had been through at Canes and Chains and in Jack's cellar, Philippa could not believe that this would present any serious challenge. And if Steve was a member of their organisation, she certainly wanted to be in on it too. 'So do we start straight away?' she asked.

'No need for that,' said Tony. 'Why don't you and Steve have a drink first?'

'What a great idea!' said Steve, obviously relieved. He went over to the drinks cabinet set into the wall and picked up a bottle of brandy. 'In fact, drinks all round would seem to be a good idea,' he added, and poured four generous measures into glasses which he handed out around the room. Philippa took hers over to the large sofa which ran against one of the white-painted walls and waited for Steve to join her.

'So you enjoyed our last little get-together, Philippa?' asked Tony when they were all seated.

'It was – interesting,' she replied, trying to sound enigmatic. 'Of course, it wouldn't have been half as interesting if I hadn't met Steve.'

'So I would imagine,' said Tony. 'And you weren't shocked to find out what was really going on there?'

'Shocked is the wrong word. Surprised – taken aback, maybe. But I suppose I would have been shocked if Jack and Jenny hadn't done such a good job of introducing me to the positive side of corporal punishment. In a way, I think it would have spoiled the party for me if I had known what was going to happen – I might not even have gone to it.'

'Well we, and especially I, can only be grateful you did,' said Steve, squeezing her hand reassuringly.

As they drank, Philippa asked as many questions as she dared about the club. She learnt that it had upward of 300 members, and that meetings and parties – hosted by members – took place all over the country. None of the three men was as yet prepared to reveal the identity of those involved, as many of them were influential or even – Tony hinted – famous, and were therefore insistent that their personal details should remain confidential.

'So,' she said, finally, 'what would be expected of me if I were to become a member?'

'You'd be expected to enjoy yourself,' said Tony, with a grin. 'Anyway, we'll tell you more once you've passed the test and become a fully-fledged club girl.'

Soon enough the glasses were drained, and there was nothing more she could do to delay the awful moment. The more she thought about it, however, the less awful the prospect seemed to her. She understood that the initiation would be a painful and humiliating experience, but the thrill she was experiencing was indistinguishable from that which she'd felt when she had been on her way to visit Paul, knowing his parents were out and that they were going to be making love in less than an hour's time. She could not deny it to herself any longer – she was excited at the prospect of a spanking.

'So, shall we start?' she said. The men looked at each other, a little taken aback by her forwardness. 'I mean, you don't want to sit here all night when there's a willing female bottom to be smacked, do you?' And she stood up, placed her empty glass on the coffee table, and smoothed her dress down over her curvy figure. 'How would you like me?'

'Bending over, of course,' David told her, 'and I think that dress, lovely though it is, would be a little too tight to pull up. You'll have to take it off.' Steve still looked slightly nervous, but David seemed completely sure that the orders he was giving would be obeyed.

And so they would, Philippa told herself. Reaching behind her she slowly unzipped her dress, then wiggled her shoulders to allow the garment to fall forward. She slid each of her arms free of the shoulder straps, and then peeled off the rest of the dress, gradually exposing her strapless bra, and then her black bikini briefs, suspender belt and stockings. She heard all three men draw in their breath, as her nubile body came into view.

She let the dress slip to the floor, stepped out of it and carefully folded it, then placed it on the sofa behind her. Steve looked down at it, before gazing up at her beautiful, semi-naked body, and she smiled back down at him to show him that she had no problem with what was happening. Then she turned back to David and Tony, placed her hands on her hips, and pulled her shoulders back. 'So who's first?' she asked, confidently.

'Me, my dear,' said Tony. David said nothing, but sat back in his chair with his legs crossed and his fingers steepled, a slight smile playing across his thin lips. 'If you'd just like to stand in the centre of the room,' continued Tony.

Philippa obeyed. Tony stood up and looked at her, a glint of desire clearly visible in his eyes. She expected him to approach her immediately, and so she was surprised to see him turn and walk towards the window, next to which a small dining table and two chairs had been placed. He picked up one of the chairs and returned to where Philippa was waiting for him. Now she understood exactly what was going to happen.

She watched as he positioned the chair so that both of the other men would have a good view – Steve of her face, and David of her bottom. Sitting stiffly on the chair, Tony put his hands on his knees then looked expectantly up at the waiting girl.

Philippa stepped towards him and he straightened his back, taking his hands away from his knees to create a space for her across his lap. She stood on his right, looking down at his legs for a few seconds before taking a deep breath and stretching forward. She felt the cloth of his trousers as it came into contact with her bare thighs, and then the soft wool of Steve's thick carpet under her own palms, which shot forward to support her weight. Her head swirled slightly as the blood rushed to it, then settled as she adjusted her position in order to get as comfortable as she could. Her legs were stretched straight out behind her, feeling more tense than any other part of her body. She looked up at Steve and smiled again, a little more awkwardly from this undignified position, and was rewarded with a reciprocal smile from him.

She twitched as Tony's left hand began to rub the small of her back before coming to a halt and lightly gripping her right side just below the ribcage. Then his right palm stroked over her upturned bottom. From there he also explored the tops of her thighs, and then moved down as far as her knees in long, swirling movements of his arm, his touch gentle and smoothing, almost as if he were trying to get her to forget what was about to happen next. And after no more than a minute of this treatment, it happened.

His hand left her legs and she guessed it must be raised above his head. A few seconds later, she knew it had been, as it had then come smacking down on the right cheek of her cotton-covered behind. The pain was not as intense as it had been in her previous spankings, and she asked herself why – was it because of the protection offered by her briefs? Might it be that Tony was taking pity on her and starting off gently? Or – she hardly dared think it – might she be getting used to the feeling of having her bottom smacked? Another spank landed on her left cheek and she shuddered, and then a third fell on her right side before the left got the same treatment. She suspected, though she could not be sure, that the latter two strokes had felt a fraction harder than the first two. Five and six were a little harder still, and she realised that Tony was indeed building up his momentum. He was also building up a solid erection, she thought, if the bulge she could feel against her left thigh was anything to go by, and she wondered if Steve and David had similar swellings. This thought stayed with her, and as the spanking continued, she found herself fantasising about what use they might be putting them to later on.

She began to grunt and groan as the punishment continued for about another five minutes, and then stopped as quickly as it had begun. 'Time for these to come down, I think, young lady,' came Tony's voice from somewhere above her, and she felt his fingers slipping inside the waistband of her knickers. She lifted her hips to aid the removal of the wispy black garment, and felt it slide down over her bottom to her knees. Then she kicked her legs a little in anticipation, as her bottom lay totally exposed and defenceless across Tony's lap. She cast another upward glance at Steve, who was drinking in every detail of the lascivious sight before him. She could only imagine the sort of view David was getting.

Once again, Tony smoothed her bottom cheeks with his palm. This time she flinched a little as his hand gently touched her now-glowing flesh. Then it left her again, and she knew that battle was about to recommence.

His hand smacked down again, and then once more, taking up the left-right rhythm he had used so far. But now it hurt more, his hard palm making more solid contact with her tender flesh. She began to moan louder than before, wriggling to try and get some kind of relief. Tony's response was to grip her waist tighter with his left hand. 'Come now, Philippa,' he chided her. 'Our girls don't usually make a fuss just because their bottoms are being smacked. They save their crying for the cane or strap.'

His words had a chilling effect on her. 'No sir, sorry sir,' she mumbled, and tried to pull herself together. How much she still had to learn! And she did not want to let Steve down, or Jack and Jenny for that matter.

The spanking continued, with the slaps getting harder each time until it felt like the centre of each of her cheeks was on fire, but now she was not tempted to make any noise or fuss. Instead she gritted her teeth, and her fingers gripped the carpet ever tighter, as if she could conduct the sharp stinging pain of each spank down into the floor. She could not of course – the pain in her bottom simply grew with each second. And so did the bulge in Tony's groin. She was not so far gone she did not notice that.

She had no idea how long she had spent over his lap, when the spanking finally stopped. She guessed it must have been a good ten minutes since he had pulled her knickers down, and about fifteen in all, but she could not say for sure, and she certainly was not going to embarrass herself by asking. But stop he eventually did, and she was allowed to rest for a few seconds, presumably so that they could both get their breath back. 'Well, I think that satisfies me that you're up to it,' he said. 'Now all you have to do is convince my colleague, and you're a fully-fledged member.' It sounded so easy when he put it like that, but she knew a second dose would be just as hard, if not harder to take. Tony pulled her from his lap, and placed her back on her feet. She noticed his eyes lingering on her pubic area before she pulled her panties back up to cover it. Stepping back from the chair to allow him to stand up, she reached back and rubbed her tender flesh through the thin garment. For a moment, it felt good, but she knew the relief would only be fleeting. And there was more to it than simply pain. The spanking had lit a fire in her loins, and she needed some male attention of a different kind, specifically from Steve, to put that fire out.

But first, David had to be persuaded that she was a worthy candidate. He had taken his place on the seat, and was looking at her expectantly. His face had a severe, cold edge to it, and she knew she would not escape lightly. Still, she had come this far, and going back was no longer an option. Submissively, she laid herself across the proffered male lap, and squirmed into place.

She was surprised, although not overly, to find her underwear being pulled down again, this time to her ankles. 'I think you've had quite enough time to get warm, Philippa,' David's commanding voice rang round the room. 'So we can get straight down to the real business.' As Tony had done, he gripped her around her middle, but his was not the light steadying hand. Instead it was firm, almost vice-like. There was no way she was going to wriggle out of this spanking.

His hand rose and fell with a loud smacking sound, right across her bottom. She let out a little cry of anguish, even though she had tried to keep herself quiet. It had just hurt too much, and it had barely subsided before the second blow landed, stinging her opposite cheek in exactly the same way. David continued regardless of her obvious discomfort, as she closed her eyes, threw back her head and sucked in great lungfuls of breath between slaps. Once she raised her head and opened her eyes to see how Steve was reacting to her punishment. She found him looking at her with obvious discomfort, but he showed no sign of being about to intervene. Good – the last thing she wanted at the moment was an over-protective boyfriend, when she was doing this partly to please him. But she was also trying to prove something to herself. This sort of thing turned her on – she was sure of that, now – and if a hard spanking like this made her feel horny, then there could be no doubt about it.

David continued relentlessly, his heavy palm crashing down on to Philippa's unprotected bottom, time after time. The pain grew, and she felt she could contain herself no longer. Her cries of distress became louder, but David did not seem concerned. He went on spanking her harder than ever.

Then, just when she had thought she was going to have to beg him to cease, or try to fight her way up, he stopped. She felt the tension flood from her body as the burning in her bottom gradually diminished to a healthy glow. It's amazing how quickly that happens, Philippa thought. Then she realised that her eyes were filled with tears, and that her breathing was laboured. She became aware of David's hand stroking her once again, rubbing away some of the ache. Then his powerful and intimidating voice broke the eerie silence which had suddenly filled the room.

'I think that will do for now. Yes, Philippa, you'll be quite an addition to our little society.' And he took hold of her shoulder, and then swept her upright with one movement of his left arm. She wobbled a little as she was set back on her feet, then regained her balance. 'Tony and I will leave you now – I imagine you'd like to be alone with Steve. We'll be in touch soon.' And he rose, his severe face looking down on her from his superior height. 'Welcome.' And he stooped to kiss her on the left cheek. Then he turned and walked to the door, closely followed by Tony, who also kissed her goodbye, adding his congratulations.

Steve followed the two men, and Philippa heard the front door open and then close after a few words of goodbye. Then he returned. He closed the door, but instead of approaching her, he leant back against it. A sheepish and apologetic look had replaced his previous air of confidence.

'Sorry,' he said. 'You must really hate me now, but it was the only way I could think of to get you into my life the way I have to have you.'

'And why should I hate you for that?' she replied, trying to sound as if nothing in particular had happened that evening, even though her throbbing bottom was a reminder to her that this was definitely not the case.

'Setting you up like that. Not asking you first. More Jack's style than mine, but the organising committee does insist on some pretty stringent security measures. Most of them are totally unnecessary in my opinion, but there you go. Rules are rules.'

'Don't worry about it. The main thing is, I passed. God knows how, though – David doesn't mess about, does he?'

'No he doesn't; that's why he went second, so you'd be nice and warm when he got to you. Is it very sore?'

'Incredibly, although it is becoming more of a warm ache now.'

'Well, I can certainly do something about that. Go and lie down – the bedroom's through there – and I'll fetch some cream for you.'

At last, she thought, he's going to get me into bed, but she said nothing as he disappeared into what must have been the bathroom, and she headed into the room which he had indicated.

Steve's bedroom was as plush and tasteful as the rest of his flat. Dark blue sheets contrasted with the lighter tones of the walls and ceiling. Apart from the large double bed and small table next to it, the only furniture was a chair. Two large wardrobes ran along the opposite wall, an electric fire set between them. Philippa used the dimmer switch to adjust the lighting to a suitably romantic level, before stripping off her panties and lying

207

face down on the bed, revelling in the softness of the duvet. She lay there for a few seconds before deciding to reward Steve with a real treat. Standing up again, she unclipped her bra and threw it on the floor with her knickers. It was soon joined by her shoes, her suspender belt and her stockings. Now totally naked, she lay on the bed again and waited.

A minute or so later, the door opened. She looked back over her shoulder to see him wearing a striped dressing gown. 'I thought you'd feel more comfortable if I were wearing fewer clothes as well,' he began, before catching sight of her naked body. 'And you obviously agree!'

She said nothing, but smiled at him. He walked across the bedroom and sat next to her on the mattress. She saw a bottle of something in his hand, and arched her back to bring her bottom into prominence. He squeezed some of the liquid on to her tender flesh, and she was surprised to find it was not the same cold cream Jenny had treated her with. Instead it was a delicately scented oil, a little warmer than she had expected. Nevertheless, its soothing effect was immediate, as it sank into her skin and filled the room with its soft aroma. 'Mmm, that's good,' she murmured, resting her head on her folded arms and closing her eyes.

Steve continued to massage the oil into her bottom until it was completely covered, and it felt slippery and slick. Then, without being asked, he began to work his way up her back, spreading the viscous fluid across her body with gentle sweeping strokes of his hands. Philippa felt as if she were melting into the bed, and nearly nodded off a couple of times.

But eventually Steve stopped. When she realised this, she turned to see what he was doing – and found him standing over her, removing his dressing gown. He was naked and ready underneath. Now, she told herself, now was the moment she had been waiting for all evening.

208

She knew she wanted to make love, and she knew exactly how she wanted him to take her. Stretching her limbs beneath her, she pulled herself up on to all fours, pushing out her bottom and parting her thighs. Steve took the hint, and climbed on to the bed behind her, kneeling and taking hold of her hips. He let go for a second and she heard a small piece of paper being torn, and then, a few seconds later, he took hold of her again as his sheathed penis nestled against her labia.

Philippa gasped and rubbed herself against his tool. She heard his breath being sharply drawn in, and his fingers gripped her waist even tighter. 'Now,' she groaned. 'Now. I need you inside me!'

Steve did not disappoint her. He pushed forward, and she let out a long, low sigh as he filled her. For a few seconds they both stopped, savouring the exquisite union, and then they started moving again, almost simultaneously, Steve withdrawing then pushing back inside her. She set up her own rhythm to counter his, beginning to move her hips in small circles as well as back and forth, to maximise the sensation of Steve's cock inside her.

Steve's pumping became quicker and more determined, his strokes shorter and almost frantic. Philippa knew he did not have long to go but was herself near to a climax. The pain of the spanking had dissolved into the ecstasy of their union, and it heightened every sensation she was feeling. Steve leant forward to take hold of her breasts, and she squealed as his palms pressed against her erect nipples and his fingers dug into the softness around them. She felt the blood rush to her vagina, and instinctively slapped her bottom back against his groin.

That was enough. She felt the explosion in her vagina and the ecstasy rippling out from its very centre. She gave another long, low growl of satisfaction, and then another as, moments later, she felt Steve's organ twitch violently inside her, and then surge into a sudden burst of life. Then it gradually became still.

They rolled together on to their sides. Philippa was exhausted but gloriously happy. The glow in her bottom now seemed to have spread throughout her whole body. She felt warm and safe, with Steve's strong arms wrapped around her, and his softening penis resting against her buttock, his breath blowing gently on the side of her face. She began to doze, then fell into a restful sleep, stirring only once before the morning, when she felt Steve move beside her and carefully pull the duvet over them. For the first time since she had arrived in London, she really felt as if she had come home.

Ten

Almost another two weeks passed before Steve called her again, and Philippa began to think she had been forgotten, or worse still, deliberately discarded. Jack and Jenny had asked no awkward questions when Steve had brought her home the Saturday morning after their date, although she did exchange a few knowing glances with the other girl.

She passed the fortnight's interlude enjoyably enough, however. Jenny came to her room at around bedtime most nights the first week, bringing a different toy each time. Philippa added amongst other things the martinet and several varieties of whip to the range of implements she had learnt to receive and use herself, enjoying the powerful feeling of having Jenny's pale, sculpted cheeks raised and offered to her as the girl lay on the bed with her nightdress rucked up around her tummy, just as much as she relished being on the receiving end herself. But at the end of each session, when Jenny told her she was heading for Jack's room for some 'comforting', Philippa declined the invitation to join them. Much as she relished the feeling of a pair of male hands on her when her bottom was hot and sore, she knew she really wanted them to be Steve's. She did, however, accept the loan of one of Jenny's most powerful vibrators, and spent the dark night whiling away the hours dreaming of him as she brought herself to the peak of pleasure over and over again.

She had almost given up hope when Steve finally called. It was early on a Thursday evening, and although Jenny had got home, Jack was not yet there.

'Hello? Oh, hi, how are you?' Philippa heard Jenny enthuse into the phone when she answered it. 'Oh, fine – the usual – nothing much, really. Yes, I'll just get her, she'll be delighted to hear from you. I guess you must have had a great time the other week.' By now, Philippa had raced into the hall, guessing who it had to be. Nevertheless, Jenny still mouthed the name 'Steve' at her as she handed over the receiver, before slinking off into the lounge.

'Hello?' said Philippa, unsure as to how she should start a conversation with a man for whom she had such strong feelings.

'Hello, Philippa,' his voice crackled down the receiver. 'I bet you thought I'd abandoned you.'

'No, of course I didn't,' she lied. She might be falling in love with him, but she did not want him thinking he had her on a string. 'I knew you'd call.'

'I intended to, but I got called away this week, to France on urgent business. Yes, I know they have phones there, before you say it, but I just couldn't get away from all the meetings and stuff I have to deal with to make a living. Companies pay an awful lot of money for good PR, but they expect blood in return.'

'Hey, you don't have to explain yourself to me,' said Philippa, secretly glad he was at least trying to.

'Anyway, I'm here now, and I was wondering if I could come over to see you. Of course, I want to see you anyway, but I have important news from the club for you as well.' Philippa's heart skipped another beat. 'Philippa? Are you still there?'

'Yes – yes, of course I am,' she said, still fighting to take in what he had said. This was it! They must want her! 'Why don't you come over tonight?' she suggested, silently praying that he would accept this invitation.

'Sounds great,' said Steve. I'll be there about 9.30. See you then.' They whispered their goodbyes, and Philippa put the phone down. Straight away, she rushed into the kitchen, where Jenny was making herself a coffee. She told her friend everything as quickly as she could, about what had happened on her previous date with Steve, about being offered membership of the spanking club, and about what she had had to do to earn it. Jenny listened, affecting wide-eyed innocence, as if this were the first time any of this was being revealed to her, and when Philippa told her Steve was coming round in an hour and a half's time, she immediately promised that she and Jack would get out of the way. This, of course, gave her the perfect excuse to insist that Jack treat her like a lady rather than a naughty schoolgirl, if only for that evening, and take her out for a decent restaurant meal. He seemed to guess something was afoot, but decided not to risk incurring his female housemates' wrath by trying to get to the bottom of it.

Philippa went up to her room to prepare herself. She showered, but decided that she would not go over the top for this evening. After all, Steve was just coming around for a chat. She selected a blue skirt and blouse, striking a tone somewhere between the office and casual home wear. She wondered whether she should cook something for him – but what if he had other plans for them this evening? As she fastened the last button on her blouse, her eye fell on the large gym shoe which had been left in the corner of the room after last night's session with Jenny. Should she gather up the implements and put them out of sight? Or should she deliberately leave them lying around so he could make free with them if he wanted to? They did have the place to themselves this evening, after all. Quickly she lifted up the back of her skirt, and pulled her knickers down as far as the tops of her hold-up stockings. Turning her back to the mirror, she checked her bottom for evidence

213

of this week's excesses. Jenny had not been too severe. Her skin appeared to be unblemished. Would he like that? Or would he like to see physical proof that she had been busy trying to learn to take as much as she could? Just as she turned this question over and over in her head, the doorbell rang. He was fifteen minutes early.

She dashed downstairs and flung open the door. He stood on the doorstep, dressed casually in jeans and a rugby shirt. He looked her up and down and smiled. 'You look gorgeous,' he said softly.

'Thanks. Oh, come in.' For a moment she had been taken aback simply by the fact that she was seeing him again, but she quickly regained her composure. She led him into the living room, and told him to make himself comfortable while she made coffee for them both. When she returned, he was sitting on the sofa leafing through one of the lifestyle magazines Jenny habitually left lying around the house. He thanked her as he took the cup, and she joined him on the couch.

'Once again, sorry for springing that surprise on you,' he said, as he slipped an arm around her shoulders.

'Hey, stop saying you're sorry for giving me such a memorable time. We both got off on it, and that's the main thing.'

'Well, it could be just the beginning if you want it to be.' She looked up at him expectantly. 'David and Tony were impressed. So impressed in fact, that they've asked me to invite you to a party this weekend.'

She had been expecting something like this, but for a couple of seconds she was still rendered speechless.

'You mean,' she said when she finally found her voice again, 'like the one where we met?'

'Like it, but not exactly the same. It'll be smaller – more of an intimate little *soirée*.'

'How many people will be there?'

'Six in all, three men and three women, ourselves included.'

'And what would I have to do?'

'Well, you could expect to have your bottom smacked by all the men to begin with. Then there'd be a variety of implements which could be used – canes, straps, paddles, maybe even riding crops.'

'And if there's something I really don't like the look of?'

'Any limits you set down will be completely respected. One of the other men will be a committee member; a kind of referee to make sure everything stays within reasonable bounds. What do you say, Philippa?'

'I – I'm not sure.' Her heart was pounding, telling her to go ahead, seize this opportunity to travel further into Steve's world with him. But her head held her back, and he could tell.

'Don't say yes now,' he said softly. 'Sleep on it, let me know in a couple of days. No one expects you to leap into this without thinking it over.'

'OK, if you think that's for the best, then I will.'

'But in the meantime,' he went on, a mischievous glint in his eye, 'why don't we take up where we left off last time? It might give you something else to think about.'

'You mean, here? Right now?' she murmured.

'Right here and right now,' he said firmly, taking her coffee cup away from her and setting it down next to his on the table. 'I think it's high time that naughty behind of yours was given a reminder of its proper role in life.' Philippa sighed as she felt herself being pulled over Steve's lap and had her skirt lifted up behind her. If only he knew what she'd been up to all week, she thought, then took a deep breath as his palm came slapping down on her right cheek, just below the leg of her knickers.

Three hours later she lay in bed. Steve had left about an hour ago, after a session they had both found rewarding. She had shown him her ability to take the cane, eighteen strokes landing on her sore bottom as she touched her toes, naked in the centre of the living room.

215

The sight of her like this had been too much for him, and he had taken her there and then. They had retreated to Philippa's bedroom for a slower, more leisurely union, and had then lain silently in each other's arms for a while. Then he told her he had to go home, and she had not questioned him. They did not want to live in each other's pockets, and besides, she wanted to maintain a little distance between her private life with Steve, and the games she was currently playing with Jenny, if only temporarily.

As she lay drifting towards sleep, she thought about his invitation. Her bottom felt a little raw against the sheets, but the glow was a pleasant one, mingling with the relaxed feeling throughout her whole body, the after-effect of terrific sex. Her heart told her head to go to hell. First thing in the morning, she would call Steve and tell him she wanted to go.

Saturday night came, and Steve was there to collect her as before. She chose a green cocktail dress – simple but elegant – worn over a matching jade green suspender belt and panties, which she had teamed with classic black stockings.

They exchanged pleasantries about the working week as Steve drove through the suburbs towards London. This time, though, he did not head into the city itself, but pulled into a small street of well-kept houses to the south west. He steered into a parking space, his Porsche not looking at all out of place amongst the smart cars lining the kerb on both sides of the road. Philippa swung her legs carefully out through the open door, and got up graciously. She was becoming good at getting out of sports cars without losing her modesty, she thought! Steve locked the car and joined her on the pavement. 'This way' he said, and gently took her arm.

He led her to a large, modern house set a little further back from the rest of the street. Her mind flashed back to the time she had unwittingly attended a party like

216

this. How far she must have come to be going in full knowledge of what was going to happen to her. But how much further did she still have left to go?

Steve knocked on the door, and it was quickly opened. 'Steve!' A genial looking man in his mid-forties stood framed by the light from the hall. His hair was grey and receding, but cut short so as not to look unattractive. 'Good to see you – and this must be Philippa.' She shook the large hand which was proffered to her, as she crossed the threshold ahead of Steve, and she wondered how well her bottom would get to know it before the end of the night.

'This is Greg,' said Steve, as their host took their coats and placed them in a cupboard. 'He's on the committee, and has very kindly volunteered the use of his home for tonight's fun.'

'And it *is* going to be fun,' added Greg. 'The others all got here about fifteen minutes ago, so we can get started soon. But go and join them in the living room and have a drink, first.'

Steve and Philippa did as he had suggested, and found three people sitting in the large, warmly-decorated living room. The little group, two women and a man, looked up and smiled as they entered. They all said hello to Steve, and then one of the women stood up. 'Philippa? I'm Claire, Greg's wife. Nice to have you along. Can I get you both a drink?'

Philippa nodded and asked for a gin and tonic. Claire looked to be about fifteen years younger than her husband, and was very pretty without being classically beautiful, with shoulder-length brown hair tinged with a trace of red. But the main thing Philippa noticed about her hostess was her choice of clothes – jeans, a sweat-shirt and a pair of moccasins. She glanced at the other woman, a blonde in her mid-twenties called Lorna, and saw that she was similarly attired. Philippa felt a little overdressed, but no one else seemed to be bothered by what she was wearing, and so she said nothing, taking her drink and sitting alongside Steve on one of the two sofas in the room.

They sat and chatted pleasantly for about a quarter of an hour. The third man in the group, introduced to Philippa as Keith, was smartly dressed, in flannel trousers and a red blazer, similar to those which Steve had chosen to wear for the evening. Even Greg was wearing a tie.

Half an hour later, the drinks were finished and Greg stood up. 'Ladies and gentlemen, I believe it's time to start the evening's festivities. Claire, would you please take the ladies upstairs? Take special care of Philippa – remember, it's her first time and we want her to enjoy herself.' Philippa looked puzzled, but Claire and Lorna stood up. Claire took Philippa's hand, gently pulled her to her feet, and led her to the door through which Lorna had already disappeared. Philippa looked questioningly at Steve, but he simply nodded and gave her a half-smile. Obviously she would just have to go with the flow, and put herself completely in the hands of these people, a prospect she found both alarming and highly exciting.

Claire led her into the hall and up the stairs, and she couldn't help but admire Lorna's retreating denim-clad posterior. On reaching the top of the stairs they all turned the corner on to the landing, and passed two doors before reaching a third through which Philippa was taken. She found herself in the master bedroom, which was both large and comfortable, and had a queen-sized double bed as its centrepiece. And when Philippa saw what was on top of the duvet, she began to understand why her companions were so casually attired at this point.

Piled on the bed was a heap of clothing, though not the contents of an average wardrobe. Even to Philippa's inexperienced eye, it was clearly a collection of outfits which had not been designed to be worn in public; only the most broad-minded and discerning members of everyday society would have appreciated these. She had seen clothes like this before in Jenny's wardrobe.

'That's a lovely dress you're wearing, dear,' said Claire, 'but I think the boys would be a lot happier if you were to reappear in one of these. Didn't Steve explain everything to you?'

'Er – no, he didn't,' said Philippa, blankly, although she was getting a good idea as to how the evening was going to progress.

'It's simple,' said Claire. 'Just dive in and grab whichever outfit you fancy. We take it in turns to go downstairs, and the men react according to whatever we've chosen.'

'It means they have to do some of the work,' said Lorna. Philippa turned to see that the slim blonde had already stripped down to her bra and panties. 'Sometimes we give them marks out of ten for imagination, technique and acting ability – now what have we got here, Claire?' And she began to rummage in the pile of garments. Claire stepped back and pulled her sweatshirt off over her head, exposing a large pair of breasts supported by a generous lacy bra. She dropped the sweatshirt on to the floor, and then unfastened her jeans. Philippa knew it was time to stop being the odd one out and, slipping her shoulder straps down and unzipping her dress at the side, she slipped it off, being careful to lay it uncreased on a chair in the corner of the room.

'Hey, you've got a great figure,' said Lorna, turning away from the bed with an armful of clothes. 'How often do you have to work out to stay in such good shape?'

'Well, I don't, really – I've always been able to eat what I like. I'm just lucky, really.'

'I'll say,' said Claire, turning to take a look at Philippa for herself. 'The boys are going to love you. Steve's a lucky dog.'

'Thank you,' said Philippa, feeling a little self-conscious and diving into the clothes to hide her blushing face. She could sense Claire standing next to her, making her own choice. It didn't take her long to find what she was looking for, and she moved away from the bed.

Philippa went on rifling through the pile, not really knowing what she was looking for. Then her eyes lit on a hat lying by itself near to the pillows. She reached out and picked it up. Making a spur of the moment decision, she turned the pile over until she found the rest of the costume to go with it. Triumphantly, she held the policewoman's uniform up to the light to examine it. Secretly, she had always wondered how she would look in one of these, and now at last she had the chance to find out.

She turned to find that Claire and Lorna were both almost fully dressed. In a parody of her status as hostess, Claire had chosen a maid's uniform, similar to the one which Jenny had worn when she and Jack had seduced Philippa all those weeks ago. The low-cut neckline showed off Claire's generous cleavage to its maximum potential, and the short skirt revealed a pair of well-toned, if larger than average thighs. She was arranging her hair under the little white cap which completed the outfit. Meanwhile, Lorna was buttoning the second shoulder strap of the old-fashioned grey gymslip she had put on over a white blouse. A striped tie was loosely knotted around her collar, and she was already wearing little white ankle socks on her feet.

'Well, I guess I'm first on tonight,' said Claire, looking up at Philippa. 'Ah, you've found something. That should fit you perfectly, dear, and I'm sure you'll look a treat. I'd better go, but Lorna will give you any help you need. Just keep your ears open, and you'll get the idea about how all this works soon enough.' And she turned, picking up a large feather duster as she went, and headed out of the door.

'If we leave the door open, we should be able to hear everything,' explained Lorna, sitting on the edge of the bed to replace her black pumps. 'We don't do this sort of thing very often, because it only works with small numbers and with members who are quite good friends. Hey – you'll need a blouse to go with that tunic and skirt.' Philippa looked down to find that she did in fact have only half of the clothing necessary to being a convincing officer of the law. 'Let's see if we can find you one.'

She and Lorna began rooting through the clothes again, but Philippa stopped dead when she heard the sound of slightly raised voices from downstairs. She stood up and listened intently. 'That's the preliminary lecture,' Lorna explained. 'Don't worry, they're only doing it because Claire really gets off on it. And at any moment now ...' The voices stopped, and Philippa heard the sound of furniture being moved around. There was a pause of a few seconds, followed by the unmistakable sound of a hand slapping hard against bare flesh, closely followed by a female squeal.

Philippa looked at Lorna, but the other girl just smiled back. 'Sounds like Claire's getting her bottom smacked,' she said, 'and about time, too.' And she got up and walked to the dressing table, where she calmly began to plait her hair into two pigtails. 'Better get yourself ready,' she advised Philippa.

Philippa looked down at the clothes she was holding. They had managed to find a suitable blouse, and after laying the tunic and skirt carefully on the bed, she slipped the shirt on and buttoned it right up to the neck. Then she put on the heavy blue skirt, finding she had to pull the belt quite tight to keep the garment, which was slightly too big for her, in place. The jacket was also a little large, but at least the sleeves did not swamp her hands completely. She buttoned it up, then found the cravat in the top pocket. She stood behind Lorna to

221

look in the mirror and knot the scarf in place. 'Terrific,' said the blonde. 'They'll love you. And they'll really have got into their stride by the time you go down there.' Philippa looked nervously at the other girl, while the sounds of the punishment being meted out downstairs continued to drift up to the bedroom. They had obviously moved on from hand-spanking to using some kind of implement, as a swish now preceded each cry.

Philippa and Lorna continued to listen as they touched up their make-up, and heard the noises stop as suddenly as they had begun. The mumble of voices replaced the sound of punishment, followed by the clatter of footsteps leaving the living room and coming up the stairs. A few moments later, Claire came back into the bedroom, and Philippa and Lorna turned to look at her. She was rubbing her bottom through her skirt, and although her eyes were slightly tearful, they also had a new twinkle about them. 'Wow!' she said. 'They're on form tonight!'

'Well, don't just stand there,' Lorna said to her. 'Let's have a look.' Slowly, Claire turned around and lifted her skirt. Very gingerly, she pulled down her knickers, taking care to lift them clear of her cheeks first, and Lorna and Philippa stared at her bottom. It was completely crimson, and about two dozen weals were clearly visible across both buttocks.

'Cane,' she explained, looking back over her shoulder, 'and they weren't messing about, either.'

'We can see that,' said Lorna. 'How many?'

'Twelve from each, after the spanking. And no rubbing allowed in between. But you'd best be getting yourself down there, sweetheart. You've got until they finish the refills Greg was dishing out when I came up.'

'I'd better go then,' said Lorna. Then she got up and skipped lightly out of the room and down to her fate, leaving a wide-eyed Philippa staring after her.

'She loves to get into character at these theme par-

222

ties,' explained Claire, bending down to remove her panties altogether. 'That's her schoolgirl walk – a bit too theatrical to be real, of course – but then that's the whole point, isn't it?' And she turned as she unzipped the maid's dress, allowing it to fall forward. Having discarded her bra before putting on her costume, she now stood naked except for her stockings, suspenders and high heels, and Philippa found herself looking at her for a little too long for it to be taken as a natural, friendly glance. 'Anything I can do for you Philippa?'

'I – I'm sorry!' she blurted out, horrendously embarrassed as she suddenly became aware of what she was doing. Frantically, she turned away from Claire, only to find herself looking at the older woman's reflection in the dressing table mirror. Claire was walking towards her, and her naked breasts were wobbling as she moved. Then she gently placed her hands on Philippa's shoulders.

'No, I mean it,' she whispered. 'You must be very frightened at the moment. Is there anything you'd like me to do to make you more at ease?' Philippa thought about all the fun she and Jenny had been having lately.

'Thanks, Claire. Maybe just a kiss.' No sooner had she spoken than Claire's mouth had closed on hers, softly at first, then opening wider as the kiss deepened into a passionate exchange of affection. As their tongues touched, they heard Lorna's spanking begin downstairs. Then Claire started as Philippa's hand found one of her sore, fleshy cheeks and began to rub it.

Half an hour later Lorna returned to the bedroom, stiff-legged and red-eyed, but smiling happily to herself. Claire had wrapped herself in a dressing gown and was innocently rearranging the duvet. Philippa was now seated in front of the dressing table, brushing her hair in readiness for the WPC's cap she was about to put on. They both looked round as Lorna reappeared. Her regulation blue knickers were in her hand, while the other was beneath the gymslip, massaging her bottom. 'Cane again?' asked Philippa, anxiously.

'Leather paddle,' replied Lorna. 'With a vengeance. Especially your Steve. Have you ever tried dressing up for him like this?'

'N – no, never,' Philippa stammered, wondering what she was about to find out about him.

'Well, give it a try sometime – if you fancy a real walloping, that is,' said Lorna, throwing her unwanted knickers on the bed and then beginning to unbutton her gymslip.

Philippa turned back to the mirror, and picked up the hat. She began carefully to balance it on top of her hair, which she had swept up into a bun to match the smart appearance of the uniform. Claire came and stood behind her. In the glass, the women exchanged a significant look. 'Don't worry,' Claire said quietly. 'They all know how green you are at this, and your own boyfriend won't let you come to any real harm. You can relax a little.'

'I don't really want to relax,' she answered. 'I think it's being wound up and tense which makes all this so exciting for me. Is it time yet?'

'As soon as you're ready. No rush.'

'I'm ready now. No point in putting it off, is there?' And she stood up to go to meet her fate, with kisses from both Claire and Lorna to wish her luck.

Her legs trembled as she reached the foot of the stairs. She thought back to Claire's words of reassurance. Claire was right, of course – one of the three men in that room was the man Philippa thought she was in love with, and he would not let her get into anything she could not handle, would he? And besides, how much more severe could this be than what she had gone through in that room at Canes and Chains, when she had been chained up and subjected to the ministrations of her mysterious tormentor?

224

The living room door was closed. She thought about opening it, then realised that this was all part of the game. She knocked timidly. 'Come in!' called a gruff voice. She thought it was Greg's, minus the genial welcoming tones he had used earlier, and she felt her palms begin to sweat as she turned the handle and walked inside.

The first thing she saw was Greg standing imperiously in front of the fireplace. She looked to his side and saw Keith looking very relaxed in a small armchair. She desperately cast her eyes around the room and finally located Steve, sitting almost behind her at the dining table. Clearly he was going to allow the others to dictate the pace of this session, even if he was overseeing it.

Greg and Keith both smiled when they saw the outfit she had chosen.

'Aha!' said Greg. 'What have we here?'

'I think we have a policewoman who has committed a serious breach of the rules,' said Keith, his voice soft and almost kindly. It would have had a reassuring feel to it had she not known exactly what he was planning for her.

'Is that so?' Greg went on. 'So, what have you been up to young lady? Planting evidence? Handing out too many parking tickets? Non-regulation items on your uniform?'

Philippa realised this was her cue to confess. 'Yes, sir – all of that,' she mumbled meekly. 'I'm sorry, sir – how are you going to punish me?'

'Well, how do you think you should be punished?' asked Keith.

'Will I be demoted? Thrown out of the force?' She was getting into the spirit of things now.

'Well, you could be,' Greg told her. 'But there is an alternative.'

Time to go, hook, line and sinker, she guessed. 'There is? What's that, sir?'

'Will you submit to a dose of corporal punishment? Purely for your own good?' said Greg.

'Corporal punishment?' she repeated, pretending not to understand, as she imagined her character would not.

'Spanking, my dear. We take you across our knees and smack your bottom. Your bare bottom,' Keith explained to her slowly.

'Spank my – oh my goodness, I've never been spanked before!' she burst out, trying hard not to grin as she lied. The men's expressions told her she was doing well so far. Maybe she should have kept up her interest in acting after being in all those school plays.

'It's the only way to keep your job,' Greg said, sounding for all the world as if he were serious. 'Do you agree?'

'I suppose I don't really have a choice,' she said, trying to sound miserable. In reality, her heart was pounding at the prospect of being dealt with in this way.

'Very well,' Greg said, gravely. 'Steve, would you bring me a suitable chair, please?' Steve carried another of the dining chairs to the centre of the room. Philippa remained in the middle of the carpet, playing nervously with her hands, but as he walked past she looked up at him. He gave her a reassuring smile, then set his face back into that of a dispassionate disciplinarian. Setting the chair down about a foot away from her, he returned to his own seat.

Greg strolled over to the chair and sat down. He was obviously going to give her the first dose. He looked up at her, expectantly. 'Get across my lap, WPC,' he said, darkly. She moved around to obey, feeling the tunic ride up a little as she stretched, cat-like over Greg's lap. Her hands sank into the soft white wool of the carpet as she wriggled and squirmed into exactly the right place. She felt her heavy skirt being lifted and Greg's hands roaming over her knicker-clad behind. Raising her head slightly, she saw Steve looking down at her, his face a picture of happiness. She knew she had pleased him, and lowered her head again to stare at the floor and accept her punishment.

Greg started the punishment over her panties, but soon slid them down to her knees so that his heavy hand might drum out a loud beat on her unguarded bottom. His strokes were painful enough, driven, as they were, straight down on to her cheeks. Steve, she had noticed, favoured an upward sweep, sending the most delightful quivers through her rear end. How strange, she thought, to find herself in this situation, actually comparing how different men like to smack her bottom. She wriggled and moaned as Greg's slaps became harder, and the intense but momentary pain of each blow became a dull ache.

Just as she was beginning to get a little uncomfortable, he stopped, and she let her breathing return to normal as he stroked and soothed her tingling cheeks for a couple of minutes. 'Right, time for your second dose,' he announced, and she felt his strong hands helping her back to her feet. Instinctively, she held up her skirt, and made no attempt to replace her underwear. After all, she told herself, what would be the point?

Greg got up and was quickly replaced by Keith, who had removed his jacket and rolled up his sleeves in readiness. He was obviously keen to get on with it, as Philippa found herself back in position in a trice. Keith wasted no time in stroking her, but began spanking her straight away. Now she noticed a different technique again, one which used the fingers as much as the palm of the hand, and which involved the arm being moved with something like a whipping motion. The pain of each individual smack was not as great as it had been with Greg, but the cumulative effect was a sting which seemed to penetrate much deeper into the flesh of her already-sore bottom. Pretty soon, Philippa was groaning and muttering, although more to herself than to the man chastising her.

Through the haze of emotions and sensations, she heard Greg's voice. 'Another half dozen, Keith, and then we ought to let Steve show us how his girlfriend really likes to be spanked.' Steve's girlfriend. The words were music to her ears and bore her effortlessly through the last flurry of spanks from Keith. As a final refinement, he hauled her knickers down to her ankles and then off altogether before allowing her to get up so that he could vacate the chair.

Now Steve crossed the room again, and occupied the punishment seat. 'Come on, my dear,' he said firmly. 'Let's show these gentlemen how well we take our punishments.' Obediently, she got across his lap, settling herself comfortably into place once again. She could feel his hardness pressing against her crotch through his clothes and ached to feel it inside her. But her spanking had to come first.

Steve laid it on with the same severity he had used on her the last time, when he had visited the house to invite her here this evening. He settled into the comfortable rhythm to which she had become accustomed, and her bottom twitched as her excitement grew. She had, of course, been spanked in front of Steve on the night of her audition for the club, but this was the first time that he had dealt with her before an audience, and she was finding it to be incredibly stimulating.

Steve increased the intensity of the spanking by degrees, and the thrill grew for her at the same rate. As she rolled slightly on his lap, she felt her labia begin to move against each other. Already lubricated, she knew she would reach orgasm with very little encouragement. But Steve either did not sense this, or would not allow her to go over the edge just yet, for he stopped and gently eased her back up on to her feet.

Philippa found that her face was wet, and realised she

had been brought to tears without being aware of it. Steve stood up and walked back to his place in the corner of the room. How she wished he had been able to kiss her, but that would not have fitted in with the fantasy they were all acting out.

'Now,' said Greg, 'take your skirt off.' Without pausing to question him she obeyed, unzipping herself and letting the dark garment fall to the floor. Bending down to pick it up, she felt her bottom smart as the skin of her cheeks tautened. She folded it neatly and hung it over the back of the chair, aware that the three men would be focusing on her pubic mound, framed by her suspenders, and wondering if they could guess how moist she had become. Finally she stood upright, with her hands folded behind her back to ensure that her sex was exposed to their view. Greg walked over to a chest of drawers and opened the top one. He delved inside it, and pulled something out of it. Turning triumphantly to face the rest of the room, he showed them all the tawse.

It was large – bigger than the one previously used on her by Jack and Jenny, and its tail was slit into three strips. Greg smacked it lightly against his left palm, using minimal force, but even then it still made a wicked sound. Philippa gulped. 'I believe you're due a dose of the strap, WPC,' announced Greg. 'And not a light one, either. Twelve –'

'Twelve!' she exclaimed.

'– Twelve from each of us,' Greg finished.

Philippa took a deep breath. She had prepared herself for something like this, but now she wondered if she could take that much. But she had to – for Steve's sake. She could not let him down in front of his friends. 'Very well, sir,' she mumbled meekly. 'Where would you like me?'

'Bend over the back of the chair. Make sure your bottom is stuck right out for us.'

Philippa did as she had been instructed, walking stiffly

as the effects of the prolonged spanking continued to make themselves felt. She bent herself over the back of the chair and gripped the seat, parting her legs lasciviously in an attempt to send an unspoken message to Steve. Greg took up position on her left side.

Philippa felt him move as he raised the strap. She closed her eyes and prepared herself for the pain, but when it arrived it was far more intense than she could ever have imagined. The tawse landed with an ear-splitting crack right across the centre of her bottom, reigniting the burn of her spanking. 'Aah!' she cried, her knuckles turning white as she tried to find a way – any way – of dealing with the pain. But at the same time, there was excitement, a feeling of heightened eroticism as she put herself on display for the enjoyment of these men.

The second stroke landed higher but just as hard. Philippa rolled her hips from side to side to try to gain some relief, much to Greg's evident amusement. 'What a delightful little dance,' he laughed. 'You must really be enjoying yourself, my dear.'

'Enjoy' was not quite the word Philippa would have used – at least not yet – but she had no intention of backing out. She steeled herself for the rest of her discipline, and managed to hold back the cry which threatened to burst from her lips as the third stroke seared across her cheeks.

She did her best to remain silent as Greg continued with the strapping. Finally, he counted off the twelfth and she breathed a sigh of relief, even though she knew it could only be short-lived. Sure enough, Greg handed the tawse to Keith, who took his place by her side. She felt his left hand resting on the small of her back, and knew the leather was being raised once again. A few seconds later it landed, and she bit her lip to hold in the scream once again.

Keith delivered his dozen with brisk efficiency, his

230

blows landing at ten-second intervals, and aimed precisely to cover every inch of her bottom. She was forcing low moans through her clenched teeth by the time the last one landed, and she knew she had a few more seconds to regain her composure.

Now it was Steve's turn. She wondered if he would be as severe as the others, or if he would be lenient. Maybe he would be even harder, not wanting to appear to show favouritism. She felt her breathing grow deeper as he arrived to take up the strap.

He stood as Greg and Keith had done, resting his left hand gently on the curve of her back, and then ran the strap smoothly over her cheeks. She winced as the leather touched the sorest parts of her flesh. 'Ready, sweetheart?' Steve asked, gently.

'Yes,' she sighed weakly.

The tawse landed with a heavy smack, and she was unable to suppress a cry, although she had found it as exciting as it had been painful. She braced herself for the second lash, which arrived ten seconds later and was just as harsh. If anything, Steve was being more severe than the others, but she knew that she had to accept whatever he chose to do.

He continued relentlessly, wielding the long strap like the expert he so obviously was. Philippa guessed that if she was going to have any kind of long-term relationship with this man, she was going to have to become very good indeed at taking this kind of punishment. She hoped she had made a good start. Apparently she had. The twelfth blow landed and she gasped out her relief. She felt Steve's hand on her shoulder, pulling her upright. When she was standing up straight, he placed a finger under her chin and he tilted her face up a little, to allow him to bestow a gentle kiss on her lips. She looked into his eyes, and loved him more at that moment than she had ever done before.

'Your punishment is at an end for the time being,

Philippa,' said Greg, as Steve handed him the strap and returned to the far side of the room. 'Have you learnt your lesson?'

'Yes sir,' she breathed, knowing she had to keep up her WPC act until she left the room.

'Very well. Go back upstairs and choose another outfit. And send my disobedient wife back down. I think it's time she got another dose. And take this – you've earned it,' he finished, handing her a large brandy.

'Yes, sir, thank you, sir,' she answered, taking the glass in one hand and picking up her skirt and knickers with the other before leaving. So she was to be given a second measure. She wondered if she would be able to stand it as she mounted the stairs.

She walked back into the bedroom to find Claire and Lorna in new costumes. Claire was wearing what appeared to be a PVC version of a nurse's uniform, with its skirt a little too short to be authentic, though it did at least show off her stocking tops and black suspenders. It was also cut very low at the front, so that her generous cleavage was revealed. Lorna had opted for a tight leather mini dress, which flattered her neat curves beautifully.

'Well done,' Claire said as she walked in.

'You heard?'

'We both did, from the landing.' Philippa blushed at the thought of the unseen audience. 'Don't worry, we wanted to keep an ear on our men anyway. But we were impressed with your performance. Turn around.' Philippa obeyed dutifully, and jumped as Claire reached out and stroked her scarlet bottom. 'They didn't hold back, did they? I think you've taken more than either of us tonight.' And she gave Philippa a slap across both cheeks, not hard, but nevertheless enough to make her wheel around and squeal with shock. 'So my husband wants me downstairs, does he? I guess I'd better go, then. You can use the bathroom to redo your hair and

232

make-up, then choose another outfit for your second performance. See you soon.' And with that, she headed back downstairs to meet her doom for the second time.

Philippa shut herself in the bathroom, feeling the need to use the lavatory as well. While sitting on the bowl, she touched herself gently, fingering her engorged clitoris and moaning as she caressed the sensitive little bud. She was tempted to bring herself off again for the second time that evening, but told herself that she would need all her strength to get through another session of severe corporal punishment. Having washed her hands, she began to fix her tear-streaked and tousle-haired appearance, and as she did so, the sound of Claire's second punishment began to drift up to her.

She took her time, wanting to reappear perfectly kempt. As she opened the bathroom door, Claire was climbing the stairs, naked now, her nurse's outfit clutched in her right hand, as she used her left to massage her bottom cheeks. 'Perfect timing, Philippa,' she said, on seeing her emerge from the bathroom. 'My arse needs a nice, cool soak and it needs it now.' Philippa smiled, and moved aside to allow her hostess in, just as Lorna sauntered past them on her way downstairs. Philippa watched her behind wiggling provocatively until she reached the hall, and then she turned and headed back to the bedroom.

She began to look through the pile of clothes in search of inspiration, knowing it wouldn't be long before her presence was again required downstairs. She pulled out one or two garments, but none of them fired her imagination, and some were just too big or too small. She tried to see it from the men's point of view – what would they like to see her wearing? It must be quite challenging for them to think up their responses to the costumes the girls chose. Although not so challenging that it was impossible she reflected, as the sound of Lorna's chastisement reached her ears. She pondered the problem as she examined a white toga-like tunic, presumably meant to turn the wearer into a Roman slave girl. The sheet-like tunic did not look as if it would cover much of her modesty. But after all, she thought, that was the point. Suddenly she had an idea – one which would surprise the men, and bring the party to a stunning conclusion. She stood up and stripped off her blouse, then unclipped her stockings and began to roll them down.

Lorna and Claire returned to the bedroom at about the same time, the former with her leather dress raised to her hips, crudely exposing her lower half with its naturally blonde pubes, and the latter wrapped in a short silk kimono. They found Philippa sitting on the edge of the bed, her legs crossed, calmly finishing her brandy. She wore nothing but a smile.

'Cutting it a bit fine, aren't you?' Lorna asked her. 'What have you chosen for your finale'

'This,' she replied, knocking back the half-inch of her drink and standing up. 'The outfit I think the boys want to see me in most of all – my birthday suit.'

'Well I'll be!' said Claire. 'I never thought of that before!'

'Do you think they'll buy it?' asked Lorna.

'Let's find out,' said Philippa, setting down her glass and walking out. She did not look back at the other women, but she felt their eyes upon her as she left.

She reached the living door once again. Straightening her back so that her breasts and erect nipples jutted out proudly, she knocked. The house was warm, Claire having turned the heating fully on, but Philippa still felt goose bumps all over her body. As before, she was called in by Greg, and she opened the door.

The three men were in the same places as before. Their eyes widened as she walked in, and she saw Keith's mouth open slightly. Greg's brow furrowed, and then he smiled wickedly. Philippa looked over towards

Steve. He was also smiling, a little more enigmatically than Greg, she thought. 'You wanted to see me, sir?' she said, trying to appear unconcerned about her nudity or her fate.

'Yes, yes, I – er, we did.' Evidently she had managed to slightly wrong-foot Greg. But not for long. 'We wanted to talk to you about your scandalous behaviour, but it seems we have quite a bit of work to do, judging by the brazen way you choose to appear before us. A good spanking, followed by a caning, would seem to be the only solution. Are we agreed, gentlemen?'

'Here, here,' said Keith.

'Absolutely,' added Steve.

'So Philippa, shall we begin?'

'Yes, sir,' she said without emotion. She could see the long yellow cane with its curved handle propped up beside the fireplace. 'Over your lap again?'

'Of course.' Greg took his place on the chair, and Philippa felt every eye in the room take in her naked curves as she walked slowly towards him and laid herself across his lap.

Greg's spanking was brisk and painful. It lasted about five minutes, after which she was summarily handed over to Keith, who delivered his share of the chastisement very enthusiastically. Finally she went back over Steve's lap, revelling in the hardness she could feel in his groin through his loose trousers.

For her caning the chair was removed, and she was instructed to bend over in the centre of the room, clutching her ankles with her feet apart. She found the position difficult to reach, and deeply humiliating once she had assumed it. And yet, she also felt a definite sense of exhilaration. She was doing this for Steve, and he loved her for it.

Greg stood beside her with the ominous cane in his hand. She could see him as she peered back between her legs. What he could see of her, she did not like to think.

He had just begun to line up the vicious looking rod against her taut skin, when suddenly he removed it. 'This is just too good for the other girls to miss,' he announced. 'I think they should join us.'

'Why not?' agreed Keith. 'That is, if Steve doesn't mind.'

'And why should I mind?' said Steve. 'After all, they've probably been running around naked in that bedroom all evening. Goodness knows what they get up to in there when we can't see them.' Philippa took a deep breath, and hoped none of the men would find out. 'Anyway, I say let's get the other two down here.'

Greg walked to the door, opened it and shouted up the stairs to Claire and Lorna, sternly informing them that they were wanted downstairs immediately.

The pair dutifully arrived, Claire still in her robe and Lorna now dressed in her bra and knickers. Philippa heard them both gasp as they came in and saw her vulnerable and uncomfortable position. 'We thought you'd both enjoy seeing Philippa get her just desserts. Are we right?'

'Oh, most definitely,' agreed Claire. 'She's beautiful standing up, but like that she's simply gorgeous.'

'Wonderful!' Lorna added. 'Are you all going to cane her?'

'We certainly are. Twelve each,' Keith replied, with a little too much enthusiasm for Philippa's liking. She kept silent, knowing that, short of calling a halt to the game, there was nothing she could say to improve her situation. She could feel the flush of burning embarrassment as she awaited the inevitable in front of this small crowd.

The cane tapped twice against her tight bottom. Then it was drawn back. She even heard Greg's deep intake of breath. She closed her eyes and wished already that she could be at the other side of this ordeal. Then, there was a terrible swishing noise, and suddenly a line of fire was drawn across both her moons. At least that was how it had felt to her. 'Aagh!' she screamed, unable to contain herself.

'I don't think she's going to make it,' she heard Lorna say.

'I think she will,' Claire chipped in, 'and I think she should count them, even if she is new.'

'Good idea,' agreed Greg. 'How many was that, Philippa?'

'One – one sir,' she groaned, her breathing returning to normal. From where her head hung, her breasts and nipples looked extraordinary, dangling before her, and her vagina felt pleasurably as though it were on fire.

'Good,' said Greg. 'Let's see if we can keep it up.' The cane sang through the air again.

'Oow! Two, sir,' she called out, trying to sound enthusiastic. She heard giggling from Lorna and Claire. 'Aah! Three, sir!' And so it went on, until Greg had delivered all twelve of his strokes. He stepped back, and she sensed Keith taking his place. She heard him swipe the cane experimentally a couple of times, and then it was lined up against her bottom once more.

A second or two later, she felt it land across her cheeks again. 'Thirteen, sir.' She had no idea as to whether they wanted her to begin again at one, or to carry straight on, and so she opted to do the latter. Keith delivered his share of the strokes with calculated deliberation. He was obviously good at this. And men could apparently wield a cane much harder than poor little Jenny had been able to when she had been demonstrating it to Philippa.

Philippa continued counting, glad to have something else on which to concentrate her mind, other than the punishment being ruthless administered to her backside. Keith left longer gaps between strokes than Greg had done, allowing her longer to recover but making the experience last that much longer, too. Eventually, though, he too had given her his dozen.

237

Philippa waited for Steve to take over. She opened her eyes, blinking away the tears which now filled them. Through her legs, she saw Greg and Claire standing directly behind her, appearing to her to be upside down. Greg was embracing his wife, with one of his hands slipped inside her robe, clearly massaging her breast. For her part, she was blatantly caressing his crotch with her hand, her fingers busily stimulating him. They kissed long and deep as Philippa watched.

Then Steve was beside her. She gasped as she felt the cane again, but this time, not rested across her twin mounds. Instead, Steve was playing the very tip of the implement over her vaginal lips. He worked it along for a few seconds, gently parting the flesh and bringing her arousal up to fever pitch, and when the thin, blunt malacca tip touched her clitoris, she nearly toppled over. All too soon, though, he stopped teasing her and removed the cane from between her legs. Philippa closed her eyes again, and tried to compose herself.

She felt the rod being aimed, and readied herself for more pain. 'Ugh! 25, sir. 26, sir. 27, sir.' The caning was relentless. Steve's aim was also good, better even than Greg's or Keith's had been, as far as Philippa could tell. She counted off each stroke through gritted teeth, until, finally, she reached the magic number. '36, thank you very much, sir!' she finished, allowing herself the indulgence of this little dramatic flourish.

She stayed locked in position, blinking until her eyes cleared, and praying silently that her punishment was indeed over. Her head was swimming, and she felt an immense sense of relief when Steve's hand appeared on her shoulder and drew her gently upward. He turned her towards him and they embraced, kissing deeply, their hands roaming over each other's body, his fingers gently twisting her nipples, and his palms slowly rotating her breasts. Eventually, they broke away from each other. Philippa leant back and looked around to see if the others were still watching her. She found they were not, and instead, she soon found herself watching them.

Keith had returned to the armchair, where Lorna had joined him. She sat on his lap, with her arms around his shoulders. Her bra had been removed, and Keith's lips were now locked around her left nipple, his eyes closed as he sucked noisily on it. She, meanwhile, was running her fingers through his hair, with an expression of pure bliss on her face. Keith's left hand was wrapped around her waist and his right was in between her thighs. The gusset of Lorna's briefs had been pushed to one side, and Philippa could clearly see that Keith's first three fingers were buried deep between her labia. Lorna's breath was coming in long deep sighs, as Keith increased the friction.

Then Philippa turned her attention to Claire and Greg. Claire was now kneeling before her husband, her kimono open to expose her naked body. Greg's trousers were also undone and as Philippa watched, Claire sucked lustily on his erect member, cupping his testicles in her left hand, while the fingers of her right encircled the base of his shaft. Her head bobbed back and forth, and her lips worked hungrily as she warmed to her task. Greg's face was a mask of passion as he looked down on his wife and rested his hands tenderly upon her head.

Philippa was mesmerised by the scene. Then she heard a zip being unfastened and turned back to Lorna and Keith to find that they, too, were getting serious. Lorna had slid herself further on to Keith's lap and had freed his erect penis. She masturbated it slowly, her long fingernails gently tracing lines up and down the sensitive flesh.

Philippa's concentration was suddenly broken by Steve's lips on the nape of her neck. She turned to embrace him, kissing him deeply on the mouth once again. 'They seem to be enjoying themselves,' she whispered, 'why don't we join them?'

239

'Why not?' Steve answered. Taking Philippa by both hands, he drew her over to the large sofa, and laid her upon it. He knelt beside her, and covered her body in little kisses, concentrating on her breasts and stomach, and finally administering a number of little licks on her damp labia. She simply lay there, her head thrown back and her arms raised in pleasured abandon. Then Steve's mouth suddenly broke away from her, and she raised her head to see why. She saw him standing up and unbuttoning his trousers, and felt a glow of anticipation spread through her body.

His hard penis bobbed into view as his boxer shorts joined his trousers on the carpet. 'I love you, Philippa,' he said, in a low, hoarse voice, 'and I want you so much.'

She eased her legs over the edge of the sofa, parting them wantonly. The roughness of the material against her skin reminded her of how sore her bottom was, but that only added to the intensity of the emotions she was feeling at that moment. Tenderly, Steve spread her thighs, and manoeuvred himself between them. She saw his glans moving ever closer to her pouting labia, until it was perfectly positioned. He paused for a second, and then pushed forward, and she threw her head back as she felt him fill her to the brim. 'Mmm!' he groaned, 'you were ready for that, weren't you? Your pussy's always so nice and wet for me.'

'All the better to fuck you with,' she gasped in response, as he began to buck and writhe between her legs. 'Aah! Oh God, *yes!*'

She was vaguely aware of similar cries coming from the couples behind them, but by now, she was past caring about them. All that concerned her was Steve, and his cock between her thighs. He leant forward to give her a kiss as he continued to thrust and pull, and she returned it with passion. She was on an erotic high which had been building throughout the evening, and now she had only a little further to go before she attained total sexual satisfaction. Then, suddenly, she knew that she was there.

'*Yes!*' she hissed, her voice wavering as an intense orgasm, the like of which she had never even come close to experiencing before, shuddered through her. The aftershocks were still coursing around her body when she felt Steve's erection begin to twitch and pulse inside her. He gripped her tightly around her waist, and took as much of her left breast as was possible into his mouth, and she cried out, as this sudden stimulation sent her once more over the edge to another, smaller, but no less gratifying orgasm. Steve chose that moment to follow her, driving his hips in short sharp spasms as he too fulfilled his sexual destiny for the evening.

They lay locked together for some time. Theirs had been a quick passionate bout – that of lovers still new to the surprises the other held. By way of a contrast, the other two couples, more experienced and far more familiar with one another, were only just beginning to reach the point of ecstasy. Philippa thought she heard Lorna cry out and imagined Keith's fingers still lodged in her entrance, now working frantically. Would she bring him off with her hand, she wondered, or slide down between his legs to take him in her mouth? She knew Claire had already chosen that option, and Philippa imagined that she could still hear the smacking of Claire's lips around Greg's cock, along with his animalistic grunts of encouragement.

She looked up at Steve, his face, now serene, peaceful and satisfied. He seemed to be in a daze, too tired even to withdraw his limp penis from her vagina. She slid her arms around and kissed him. He opened his eyes and smiled down at her. 'Thank you,' she breathed softly.

'For what? I should be thanking you.'

'No, I owe *you* one. For getting me here.'

'Here? You mean to the party tonight?'

241

'No, for getting me this far. For showing me how much I've achieved, how far I've come.'

'If only you knew how much further you can go, Philippa,' he said. 'But we've got all the time in the world to get you there.' And he leant down and kissed her.

Eleven

At seven-thirty on Monday morning, the post arrived. Philippa, late for work and already pulling on her coat, scooped it up, and shoved everything addressed to her into her bag, before hurrying out of the house.

The morning was busy, so much so that she hardly had time to think about what had happened to her at the party at the weekend, let alone the bundle of unopened envelopes. It was not until lunchtime when, sitting alone in the small café opposite her office, with a coffee and a cheese roll, she thought to examine this morning's correspondence more closely. As expected, it contained unwanted communications from her bank and credit card company, along with a selection of impersonal junk mail. Making a mental note to toss most of it into the recycling bag back at the office, she reached the last letter in the pile and stopped.

It was a personal letter – as opposed to a computer printed circular or bill – and the small white envelope was addressed to her in a neat fountain pen hand. She examined the post mark and found that it had been sent the day before from West London. Unable to garner any more clues from the outside, she slid a thumbnail into the flap and tore it open.

She pulled out a sheet of crisp, high quality writing paper, the kind usually used for formal invitations, which had been folded in four to fit inside the envelope. She opened it out, and found a few lines written in the

243

same hand and bold black ink as the address had been, and, taking a long sip of her coffee, she read the intriguing paragraph:

Dear Philippa,

Forgive me for not speaking to you personally at this time, but if you choose to go on all will be revealed. You have begun to explore the limits of your own self, to taste the life which could be yours. You have come a long way in a short time. But now I offer you the chance to take the next step on your journey. For people like us, trust is everything. Please trust me. If you wish to know more, be waiting at your house at eleven tomorrow morning. And please say nothing to your friends. If you choose not to be there I will understand, but I am guessing that you will be unable to resist the chance to discover more about yourself than you know already. I look forward to seeing you.

A Friend.

Philippa read and reread the letter over and over again as she finished her snack. She did not recognise the handwriting, which ruled out Jack and Jenny, but it could have been from anyone else at all. How many members had Steve said the spanking club had? About three hundred? Maybe it was from Dave or Tony, the two men who had auditioned her, or from Greg or Keith, from the party – it could be from any one of them.

She spent the afternoon pondering what to do about the letter, turning over the possibilities in her mind. It sounded plausible, going by what she had experienced so far, but it did not sound very safe. Why could she not tell Jack or Jenny, or even Steve, about it? Would she be taking a risk by going? Would she be taking a risk by not going, or possibly failing a test which would result in her being barred from the wonderful world she had discovered? That she would not be able to bear. By four o'clock, she had decided upon a course of action. She went to her supervisor and booked the next day off. She told herself she would wait in the house until whoever it was arrived. If she did not like the look of them or of what was happening, then she would call a halt to it right then and there.

The following morning, she got up at her usual time, but did not dress. 'What's up?' Jenny asked, as she appeared in the kitchen.

'I don't feel too good today,' she lied, trying to sound as convincing as possible. 'Bit of a migraine. I've got a splitting headache.'

'Are you up to going into work today?'

'I don't think so, at least not this morning. I'll take a couple of painkillers and go back to bed. I'll call the office after nine and tell them I'll come in this afternoon if I feel any better.'

'Good idea,' said Jenny. 'Best not to take any chances. Do you want me to get you anything before I go?'

'No, but thanks anyway. I'll just go and lie down.'

Once Jenny had left the house, Philippa threw back the covers and leapt out of bed. She showered and dressed, taking extra care over her hair and make-up. She was not sure why but something told her this might be important today.

By 10.30 she was ready. She sat in the living room and tried to watch television, but was unable to find anything worth watching. She went into the kitchen and switched the radio on but again she could not concentrate. She switched the kettle on to make a coffee, and took the letter from her pocket. She examined it yet again, searching the note and the envelope for some clue she had missed, but could find none. The kettle boiled and she filled her mug, then took it into the living room.

She sat drinking the coffee and watched the clock tick around to eleven. The appointed hour arrived, and she half-expected to hear the doorbell immediately. But nothing happened.

The hands of the clock moved slowly as she watched, and she wondered if perhaps she had been the victim of some bizarre hoax or practical joke. It reached ten past, and she thought about calling Jenny at work, or possibly even Jack or Steve, and explaining the situation to them to see if they had any ideas as to who had sent the letter.

When another five minutes had passed, she made up her mind to do just that. She drained her mug and was just standing up to reach for the phone when she heard footsteps on the path outside. A moment later, the doorbell finally rang, its tone sounding throughout the empty house. Philippa was suddenly very anxious, not knowing for a few seconds what to do with her empty coffee mug, before setting it down on the low table. Pausing to check her hair and make-up in the mirror over the fireplace, she rushed into the hall just as the bell sounded for the second time. No matter who it was, she must not keep them waiting; that would be terribly bad manners – what would they think? What would they do to her . . .? She gathered her thoughts, and reached for the door handle.

She could see a dark figure through the frosted glass, but could not make out any detail before opening the door. Even when she saw who was standing on her step she was no closer to having any of her questions answered.

It was an attractive young woman, about five feet four tall, with long blonde hair hanging loose around her shoulders. Her smiling lips, painted a deep red, bore a full promise. She was dressed in black leather jeans, tucked into calf-length stiletto-heeled boots, and a black biker jacket zipped up to cover her obviously luscious curves. Philippa could not tell if she was wearing anything underneath it. 'Would you be Philippa?' she asked sweetly.

'Er, yes – yes, I am,' she replied, somewhat thrown.

'Would you come with me please, miss?'

'Come with you? Where? Why?' She had not been prepared for this, and found herself playing for time to try and find out more.

'I'm afraid I can't tell you anything at the moment, miss.'

'Well, let me make a phone call, then.' Philippa now wished she had confided in Jenny, and wanted to contact her friend now if she could.

'I'm afraid I can't wait. If you want to find out more you must come with me now.' And the girl turned and walked back down the path. Philippa was faced with a split-second decision. She paused only for a moment, then grabbed her coat and ran out after the girl.

The girl reached the pavement beyond the gate and turned to see if Philippa was following her. When she realised that she was, she opened the back door of a gleaming black Sierra and held it open, chauffeuse-style. 'Where are we going?' Philippa asked.

The girl just smiled back at her again. 'I'm sorry,' she said, 'I just can't tell you.' It was obvious that there was only one way Philippa was going to get to the bottom of this. She climbed into the back of the saloon and settled herself into the plush seat as the girl closed the door behind her. Then her mysterious visitor walked round the car and climbed into the driving seat. The engine was switched on with a gentle shudder, and the car pulled quietly away from the kerb.

They drove out of the suburb and on to the main road for town. Philippa tried to keep track of where they were going, but, not knowing London as a driver would, she found it difficult to follow their route once they were in the heart of the city. Just once she asked the girl again if she could give her any idea as to where they were going, but her question was answered by no more than a shake of the girl's blonde head. Philippa tried to relax, and to content herself with the radio playing gently through the car's stereo system as she watched the streets roll past.

When she next checked her watch, she saw they had been travelling for an hour, but when she read the name of the borough on the next street sign she saw, she noticed that they had only reached North London. She had also begun to find her surroundings strangely familiar, and suddenly realised that she had actually visited this area of the capital before – on the night that Jack and Jenny had taken her to Canes and Chains.

Ten minutes later, they pulled into the actual street in which Canes and Chains had been located. This time, there were no parking spaces, but that did not seem to be a problem – the girl at the wheel simply double parked outside the building Philippa knew to be the fetish club. 'You know this place?' the driver asked, turning in her seat to face Philippa again, the engine still running.

'Yes – yes, I do,' Philippa replied, watching as another car had to steer carefully to avoid the Sierra.

'Then please go inside. The friend who sent you the letter is waiting for you.'

'But, who is it?' Philippa asked, once again unsure about this whole venture.

'I can't tell you, but you'll find out inside. Please – I can't wait here all day, miss.' Philippa opened the door and started to get out. 'I'll be back to take you home when your business is finished,' the chauffeuse told her, as she was about to slam the door behind her. Business? What business could she possibly have inside Canes and Chains, especially at this time of day? But it seemed the other girl was going to do nothing but tease with her enigmatic answers, so Philippa simply mumbled, 'OK', and shut the door.

She crossed the road towards the neat and innocent-looking building, turning back only once to watch the car drive away. If the girl did not come back as she had promised, then Philippa would at least be able to find her way home on public transport, since she had slipped her purse into her pocket before rushing out. She climbed the steps, which looked so innocuous by day, and tried the front door. It did not yield. She rang the bell and waited, but heard no sound coming from within. She rang again and waited two more minutes, but still nothing happened. What was she supposed to do now? She wondered if this was all some kind of elaborate joke. It certainly had Jack's sense of humour written all over it. She descended the steps back to pavement level and looked up at the front of the tall building. Then she looked down, and saw there was another flight of stone steps leading to a basement.

Cautiously, still expecting the front door to be opened, she walked down into the dark recess. There was another door, not as solid as the front door, with two frosted glass panels. She tried the handle experimentally. It turned, and the door swung open as she pushed it. This must be the entrance she was meant to use. Feeling a little foolish because it had taken her a few minutes to figure this out, she closed the door behind her.

She fumbled for a lightswitch, and found one by the door. Turning it on, she saw that the room was stacked high with boxes. It looked like a store room. In an institution such as this, she might have expected such a dark and dingy place to have been converted into an ultra-atmospheric dungeon, but she guessed that even a fetish club needed somewhere to store its supplies of soft drinks and bar snacks. There was, however, a second door on the other side of the room, and she headed straight for it.

Beyond it, she found herself at the bottom of a stairwell. Seeing no other choice but to go that way, she started climbing. One floor up, and she recognised the reception area which she had entered on her first visit.

Feeling a little more confident now that she knew where she was, but still a little worried by the lack of other people, she continued upstairs. What would she say if she were challenged by somebody – say if a neighbour had seen her go in and had called the police? She doubted that she would be able to come up with a plausible excuse for being in the building.

She made her way through all the rooms leading to the bar, thinking that if there was anyone here, then that was where she would find them. But, as she walked in through the door, she saw that it too seemed empty. It was also cold in there and so she pulled her jacket tighter around herself. As she peered around the large room, her eyes fell on a black riding crop lying on the bar. She walked over and picked it up, running it through her hands as she pondered her next move.

'Hello there.' She nearly leapt out of her skin, and she certainly took three paces back. Steve had suddenly appeared on the other side of the bar. 'Sorry – did I startle you?'

'Startle me? You could have bloody killed me with a shock like that!' But Philippa was more stunned than frightened. Gradually, she regained her composure and asked him the obvious question. 'What the hell are you doing here?' she said. 'I was sent a letter asking me to meet someone who said they were a friend.'

'Were you really?' he replied calmly.

A thought suddenly occurred to her. 'Did you get one too? Could it be someone we both know?' Now she had Steve with her, she knew it would not be long before the puzzle was solved. And she was right.

'Actually, Philippa, it was me who sent you the letter.'

She stared at him for a few seconds, trying to make sense of it all, but the solution had posed even more questions. 'You?' she said eventually. 'You? Why? You couldn't just pick up the phone and call me like anyone else? And why are we here? How did you get in here?

Does the Mr Big-Shot-No-Publicity-Please who owns the place know we're here? I suppose he's another of your friends, like the committee of the spanking club.' She tried to piece it together as she spoke, but nothing would fit.

'I suppose you could say that, Philippa,' he began, and then paused, obviously thinking carefully about how he would phrase the next line. 'You see, the truth is – well, your Mr Big-Shot is actually yours truly.'

'What?' she gasped. 'You mean you own this place? But I thought you worked in PR?'

'I do – well, I mean, I do that too. But I also began dabbling in a little property speculation when the market went down. I bought this place for a song, and I was going to convert it into flats, but then it occurred to me to make my hobby into a going concern, as well as creating a place where I – and my like-minded friends – could have a little fun. So, with a few backers putting in a little cash – although the lion's share still had to come from me – Canes and Chains was born.'

'But why keep it a secret?' she asked, as he moved out from behind the bar and pulled up a pair of high stools for them.

'Because PR is a high-profile job, especially at the level at which I play the game. I can't risk losing clients who would have to pretend to be mortified by the fact that I run a club for people who the unenlightened world might brand perverts. But it can be funny when I find some of those selfsame clients enjoying my hospitality here without even realising it.'

'Get away!' Philippa was feeling a little more at ease now, and replaced the crop on the bar. 'But why bring me all the way over here just to tell me about it? You know you can trust me to keep your secret, so why didn't you just tell me over dinner or at your flat, or at my place?'

'I wanted to make it an event which you'd find

exciting and memorable. Presentation is everything in advertising, after all. But I also wanted you to be in the right frame of mind for a proposal I wanted to put to you, and this place seemed my best bet in terms of creating the right atmosphere.'

'Proposal? You don't mean . . .' Her heart skipped a beat and, going by the look on his face, so did his.

'No, no – nothing like that! At least not yet.' And he quickly recovered his wry smile. 'I mean a business proposal.'

'Oh, business,' she repeated, unsure whether to feel relieved or disappointed. 'What exactly do you mean?'

'This place is beginning to do pretty good business. It only opens twice a week at the moment, but we have enough members to open it four times a week. That's what I want to do, but to do that I'd need someone to run it full time. I'd like it to be you.'

'Me!' She stared at him incredulously. 'Why me?'

'Why not you? You have qualifications, a good brain for business management – you've more than proved yourself in the job you're doing now. Why not come and do the same for me, and in a place where you can really have some fun?'

'But I know nothing about running a fetish club. And what about the staff you've already got – the girl on the door, for example? Wouldn't one of them be a better choice?'

'Probably not. They only work part-time at the moment, and none of them seem to be interested in making it a full-time thing. Besides, they don't have your business mind or experience. And I need someone I can trust – If that's not you, then who is it?' And he rested a hand gently on her knee.

'So, what exactly would I have to do?' she asked, hesitantly.

'Be my eyes and ears here. Make sure that the cellar has enough food and drink, that all the membership fees

252

are paid up, and that all the invitations and mailings about special events are sent out.'

'But what about the accounts? The tax returns?'

'Oh, my accountant deals with those. You'd just have to keep the books up to date, and give them to him at the end of the year.'

'What? Your accountant knows you own this place? How did you tell him?'

'I didn't have to. He's a member. He turns up regularly, one Friday each month. Seriously, though, if you want the job it's yours. And if you're worried about it falling through once you've quit your job, I promise you, if you don't enjoy it once you start, I'll put you in my PR firm on the same money. You're in a no-lose situation.' Philippa stared unseeingly in front of her as she tried to take it all in. Steve was silent for a while, and then he went on. 'Of course, it would have its fringe benefits, too.'

'Fringe benefits?'

'You'll be here on club nights, of course, but most of the admin will be done during the day. You'll be free to indulge yourself during the evening.'

'Indulge myself?' She was beginning to feel like a parrot.

'Indulge yourself, just like you did the night Jack and Jenny first brought you here. No, don't look surprised, I know about what happened in the private room, but I'm not angry. It just made me believe all the more that you're the person I'm looking for. In fact,' he said, rising from the stool and walking to the door at the opposite end of the bar, 'your flatmates helped me to set up a little surprise which we hope is going to convince you that this is what you should be doing with your life.' He opened the door, and Philippa's eyes widened as Jack and Jenny walked in.

They had clearly not come straight from work. Jack wore the leather jeans and riding boots that she had seen him in before, a black T-shirt completing the dark and menacing look. Jenny was following close behind him, but she did not really have much choice in this matter. She was naked except for a thick leather collar around her neck, from which ran a silver chain. Jack held the other end in his left hand. Jenny's arms were held behind her back, and Philippa guessed she had been bound in some way. Her face was cast down, her eyes staring at her own bare feet. Jack smiled as he saw the shock on Philippa's face.

'Think of this as a little test, too,' said Steve, as he returned to his seat beside her. 'I know you can handle the day-to-day running of Canes and Chains, but I'd like to see if you can run a scene to entertain our customers as well. I'm guessing you can, but I'd really like to see it for myself.'

'Run a scene? You mean, make Jack and Jenny do stuff to each other?'

'Exactly.'

'But what? What am I supposed to tell them to do?'

'Anything you like. You're in charge of them.'

'I – I'm not sure if I can.'

'Really? I'm not so sure you can't. Firstly, you wouldn't be here if you didn't belong here. Nor would they. And they've done so much for you, I think you owe it to them not to back off now, after all you've been through together. They helped you set out on this journey, now take the first step on the next stage of it with them.'

Philippa looked at the couple before her, Jack still smiling faintly, Jenny nervously shuffling her feet and still looking meekly at the ground. 'Well, I guess it won't hurt to try,' she muttered. 'But Steve, please remember I'm new to this. It's not in my nature to be bossy.'

'You'll soon wonder how you ever got by without it,' he whispered reassuringly, then said, a little more loudly, 'Take it away!'

Philippa rose and walked slowly towards Jack and Jenny. Her heels tapped on the hard floor. She stopped right in front of them, and contemplated them for a few seconds, her hands resting on her hips. Then she spoke. 'So you both knew about this little mystery today, did you?'

'Yes, Philippa,' said Jack.

'Yes, *miss*, if you don't mind. And what about her? Hasn't she got a tongue in her head?'

'She hasn't been given permission to speak yet, miss.'

'Well, I'm giving her permission now. In fact I'm ordering her to. Did you know about this?'

Jenny looked up, and Philippa saw her face for the first time since she'd arrived on the scene. She was wearing no make-up, but she still managed to look as lovely as ever. Her expression was one of trepidation, but her eyes still spoke of great excitement. 'Yes, miss, I did,' she murmured.

'So, you both deliberately kept me in the dark?'

'Yes, miss,' they chorused together.

'So you obviously both need punishing. And I think I know exactly how to do that. Jack, give me the chain.' He handed her the gently clanking silver links. Philippa took it, and stared deep into the trembling girl's eyes. 'Now go and fetch me one of those barstools, and set it in the middle of the room.' She heard his footsteps as he went back to the bar, and then the scraping of the chair legs as he did what he was told. 'Now, young lady, over you go.' And Philippa turned and led the compliant Jenny to her fate. Walking around so that the stool was between them, she tugged the chain briskly, so that Jenny had no choice but to let herself fall gently on to the padded leather surface, and Philippa saw that her hands had been restrained by means of two leather bands around each wrist which had then been padlocked together.

Slipping off her coat, Philippa adjusted Jenny's

position until she was happy with the presentation of her naked buttocks. She let the chain dangle on to the floor in front of her. 'Bring me the crop from the bar,' she instructed Jack. Her landlord, normally so aloof and in control, obeyed without so much as a whimper, walking to her and handing her the heavy leather-bound rod. 'Now, step back and give me room,' she said, curtly. 'Oh, and ready yourself to enter her when I'm done – if you're not already prepared, that is.'

Having dealt with Jack so dismissively, Philippa could feel the rush of self-confidence taking her over. She turned to Jenny, flexing the whip as she eyed the round, smooth cheeks thrust up at her. 'Prepare yourself, my dear,' she said, coldly. 'This may sting a little.' And she raised the crop behind her head, waited a few seconds, and then brought it whistling down across her target area.

It landed with a crack, and Jenny screamed. The old Philippa might have relented, might have lost her nerve, and thrown down the whip and run crying from the room. But the new Philippa knew exactly what she was doing, and that this was what both she and Jenny really wanted. She knew how painful this was for Jenny, but also what an emotional high the girl would reach before much longer. And she intended to make sure she reached it. The crop came down again, just above where the first stroke had landed. Jenny squealed again.

Philippa continued to whip Jenny almost as hard as she could, until she could feel her own sweat begin to make her blouse cling to her body. Jenny began to writhe and wriggle, her moans becoming less distinct as they got more frequent. But Philippa kept on, until Jenny's bottom was a striped and cross-hatched mess of weals. Then she stepped back and turned to Jack.

He had obeyed her to the letter, and his fly was open, exposing his hard penis. It was already sheathed, and his fingers were running gently up and down its length, teasing it as he watched Philippa flog Jenny. 'Now, Jack, take her.' He approached the prostrate girl, and grasped her by the hips before Philippa took the two of them by surprise with her next instruction. 'No, not up there; she doesn't deserve that much pleasure. Take her anally.' Jack looked up at Philippa, an unspoken question in his eyes, but Philippa's expression told him not to argue with her. Returning his attentions to Jenny, he gripped her sore buttocks, eliciting a gasp of pain from her, then prised them apart. Leaning back a little to give himself the extra height he needed, he positioned himself at her smallest entrance. He looked back up to make sure that Philippa was watching them closely, and then he pushed forward.

Jenny drew in a sharp breath. Jack grunted. They stood still for a few seconds, and then he shoved his cock a little deeper home. Jenny began to moan quietly, but still he pushed, until he was inside her to the root. He paused for a few moments, presumably to savour the sensation, and then he slowly pulled his shaft halfway out of her, before ramming back into her again. He began to get into his stride, and set a steady rhythm.

Philippa watched, fingering the crop as Jack pumped his prick in and out of Jenny's bottom. She imagined he must be enjoying himself by now – perhaps too much, she mused, which led her to instruct him to stop and pull out of her.

He stopped in mid-stroke, and turned to look at her in astonishment. 'Wh-what? Take it out?'

'That's what I said,' she told him, coolly, 'and that's what you're going to do, unless you want me to take down those ridiculous trousers and give your arse something to think about.' For a moment, he paused and seemed to be considering this as a possible option, and Philippa was not sure that she could call his bluff. Eventually, though – and somewhat reluctantly – he grasped the base of his rod in one hand, and slid its head out of Jenny's back passage. He stared desperately down at his throbbing penis, his face flushed, and then he began to manipulate it with his fingers, which were still wrapped around its root. Philippa saw him. 'Don't you dare!' she barked, shaking the riding crop at him. 'If you come before I give you permission, then you'll swap places with her and get this ten times worse than she did!'

This seemed to work. 'Sorry, miss,' Jack mumbled, as he took his hand away and clasped his arms behind his back. Now Philippa approached the prostrate Jenny, and stood in front of her. She reached down with the crop and tickled the girl under the chin with it so that she lifted her tear-filled eyes to look at her.

'If you ever hide anything from me again,' Philippa said evenly, 'you'll be back here, but on club night, with a queue of men waiting to use you like this. I am the new manageress of Canes and Chains, and I will not have members or staff plotting behind my back, do you understand?'

'Yes, miss,' Jenny sniffed, adding 'I'm very sorry.'

'We both are,' said Jack, sounding genuine enough, though his eyes kept wandering in the direction of Jenny's reddened bottom cheeks and stretched anal opening.

'That's as may be,' Philippa said, 'but I still need more proof. Jack, come here.' He obeyed without hesitation, his hardness bobbing in front of him. 'Unzip my skirt. Now lower it. Now my panties. Now take them away – and fold the skirt carefully.' Philippa stood before Jenny, her lower half clad only in stockings and suspenders which framed her pubis. 'Raise your head again, Jenny,' she said. The blonde did so, and Philippa parted her thighs and moved in as close as she could. Taking two handfuls of the girl's long blonde hair, Philippa guided Jenny's mouth to her moist labia. Instinctively, the submissive girl opened her lips, and began to apply her tongue with fast, light strokes. 'Jack,' Philippa breathed, as her own excitement grew, 'you may finish – in the orthodox hole, this time.'

'Yes, miss, thank you, miss,' he said happily, as he leaped between Jenny's sagging legs.

Suddenly Philippa felt a pair of hands seizing her breasts, and manipulating them through the damp cotton of her blouse. A solid erection rubbed up and down the cleft between her bottom cheeks, just below the point at which Jenny's tongue was busy. Philippa turned her head, and immediately found herself being kissed passionately by Steve. Her orgasm built and suddenly exploded, and at the same time she heard Jack and Jenny shout their own ecstasy as he rammed solidly into her. Disengaging herself from Jenny's hot mouth, Philippa turned and faced her lover, then sank to her knees. As she took his hardness into her mouth, she wondered if it would be like this every day from now on. My God, she thought, I hope so.

NEW BOOKS

Coming up from Nexus and Black Lace

There are three Nexus titles published in December

The Schooling of Stella by Yolanda Celbridge
December 1997   Price £4.99   ISBN: 0 352 33219 0

When English rose Stella Shawn wins a coveted scholarship to Castle Kernece, Scotland's sternest training college, she plans to fulfil her ambition of becoming a schoolmistress. More than a college, Kernece is a way of life, a fierce arena of dominant and submissive females where punishments are frequent and taken 'on the bare'. Only by her own total submission to the rules can Stella learn to dominate.

The Reward of Faith by Elizabeth Bruce
December 1997   Price £4.99   ISBN: 0 352 33225 5

Faith returns from her training to be claimed by her Master and ready to be instructed in the arts of carnal pleasure. Yet her new-found discipline will be severely tested as she enters Alex's decadent world in which Masters and Mistresses have Pleasure Slaves to serve their every sexual need. Faith joins the select ranks of the Chosen, where she has her taste for bondage and submission fully explored as she enjoys bizarre new extremes of humiliation.

The Training of Fallen Angels by Kendal Grahame
December 1997   Price £4.99   ISBN: 0 352 33224 7

Lisa and Janet are two teenagers who are driven by their insatiable libidos to discover new ways to satisfy their depraved desires. They become servants of the enigmatic Mr Gee, who lures them to his rural manor. But there is something sinister happening there. Lisa and Janet are blind to the danger they are in, intent on exploring new realms of debauchery – will they realise the risks before it is too late?

Emma's Secret Domination by Hilary James
January 1988   Price £4.99   ISBN: 0 352 33226 3
In this, the final instalment of the *Emma* series, Emma returns to London only to fall back into the clutches of her cruel former mistress Ursula. Realising that she has missed the bittersweet delights of lesbian domination, she begins finally to enjoy Ursula's attentions – but this only serves to anger and humiliate the prince, who is still her master. How will he administer the discipline she deserves?

'S' – A Story of Submission by Philippa Masters
January 1998   Price £4.99   ISBN: 0 352 33229 8
When 'S' answers an advert which seems to promise an escape from her dull life, little does she realise that her fantasies of total submission are soon to be fulfilled. Entering into a secret world of domination, subservience and humiliation, she explores the bounds of her sexuality, finally realising the depravity of her darkest desires.

Lake of Lost Love by Mercedes Kelly

December 1997   Price £4.99   ISBN: 0 352 33220 4

Princess Angeline lives on a paradise island in the South Seas. Married to Prince Hari and accepted into the native culture and customs, she has a life of ease and debauched sensual delights. When Prince Hari's young manservant is kidnapped and used as a sex slave by the cruel and depraved female ruler of nearby Monkey Island, Angeline sets about planning his rescue.

Contests of Wills by Louisa Francis

December 1997   Price £4.99   ISBN: 0 352 332 239

In Sydney, Australia, in the late 1870s, lascivious young Melanie has married a man old enough to be her grandfather. When their honeymoon is cut short by his sudden death, his will is contested by his grandson, the louche and hedonistic Ric Lidell, and his promiscuous half-sister. Ric's dark satanic looks draw Melanie to him like a magnet – but Melanie's kinky former lover is unwilling to let her walk out of his life.

Sugar and Spice – a collection of Black Lace short stories

December 1997   Price £6.99   ISBN: 0 352 332 271

This is the long-awaited first anthology of Black Lace erotic short stories. Testament to the wildness and originality of the untamed female sexual imagination, there is a variety of settings and characters here to suit all tastes – from the icy tundra of Siberia to the more familiar locations of the office and library. Only the most arousing and erotic stories have made it into this anthology.

Unhallowed Rites by Martine Marquand

January 1998   Price £4.99   ISBN: 0 352 332 220

Twenty-year-old Allegra di Vitale is bored with life in her guardian's Venetian palazzo – until temptation draws her to look at the bizarre pictures he keeps in his private chamber. Her lust awakened, she tries to deny her powerful cravings by submitting to life as a nun. But the strange order of the Convent of Santa Clerisa provides new temptations, forcing her to perform ritual acts with the depraved men and women of the convent.

Nexus

NEXUS BACKLIST

All books are priced £4.99 unless another price is given. If a date
is supplied, the book in question will not be available until that
month in 1997.

CONTEMPORARY EROTICA

THE ACADEMY	Arabella Knight	Oct
AGONY AUNT	G. C. Scott	Jul
ALLISON'S AWAKENING	John Angus	Jul
BOUND TO SERVE	Amanda Ware	
BOUND TO SUBMIT	Amanda Ware	Sep
CANDIDA'S SECRET MISSION	Virginia LaSalle	
CANDIDA'S IN PARIS	Virginia LaSalle	Oct
CANDY IN CAPTIVITY	Arabella Knight	
CHALICE OF DELIGHTS	Katrina Young	
A CHAMBER OF DELIGHTS	Katrina Young	Nov
THE CHASTE LEGACY	Susanna Hughes	
CHRISTINA WISHED	Gene Craven	
DARK DESIRES	Maria del Rey	
THE DOMINO TATTOO	Cyrian Amberlake	
THE DOMINO ENIGMA	Cyrian Amberlake	
THE DOMINO QUEEN	Cyrian Amberlake	
EDEN UNVEILED	Maria del Rey	
EDUCATING ELLA	Stephen Ferris	Aug
ELAINE	Stephen Ferris	
EMMA'S SECRET WORLD	Hilary James	
EMMA'S SECRET DIARIES	Hilary James	
EMMA'S SUBMISSION	Hilary James	
EMMA'S HUMILIATION	Hilary James	
FALLEN ANGELS	Kendal Grahame	
THE TRAINING OF FALLEN ANGELS	Kendal Grahame	Dec

STEPHANIE'S REVENGE	Susanna Hughes	
STEPHANIE'S DOMAIN	Susanna Hughes	
STEPHANIE'S TRIAL	Susanna Hughes	
STEPHANIE'S PLEASURE	Susanna Hughes	
SUSIE IN SERVITUDE	Arabella Knight	
THE TEACHING OF FAITH	Elizabeth Bruce	
FAITH IN THE STABLES	Elizabeth Bruce	
THE REWARD OF FAITH	Elizabeth Bruce	Dec
THE TRAINING GROUNDS	Sarah Veitch	
VIRGINIA'S QUEST	Katrina Young	Jun
WEB OF DOMINATION	Yvonne Strickland	

EROTIC SCIENCE FICTION

RETURN TO THE PLEASUREZONE	Delaney Silver	

ANCIENT & FANTASY SETTINGS

CAPTIVES OF ARGAN	Stephen Ferris	
CITADEL OF SERVITUDE	Aran Ashe	Jun
THE CLOAK OF APHRODITE	Kendal Grahame	
DEMONIA	Kendal Grahame	
NYMPHS OF DIONYSUS	Susan Tinoff	
PLEASURE ISLAND	Aran Ashe	
PYRAMID OF DELIGHTS	Kendal Grahame	
THE SLAVE OF LIDIR	Aran Ashe	
THE DUNGEONS OF LIDIR	Aran Ashe	
THE FOREST OF BONDAGE	Aran Ashe	
WARRIOR WOMEN	Stephen Ferris	
WITCH QUEEN OF VIXANIA	Morgana Baron	
SLAVE-MISTRESS OF VIXANIA	Morgana Baron	

EDWARDIAN, VICTORIAN & OLDER EROTICA

ANNIE	Evelyn Culber	
ANNIE AND THE SOCIETY	Evelyn Culber	
ANNIE'S FURTHER EDUCATION	Evelyn Culber	

BEATRICE	Anonymous	
CHOOSING LOVERS FOR JUSTINE	Aran Ashe	
DEAR FANNY	Aran Ashe	
LYDIA IN THE BORDELLO	Philippa Masters	
MADAM LYDIA	Philippa Masters	
LURE OF THE MANOR	Barbra Baron	
MAN WITH A MAID 3	Anonymous	
MEMOIRS OF A CORNISH GOVERNESS	Yolanda Celbridge	
THE GOVERNESS AT ST AGATHA'S	Yolanda Celbridge	
THE GOVERNESS ABROAD	Yolanda Celbridge	
PLEASING THEM	William Doughty	

SAMPLERS & COLLECTIONS

EROTICON 1		
EROTICON 2		Jun
EROTICON 3		Sep
THE FIESTA LETTERS	ed. Chris Lloyd	
MOLTEN SILVER	Delaney Silver	
NEW EROTICA 2	ed. Esme Ombreaux	

NON-FICTION

HOW TO DRIVE YOUR WOMAN WILD IN BED	Graham Masterton	
HOW TO DRIVE YOUR MAN WILD IN BED	Graham Masterton	Jul
LETTERS TO LINZI	Linzi Drew	